When Rose-Angela was born to Bridget and James Paterson, she was one of the loveliest children in the fifteen streets. With skin the colour of cream, and hair that was straight and black, no trace of her parentage was apparent other than in her eyes. For her eyes were the same deep penetrating brown as those of her coloured father.

And because of that same father, Rose-Angela was to spend the rest of her life being 'different' ... excluded from the lives of the people around her ... set apart and made to feel she was an oddity.

Not until she went to work for Michael Stanhope, the artist who lived in the house by the creek, did her life become rich and full of event ...

Catherine Cookson

Colour Blind

CORGI BOOKS
A DIVISION OF TRANSWORLD PUBLISHERS LTD

COLOUR BLIND

A CORGI BOOK 0 552 11367 0

Originally published in Great Britain
by Macdonald & Co. (Publishers) Ltd.

PRINTING HISTORY
Macdonald edition published 1968
Corgi edition published 1971
Corgi edition reprinted 1972
Corgi edition reprinted 1973 (twice)
Corgi edition reprinted 1975
Corgi edition reprinted 1976 (twice)
Corgi edition reprinted 1977
Corgi edition reprinted 1978 (twice)
Corgi edition reissued 1979

Corgi Books are published by
Transworld Publishers Ltd.,
Century House, 61–63 Uxbridge Road,
Ealing, London W5 5SA
Set, printed and bound in Great Britain by
Cox & Wyman Ltd, Reading

AUTHOR'S NOTE

The characters in this book are entirely fictitious and have no relation to any living person.

Although the setting is Tyneside, and several actual place-names have been used, the fifteen streets, Casey's Wharf, and other parts of Holborn are imaginary.

Owing to the difficulty in comprehension by the uninitiated, the Tyneside dialect has not been adhered to.

In this story I make no effort to solve a problem. The solution, if there is one, for the living conflicts, the half-castes, would seem to lie in the far, far future.

CONTENTS

PART ONE

PART TWO

PART THREE

PART FOUR

PART ONE

CHAPTER ONE

ME DAUGHTER BRIDGET

'Glory be to God and his holy Mother. Well, well I never! And it to happen on me birthday an' all! ... Did y'ever now.' Kathie McQueen threw her great head back and opened wide her full-lipped mouth and let the resounding waves of her laughter free. Her huge breasts and hanging stomach wobbled with it, and her feet, encased in the remnants of a pair of slippers, slapped at the bare floorboards alternately.

The boy, standing at the side of her chair, holding a letter in his hand, smiled up at her. He did not laugh with her, although his heart was racing and leaping inside his narrow chest. Having lived with the McQueens for four years he was used to their laughter, and perhaps it was the extravagance of it that subdued the laughter in himself, for his face rarely stretched beyond a smile. The McQueens frequently chipped him about this, saying, 'Go on, Tony, stretch your gob. Go on, give your face a day off, lad. Go on, forget about your leg; the inch you've lost on that you've got in your napper.' They meant it kindly. All the McQueens were kind to him, even Matt. But no matter how kind they were, or what they did for him, he could never laugh with them. For there was something he didn't understand about their laughter; at times it even brought a fear to him.

Into the sound of the laughter came a dull thumping on the back door, and the boy, raising his voice, shouted, 'There's someone at the door.'

'What?' Kathie brought her streaming eyes down to his. 'Someone at the door? Away then and open it.' And in the next breath she called, 'Come in, there.'

Before the boy had limped half-way to the door, it was opened, and a small girl with a coat over her head came into the kitchen.

'Me ma says can yer lend her yer gully, Mrs. McQueen?' The black coat, forming a hood about her face, emphasised the pinched cheeks and hungry eyes, and the voice, too, sounded thin and hungry as it issued from the shadows of the coat. 'She won't keep it a minute. We've got some bread and me ma's got a ticket to get some groceries. But we've got the bread now ... and ...' Her voice trailed off.

'Yer ma got a ticket? God be praised! But I thought ye got yer gully out last week,' said Kathie, reaching across the table and picking up a long bread-knife.

'It had to go back with the fire-irons so as to get the bread.' The child's voice seemed to come from more remote depths of the coat.

'Ah well, times like these won't last much longer.' Kathie handed the child the bread-knife. 'Yer Da's bound to get set on now ... cough, spit an' all. They'll be taking the blind and the deaf soon, they'll take owt during a war, God bless the Kaiser!'

Kathie's head was again thrown back, and the boy and girl stood regarding her solemnly, fascinated by the great pink and grey cavity of her mouth.

Her laughter seemed to remind her of the previous bout, and its cause, and she stopped suddenly, saying, 'It's good news we've got the day ... what d'ye think? Me daughter Bridget's on her way home.... Tell yer ma, Milly.'

'Brid coming home? Oh, I will, Mrs. McQueen.'

'An' tell her she's married, at that.... Me daughter Bridget's married, tell her, to a seafaring gentleman. Now what d'ye think of that? Go on now, tell her. And let me have that gully back!' she shouted to the departing child; 'they'll all be in in a minute, and I want it for the tea.... Eeh, Tony lad'—she turned once more to the boy—'read it again. No ... give it me here.'

She took the letter from his hand and held it at arm's length, and, pulling her chin into the rolls of fat on her neck, she said slowly, ' "Dear Ma, I'll be home on Friday night. You will be surprised to know I am married. He goes to sea. My name is Mrs. Paterson. Ma, there's something I should tell you, but I can't write it down. I'll have to come home. Love, Brid." '

The boy looked at her in admiration. He knew she couldn't read a word ... she couldn't even write her own name. But her grotesque, fat body seemed to be the storage house for everything she heard; she had only to hear a thing once to remember it for ever.

'I know what she's afraid to tell me, Tony lad.' She leant towards him and whispered with a natural frankness, 'It's a baby she's goin' to have, ye know.' She joined her arms together and rocked them as if a child lay on them. 'Ye know, like my Eva upstairs. Now there's no disgrace in having a child if ye're married and the priest's blessing on ye, is there, Tony? Now is there? But me Bridget was always the shy one.'

The boy regarded her in silence. Women with protruding stomachs were a common sight to him; he had only to walk down the back lane any time of the day to see one. In the summer he looked down on great cones of flesh hanging out from open blouses as the women sat on their front doorsteps suckling their babies. Eva upstairs had always appeared ugly to him, with her young fat and her red hair, but when her stomach had bulged she had been repulsive. And when her babies were born—for they were twins—they, too, were repulsive; and had grown more so, with their skinny bodies and rickety legs.

Yet here was Mrs. McQueen classing Bridget, his beautiful Bridget, with Eva. If Bridget had a baby, it would be beautiful like her, and its hair would be fair, and the grey of its eyes would dance at you. But it wouldn't laugh all the time, for Bridget was the only one of the six McQueens who didn't laugh all the time.

Tony blinked his eyes in startled surprise as Kathie McQueen's hand brought him a playful slap across the face. 'It's a solemn puss ye have on ye. But ye like me Bridget, don't ye?'

He nodded but made no answer. Liking was a poor word for the feeling he had for Bridget. She was the star that had filled his dark sky since the day his mother died and an aunt, his only living relative, had refused his claim on her. It was the McQueens who came forward, and without any preamble took him into their already full house. But only the fifteen-year-old Bridget brought him comfort. When they sat round the fire at night, huddled close to its often small embers, but always shouting and laughing, it was she who would sit next to him, with her arm about him. And when the lads called after him 'Hoppy on the Don!' it was she who would walk by his side, and at times fill him with curious pain when she affected to limp slightly, saying she had a pain in her hip. She championed him until he reached twelve, when he suddenly started to grow. But from then Matt had taken notice of Bridget's attentions to him. If she brought him some little tit-bit from her daily place, Matt would say, 'Stop making a blommin' fool of him. Why don't you give him a dummy?' At times there would be fierce rows, and he felt he was the cause. And the rows always took place in the wash-house, where Matt would push Bridget, and their voices, low and thick with rage, would filter into the house. One thing Tony noticed was that Matt didn't corner his sister when their father was about. And it was after one of these rows, which seemed to mount with the years, that Bridget suddenly went away. And for weeks afterwards Matt hadn't laughed.

And now Bridget was coming back, and she was married. This fact did not touch Tony's own feeling for her, but into his mind there crept a fear—a fear of Matt's reactions when this knowledge should be made known to him—and he thought, I won't look at his face when he reads the letter.

Cavan McQueen was the first to come in, his laugh in the back yard heralding his approach. The booming of his voice and the depth of his laughter were in striking contrast to the short, slight body. And his shortness was emphasised as he stood by his wife. He threw his bait tin with a clatter on to the table before bringing his hand with a resounding whack across Kathie's buttocks.

'We're set, lass. The war's only been on three days and the sods are begging us to do overtime.'

He was lifting his hand again to repeat the slap when she yelled, 'Stop it, ye little rat, ye!' Then her voice dropped to a thick caressing tone. 'Cavan lad ... guess what. Ye'll never guess in a month of Sundays ... read that.' She pulled the letter out from her blouse, then stood with her arms folded on the shelf of her stomach watching him. She saw the smile follow after the laughter, to leave his face wearing the blank, stiff look she hated.

When he made no comment she cried angrily, 'Ain't yer pleased? What would ye be wanting? The child's coming home an' she's married. Ye're wearing a look as if ye'd heard she'd been dropped with a bairn and no one to father it. She's married, man, an' all respectable—they call her Mrs. Paterson. And what's more, she got him herself. She hadn't to drag him to the altar rails like Eva had that miserable swine up there.' She flicked her eyes towards the ceiling.

Cavan rubbed his greasy hand over his moustache and said dully, 'Aye, there's that in it,' and handed the letter back to Kathie. Then, turning slowly, he went to the corner of the room, took off his coat, and proceeded to wash himself in a tin bath of hot water which was standing on a low shelf attached to the wall. He dried himself on a piece of sacking that had been hemmed into a square, and which still bore the sugar manufacturer's name across it. He took no heed of the upbraidings of Kathie as she pounced round the kitchen; he could stop her effectively whenever he wished, and she knew just how far she could go. His mind was trying to grasp the fact that his lass ... his own lass ... was married, and him not knowing. Of his four children, his heart laid claim only to one. In varying degrees he liked Eva, Matt and Terence, but Bridget he knew he loved.

13

He scrubbed himself more vigorously with the sacking to cover up the thought. Bridget had the knack of making people love her. All men seemed to love Bridget, even those that shouldn't.... His thoughts swung to his son.... That had been the trouble: Matt hadn't let Bridget live any life but that which he chose. If it hadn't been for Matt, Bridget would never have left home, to go all that way to London to work; and then to Liverpool.

Cavan stopped rubbing himself and stared down into the bath of dirty water. He was trying to see through his thoughts, but they were as opaque as the water. Yet this much he could see: if Bridget had not got married away, she would never have got married at home ... not as long as Matt was alive.

Kathie's voice, raised in laughing greeting to their younger son, brought Cavan's mind from Matt, and he turned from the contemplation of the water and threw his greeting to the lad who was a replica of himself. 'How's it gone?'

'Oh, champion.'

'Was it hard?'

'Aye, a bit. But I'll get used to it. The stink of the chemicals made me sick at first, and you get covered all over with white dust. Most of them have overalls ... can I have a pair of overalls, Ma?'

'Ye can have owt yet like, lad, if ye bring the money in.'

'Well, I'll be doing that. A pound a week, and me only sixteen!'

'Aye,' his father put in, with unusual seriousness, 'you'll be a millionaire shortly. But look out, and don't let on to anyone, for when the Government get wind you're having three meals a day they'll find some bloody way of bringing them down to one, or nowt.'

Terence took no notice of this, but said, 'Da, you said if we all got set on you were going to try for a house in the middle or top end.'

'Aye, I did.'

'Well, you'd better look slippy then, for they're being

snapped up; the men coming to work in the Barium are looking round. They want to live as near as they can.'

'Oh, there'll always be plenty of houses if ye've got the money to pay the rent. But we'll stick where we are till we see how long this war's goin' to last. It might only hang on a few weeks, and then where'll we be if we move, eh? Best forget moving for the time.'

But as Cavan sat down to his tea he was thinking as much about the possibility of moving as he was about Bridget's coming. They were both entwined in his mind; for hadn't he always promised Bridget that one day they'd move back into the middle of the fifteen streets ... or, with a bit of luck, perhaps the top end. It was a great pity they couldn't have moved before she came back, but he had learned too much from life to take a step like that without being sure the present flood of work would last. Here they had a roof over their heads. And it wasn't a workhouse roof, although he knew that the latter contingency had only been avoided by his wife's laughing tenacity and Matt's pilfering, and the pulling in of his own belt to let what food there was go to the others. But God was good, and had showered his special Providence over them, when all around, weeping women and grim-faced men had watched their last sticks of furniture being carried out by the bums before wending their heart-breaking way down the Jarrow Road to East Jarrow, through Tyne Dock and down Stanhope Road, to where Talbert Road showed the grim gates at the far end, which, once entered, a family was no longer a family but merely segregated individuals, with numbers on each of their garments. When this happened the McQueens had stood close together, defying Life's blows with their laughter. Bridget and the boy Tony hadn't laughed much, but the others made up for them.

It was said that only the scum of the earth lived in the fifteen streets, but Cavan would have considered himself one of the fortunate of the earth if he could have moved into the middle section, where the houses possessed four box-like rooms, and you went upstairs to bed; and where

15

you were the proud possessor of your own back yard, and what was more—a netty. There you hadn't to stand waiting for your turn until your bladder nearly burst, or see the bairns doing the wet dance while they waited, for he would allow none of them to foul the yard.

Here, in these two rooms that dared to flaunt the name of a downstairs house, the lavatory had to be shared with the family upstairs, although since Eva had come to live above them the situation had eased considerably. Before the previous tenant had taken the long trek to the iron gates there had been nineteen of them sharing the yard and its amenities.

When Cavan heard his quarter referred to as the 'stinkpot' or the 'buggy-boxes' his laughter would disappear, and he would yell at the offender, asking how he could expect anything else. During one of his angry spells he started a campaign against the bugs and enlisted a number of the neighbours. Paper was stripped off the walls, which were soaked with carbolic. This was quite effective if both upstairs and downstairs co-operated. But poverty dulls incentive, and the war against bugs needs to be wholesale, so many were soon back where they started. But not 42 Powell Street; for Cavan became almost a maniac with the carbolic, the smell of which permeated their clothes and food.

Cavan's thinking had reached a point where he was asking himself if it was the living conditions as much as Matt that drove Bridget away from home when Matt came in.

Matt seemed to spring into the kitchen—there was a spring in his every step. If he laughed when he walked, the combination became a beguilement, bringing the children after him and the eyes of the girls on him. His body, like his father's, was thin; but he had height with it, and a steely sinuation that spoke of arrogant maleness. His face was narrow and overhung by a thick mop of sandy hair, growing low on his brow. It was his eyes that were the most noticeable feature of his face; they were like large jet beads, and not even his laughter could lift

16

the brooding veil from them.

Kathie's greeting to him was shriller than ever, and her laughter caused Tony to fix his eyes on his tin plate; it was the kind of laughter that frightened him, for somehow he didn't think it was meant to be laughter at all.

'I'll give yer a month of Sundays, Matt,' Kathie was yelling, 'to guess what's happened. Go on: Jesus in Heaven, ye'll never guess it.'

Matt looked questioningly at his father; and Cavan returned his look, but said nothing.

'What is it?' Matt turned to his mother.

Still laughing, she said, 'Get the grease washed off yer, and come an' have yer tea—I've a steak as thick as a cuddy's lug for yer. Oh, ye'll never guess.' And her laughter and chattering filled the time until he came to the table.

'Let him have his tea,' said Cavan.

Kathie stopped her laughing and said soberly, 'Yes. Yes, I will.'

'I'm not having any tea till I know what's up.' Matt stood by his plate looking at his mother.

She looked at Cavan, and when he nodded his head she put her hand inside her blouse again and handed the letter to her son.

Tony did as he had promised himself: he didn't look at Matt while he read the letter. With great deliberation he wiped up the last of the gravy from his plate with a piece of bread, going round and round it until the tin shone with a silver gleam. Under this lowered lids he saw the letter flung on to the table. He saw Mr. McQueen, too, wiping his plate clean with his bread.

Then Mrs. McQueen's fist banging the table made him jump, and her voice nearly deafened him as she yelled, 'That's the last damn time the Cullens will get a loan of me gully. I've sworn it afore an' I'll swear it again! Here's me having to tear me own bread while those hungry hounds are lording it with me gully.'

Tony saw Matt's legs moving with unusual slowness towards the door. When he heard it close he lifted his

17

head and watched Matt disappear down the back yard and into the September dusk. Mr. and Mrs. McQueen with one accord left the table and went into the other room; and Tony was left with Terence, who, taking advantage of the situation, cut a piece off Matt's congealing steak and motioned to Tony to do likewise. But Tony took no heed; he was tense with the feeling of nervous expectancy, longing for, yet dreading the time when Bridget would be in the kitchen again.

As Matt walked out of the fifteen streets into the main road he turned the lapels of his coat across his chest to hide his dirty shirt, for he had come out without his muffler. The air was soft and close, but he shivered, and a girl crossing the road called to him, 'Hallo there, Matt—you look as if ye'd seen the Kaiser. Have they called yer up?'

The sound of his laugh was sufficient answer for her, and she went on her way, laughing too.

Laughter was easy—when everything else failed you could always laugh. Then why hadn't he stayed in the house and laughed this off? No, he'd had to make a bloody fool of himself and come out! It was the shock. Bridget married! Well, he knew she'd marry sometime, didn't he? He knew that once she got away on her own some fellow would get her. He twisted the torn lining of his coat pocket round his fingers, tearing it still farther. He'd thought that in the months following her surprising departure he had worked the whole thing out; he'd imagined he had got her out of his system, for life, although emptier, became easier without her. The tearing, mad feeling of possessiveness faded, and he lost his hate of all mankind because she was not near to bestow her smile on it. He had been mad—he could see that now. But he could also see now that he would be mad again. What possessed him? Why was it he should feel like this about her? All his life he had suffered and enjoyed the torment of this feeling for her. He could remember himself as a tiny child holding her and knowing that she was his; still a baby himself, he had washed and dressed her; no one was allowed to take her to school but himself; he had even stolen for her. He knew he would have let the others go hungry to death, and they would have done, or else to the workhouse, if Bridget's grey eyes hadn't told him that there was a gnawing in her stomach.... And now she was married, and was coming home to flaunt her catch—the bitch! She was just doing it to torment him, By God, he'd kill her! No, no! ... He wiped the moisture from his lips with the back of his hand. Whatever was the reason for her coming back, it wasn't to torment him. He would give her her due; she would never do that intentionally. Then why was she coming?

It was dark now, and he walked on through Tyne Dock, down Eldon Street and into Shields. If it had been light, he would have cut through the Deans into the park. He had been taking walks in the park often of late; to get away from the grime and muck of the fifteen streets, he had thought. Yet up to Bridget's going away he had never noticed their grimness. Vaguely he knew that to make his life bearable he needed something. Her personality, in such contrast to his, and her strange beauty had supplied that something. Now he was searching blindly to replace it. The park, in the minutest way, brought Bridget back to him. Was it its colour and cleanness?—for Bridget had always been clean. Or was it just some quiet place where his thoughts could move around her without the perplexing agony of her presence? He didn't know.

She would likely be home now, and they'd all be about her, laughing at the tops of their voices, and she would be smiling at them, that lovely wide smile. He turned abruptly and walked towards Jarrow again. After she had quietened them all, as she had the power to do, she would look around her and say, 'Where's Matt?' Yes, she would ask for him, for she knew as well as he did that some part of her belonged to him. And she could never rob him of it, husband or not.

When he passed the dock arches and reached the quiet stretch of road joining Tyne Dock to East Jarrow he started to run swiftly and lightly, with the loping grace of some forest animal. He kept on running, past the slacks where the water flapped at the bank to the side of his feet, past the Barium chemical works, where Terence had started that day, past Bogie Hill, and on to the fifteen streets.

He was panting when he reached the back yard, for it had been a long run, and as he paused behind the closed door of the yard, looking towards the gas-lit blind of the kitchen window, he was at once struck by the odd quiet that prevailed. He knew, as if he could see her, that Bridget had come. She was there, in the kitchen. Then why was there no laughing, no yelling? He looked to the upstairs window. It was alight, and he could see Eva moving back and forth with the unwieldy bulk of a child on her hip. Why wasn't she downstairs with the rest?

He turned the lapels of his coat back and straightened his shirt neck, and walked slowly up the yard. His hand hovered over the latch of the door; then he thrust it open, and with his usual spring entered the kitchen.

They were all there except Eva: his mother and father, Terence and Tony, and Bridget. They all stared at him, and the almost audible pleading in Bridget's eyes was also in those of the others. But he looked at none of them, not even at Bridget; for his eyes were riveted in stupefied amazement on the massive Negro standing behind Bridget's chair with his hand possessively covering her shoulder.

CHAPTER TWO

A SEAFARING GENTLEMAN

'Oh, it's ye, Mrs. Cullen—did ye want to borrow something?'

Jane Cullen knew it was a danger signal when Kathie addressed her as Mrs. She stood within the door, hugging her shawl about her, and looked in envy at this neighbour whom no sorrow or tribulation could affect. She guessed Kathie was a bit upset about the black man, but nothing to speak of—if it had happened to one of her lassies she would have died with shame. She said gently, 'I was wonderin', Kathie, if ye'd lend me yer boots. I've got to go into Jarrow and it's pourin', and there's not a sole on mine. If he gets the job of night-watchman I'll get meself a pair.'

'Ye've been saying that for the last year, Mrs. Cullen. If it isn't me gully, it's me boots!'

Jane looked at Kathie for a moment, then turned silently to the door.

'Here, take them.' The boots were thrust against Jane's arm, and as she took them with a low murmur of thanks Kathie remarked grandiosely, 'I'll soon be able to pass them on to yer altogether, for me daughter Bridget is buying me a new pair. She's able to buy anything she likes now she's married such a well-set-up gentleman. Did yer hear that she's setting up in the middle streets? Four rooms she'll have at that. They're down in Shields this very minute getting the furniture, and for the whole house, mind yer ... there'll be no beg and scrape for me daughter Bridget.'

Jane nodded her head and smiled weakly. 'I'm glad for

her, Kathie.'

For a second longer the two women stared at each other, then Jane sidled out, and Kathie, turning to the fire, stood grinding her strong teeth together until her jaw-bones ached. She'd let them see; no one would pity her. She had laughed longer and louder these past few days than ever before, and she had made the others laugh too, saying, 'If ye laugh, they won't pity ye, and if they don't pity ye they'll envy ye.' Cavan, Terence and even Tony had done as she bid. But not Matt.... Matt seemed to have been transfixed into silence from the moment he saw the Negro. And Eva—that big daft slobbery bitch. Kathie turned up her eyes and their venom was enough to penetrate the ceiling. Playing the respectable married woman! And getting all virtuous like—the silly sod, when her belly was full of Harry McGuire before she'd dragged him to the altar rails!

Eva had always envied Bridget; and rightly too, Kathie thought; but now she refused even to speak to her sister. And so Kathie had taken Bridget's marriage lines and held them under Eva's nose. But Eva, with an air that nearly drove her mother mad, had pointed out that a Registry Office marriage was no marriage; so besides the awful disgrace of having a black man, Bridget was also living in sin, and she'd soon have Father O'Malley on her track. And, blast her, she was right, too ... about the priest, anyway, for he had never been off the doorstep since he'd got wind of the affair.

He had managed to corner Bridget but not him ... Kathie couldn't bring herself to call her son-in-law James. To his face she addressed him as 'Mr. Paterson'; and time and again she wondered at the ordinariness of such a name for such an extraordinary man, and wondered too what in the name of God made her Bridget marry him. She couldn't get a word of explanation out of Bridget. When she asked her, Bridget just drooped her eyes and clasped her hands on her lap, and sat still and tense, until Kathie cried, 'Then why did ye come back?' And to this Bridget answered simply, 'I wanted to be near you all when he's away at sea ... and the bairn coming.'

A bairn coming. Kathie held her head between her hands. A black bairn. For it would be a black bairn, she was sure; there was too much of him in comparison with Bridget's whiteness. The child would be black both inside and out, and her Bridget would have to push a black bairn around the streets. Mother of God! How could a daughter of hers stand up under the shame of it? She rocked her head with her hands. But Bridget didn't seem to be ashamed: there she was, away now in Shields, walking openly with him in the broad daylight! Hadn't she watched her go down the street with never a look to right or left, her head held high as if she had something to be proud of? What had come over her? Why had she done it? Kathie beat the top of her head with her fist. Would the good God tell her why she had done it?

Something of the same question was passing through Bridget's mind as she faced the look of ill-concealed scorn in the eyes of the shop assistants. She had watched her husband put down the five pounds deposit and sign his name with a proud flourish on the form which was an open sesame to a choice of oil-cloths, of beds and bedroom suites, of half-sets of china and Nottingham lace curtains. Never had she dreamed that she would be able to set up house with thirty pounds' worth of furniture. She should be mad with the joy of it; but there was no spark of joy in her, only pain and pity, and gratitude and abhorrence—the pain and pity and gratitude were the feelings that the bulk of towering blackness evoked in her; the abhorrence was for herself and the thing she had done.

When they left the shop it was her husband who showed her out. Taking the door from the hand of the shopwalker he stood aside to allow her to pass. But the closing of the door did not shut out the tittering from the shop, and its sound brought an angry flush to Bridget's cheeks, and a higher tilt to her chin. They laughed at her because he treated her like a queen! If she had married one of them she would have been made aware of her inferiority for the remainder of her life, and if she had married one of her own class never would she have known the meaning of worship—not to speak of consideration; never would she have known what it was to be loved as this man loved her. Then why was she ashamed of him? Why did it take all the rallying of her forces to brave the streets with him at her side?

When they were together, closed in by four walls, with no eyes upon them, the shame would fade, and then a strange tenderness for him would fill her. Even at times a feeling she thought might be love for him would sweep over her. This often happened in the night when he woke her with his loving, for even with his passion, which lifted her into realms hitherto unknown, his love-making never lost the adoring quality that gave to it a gentleness. But she wished again and again that he would not show this gentleness to her in public, for it was this as much as anything that brought the guffaws and smiles of ridicule upon them. She wanted to tell him, but she could not bear to hurt him. She had soon found that she could hurt him with a look or a word; and she knew that she must never do this ... she must never hurt him more than she had done by marrying him. She did not blame him for marrying her—if she had been in her right senses it would never have come about—Matt had always warned her ... Matt.... She shuddered. She had Matt to face yet. Oh God, give her strength for the day when Matt would speak to her, and drag from her the reason why she had done this thing.

Her husband's hand in her arm pulled her closer to him, and his thick bell-toned voice, speaking his short-cut English, fell on her head. 'You cold? ... You shivering? ... Me, I'm big selfish beast. I take you home right away, eh?' He bent down and looked into her face. 'Eh, honey? We go home, eh?'

She smiled at him. 'I'm not cold—someone was walking over my grave.'

'Someone on your grave? ... Sh!' He pulled her still closer. 'You don't talk of graves; you make me have creeps

24

too. No grave will get my Rose.... By way, your mam don't like me calling you Rose, do she? But you Rose all through.... Bridget, it is hard sound—like—like a swear, eh?' He laughed, his head thrown up and his massive shoulders shaking.

His laugh was infectious, but the passers-by did not join in as they would have done had he been alone ... a black man and a white girl was something not to be condoned in any way. In the unmoving depths of his mind James Paterson knew this, but in the conflicting groping layers nearer the surface, where his thoughts jumped and clung to anything that would bring him a level nearer to the white man, he told himself that the looks of the women were jealousy of his Rose's beauty, and those of the men, envy of himself for his luck in possessing her.

He believed in luck ... he believed he was born lucky. Had he ever starved like other black men? No. Hadn't he been to school? Couldn't he read and write? ... By God, yes! And hadn't he always had any woman he wanted? Again, by God, yes! There were times when he had to push them off ... white women liked black men; and they weren't all women of the bars, either; no, by God, they weren't. But one thing he never had until he took Rose; and that was a virgin. He knew then that Rose must belong to no man but him. It had been hard work getting her, and he'd nearly lost his boat. It would have been the first time he had missed a trip, either through drink or women, but he had been prepared to do it for Rose.... The nagging thought came again ... would she have married him had she not discovered there was a baby coming? ... Yes; yes, she would. For his Rose loved him; and the colour of his skin meant nothing to her.

He pulled her even closer to him until he bore her weight on his arm. He wanted to lift her up and carry her through the streets; he wanted to show all men by some definite sign that she was his; he wanted to touch her and caress her. He said softly, 'We call at our own house— what you say?'

She consented readily, for anything was better than

going home when Matt would be in, and have his eyes avoid hers and his silence beat at her.

As they turned into Dunstable Street James spoke a cheery 'good evening' to a small group of men standing at the corner. They answered him in low growls, turning their heads away and becoming engrossed in each other's conversation.

And Bridget felt a desire to stop and shout at them, 'He's as good as you—he's better than you. He wouldn't let his wife trail round the bars after him to get what was left of his pay; nor yet have his beer if the bairns went naked—you lot! What are you, anyway? ... Scum ... scum.'

She was shivering again when they entered the empty house; and James, all concern for her, said, 'I know you got chill, honey—come, we go to your home—there's big fire there.'

'No, it's all right; I want to stay here awhile.' She smiled at him. 'We'll plan where we'll put the furniture.'

He responded to her, as pleased as a child: 'Oh, my, yes. Tomorrow when it all come—my!' He shook his head. 'We have our home—my Rose has a beautiful home.... And me ... between watches I sit on deck and think of you sittin' here thinkin' of me—eh?' He took her chin in his great black hand and tilted her face up to his. Her grey eyes were moist with the pity that was foremost in her mind at that moment, and he said, 'You not sad?'

She turned from him and went into the little bare kitchen, and he followed her in concern. 'You not like the house and the pretty furniture?'

The expressive, appealing gesture of his outstretched arms wrenched the words out of her! 'Oh yes, yes—it's only that I'm happy.' She sniffed and blew her nose. 'I always cry when ... when I'm happy.'

As his laughter resounded from the bare walls she knew that in a way she had spoken the truth, for she would be happy in this house with all her lovely furniture. She would have four rooms all to herself, and a back yard to herself, and she could bolt the door and be shut away from people. Apart from those looking down on the yard out of the windows opposite, no one would see her if she did not wish it. And she would have the added comfort that her people were near if she wanted them. Oh yes, she would be happy. She was happy. She could believe it; for now they were alone together.

The soft light that had been the magnet that first drew him was in her eyes, and he pulled her away from the window to the dark corner near the fireplace.

'You love me, Rose?'

She nodded.

'Always?'

She nodded again.

'No other man, ever?'

She shook her head.

'Not when I'm away at sea, like some white women?'

'No, no, never that!' Her protest was vehement.

His enormous lips slowly traced the outline of her face. The moving black blur filled her with such conflicting emotions that she became faint under them. His unfinished words ran into one another, forming a lulling drawl. 'Rose love ... my beautiful Rose. No other woman in world like you.... You marry me 'cause you love me. You don't mind colour, and our baby ... my baby, she be a girl; we call her Angela, eh? like angel.... Rose Angela.' His fingers moved down the waist-band of her skirt and pressed gently on her stomach. 'I feel her heart-beat ... she'll be like you, Rose ... white and beautiful with long limbs and...'

The sound that checked his words was of someone breathing. They both remained still, pressed close against each other for a second longer, listening to the hiss of the indrawn breath. James turned slowly, but Bridget almost jumped into the centre of the kitchen at the sight of the priest standing in the front-room doorway.

If it had been an ordinary man, James would have demanded 'What the hell you up to, eh?' before, perhaps, whirling him through the air into the street. But a priest to him was not a man, so he said with laughing irony,

'Why, sir, you near scared me white.'

The priest looked from James to Bridget, and the expression in his eyes bore down her courage. Her head drooped and the old childhood fear of him overcame her.

'I told you to bring him along to the vestry.' Father O'Malley might have been speaking of an animal, and his words seemed to have been pressed thin in their effort to escape his tight lips.

'I ... I didn't tell him, Father.'

James looked enquiringly from one to the other. Although he didn't like the tone the priest was using to his wife, nor the way he was looking at her, the smile still hovered about his face. Bible-punchers were funny; all bible-punchers were quaint men.

Father O'Malley again addressed Bridget. 'You have told him what must be done?'

She shook her head, her eyes still directed towards the floor. 'No, Father.'

The priest adjusted his thick glasses and brought the pin-points of his eyes to bear on James. 'You must be married; and you must take instruction.' He separated each word, and the effect was very much that of James's stilted English. 'I will marry you on Saturday morning at eight o'clock.'

'Marry? ... Me? ... We be married?' James looked in perplexity at Bridget's bowed head. The smile had left his face, and his body was stretched to its fullest height, making the small priest appear like a dwarf in comparison. 'What you mean, married? I got paper all signed— we married.'

'Not in the eyes of God. A Christian marriage cannot be performed in a Registry Office; and you must take instructions to become a ...'

'But me am Christian.' A patient smile began to hover around James's lips; he felt he knew now why the priest was so concerned. 'Why, sir, I was baptised—yes, yes, I know all about Christ Jesus.... Mr. Edwards, he very good missionary—splendid fellow, he learned me Jesus Christ all through, and what those bloody Jews did for him. A good man, Jesus Christ.... Yes, me Christian all right.' James's smile widened, spreading the corners of his mouth to meet the expanse of his broad nostrils. 'You no need worry 'bout me.'

'The missionary wasn't a Catholic—it isn't the same. This is your fault!' Father O'Malley hurled the accusation at Bridget.

'Here, here! You no speak to her like that.' James stepped to his wife's side and placed a protecting arm around her shoulders. 'You man of God all right, but you no speak like that, please. You mean me isn't Christian 'cause me not Catholic-Christian? Christ Jesus all kinds Christian. The Catholic Father he came and play chess with Mr. Edwards, and laugh fit to bust over jokes. They both Christian men. Once Catholic Father say to me I am name same's Christ's brother, and I should be fisherman. Always that stay in my head. An' one day I leave my home for the water. Me was never fisherman, but me always on water.... That Catholic Father was good man. He know me Christian all right.'

'Be quiet!' The sharpness of the command whipped the returning smile completely from James's face, and his scalp moved, shifting his mop of wire curls from side to side. The priest went on, looking now with open contempt at Bridget, 'This is no marriage and you know it. You have sinned enough already, and we naturally as night follows day retribution will come upon you. Your only atonement can be too ensure the safe keeping of the soul of your child; and God knows it will need that to be in safe keeping. Be at the church at eight o'clock on Saturday morning; and I will take him for instruction whenever he is in port.'

'You what, by God!'

James made to follow the priest as he went through the front room, but Bridget clung on to him, crying, 'Please, James ... James. Don't for my sake.... James, we will see Father Bailey ... he's different ... he'll explain to you.'

James became still. His eyes were puzzled and sad as they looked down into hers. 'You no want us do this thing—to go be married again? If we do this, no dignity left. Mister Edwards always say "Keep dignity", and here I feel'—he pointed to his chest—'dignity be gone if we do this. We married all right in here'—he pressed his hand on his heart—'I know we'm married all right.... Very much married. But him, he say we not married at all.'

Bridget's mind suddenly cried at her, Oh God, if only Father O'Malley was right, and it was no marriage! But it was a marriage all right. The night she had slept with James hadn't made it a marriage; but when a man with a greasy collar had mumbled some scarcely intelligible words over them and they had written their names in a book, that had made it a marriage. Why? but why? The cry against man's social order that had rung through unhappy unions down the ages found only one answer in her mind, You've made your bed and you'll have to lie on it.

She said to James, repeating the formula that had been drilled into her at school, 'The Catholic religion is the only one true religion.' Then she added, 'You've got to be married in the Catholic Church before—before it's all right with God.'

It was a bright Saturday morning and the streets were warm, and women, the respectable ones, were kneeling on the pavement washing their steps. Some were covering a large half-moon of the pavement with bath brick, taking care to get a smoothness in the distribution, regardless of the fact that within an hour, perhaps less, the feet of the children would have stamped it black; clean patches seemed to draw children like magnets. But this morning the women turned from the daily sign of their respectability to stare at Kathie McQueen and her man Cavan, all dressed up ... and Kathie in her funeral coat too! One after the other, after answering Kathie's loud greeting, they knelt back on their heels and stared after her swaying figure encased in the tight black satin coat, and at Cavan, who from the back appeared like a boy walking with his mother, and silent, too, like some boys who are forced to walk with their mothers on some disagreeable errand, for he gave no greeting to the women, nor yet cast a glance at them.

'We are off for a jaunt with me daughter Bridget and her man.' Kathie threw this information to the last remaining women in the street, before they turned into the main road.

'And what better morning for it, eh?'

And the women answered back, 'None better.'

In the comparative quietness of the main road Cavan, still looking straight ahead, said, 'Ye're foolin' nobody but yersel'.'

And after a moment's silence Kathie replied, 'That's as may be; but I'll not have their pity ... see?' She turned her head aggressively on him. 'They'll think as ye want them to think, in the long run.... I've seen it afore ... it's always the way.'

They walked on in silence again, and Kathie adjusted her large satin-covered hat that had once been black but was now a variety of shot greens, then hitched her coat into an easier position under her breasts, and hoped as she did so that the button wouldn't give way; and she cursed Father O'Malley at the same time. If he had to marry them again he could have waited a bit; and with Cavan in work she might have got herself a coat, for this one had seen its day. Eighteen years it had been on the go, and it second-hand when she got it. She'd had her nine-and-six worth out of it, and many a proud moment it had given her, for hadn't it come from a big house and been worn by a lady? You only had to smell it to know that. But she never thought she'd wear it to go and see her daughter married a second time to a nigger. The humiliation weighed her down and caused her greetings to the step-washers in Dunstable Street to be even louder. And when she knocked at Bridget's door the satin of the coat was rippling and changing its greasy hue with her laughter.

The door was opened instantly, as if Bridget had been waiting for her knock, and Kathie was unable to keep up her laughter to cover her annoyance when Bridget, without a word, stepped into the street, and James, looking more massive and black than ever because of the stiffness of his body and the sombreness of his face, followed her. He, too, gave them no greeting; but locked the door; then, taking his place by Bridget's side, walked down the street, Kathie and Cavan following.

Kathie yelled at Cavan; she yelled to the step-cleaners again; she yelled to no one in particular; and some of her words, even to herself, were unintelligible.... To be turned back at the door like that; not to be asked in and given a drop of something to help things along a bit. God knew that at ordinary funerals and weddings you needed something; and this was no ordinary wedding; yet not a drop of anything. What were things coming to, anyway . . .

The church was empty when they arrived, and self-consciously they filed into the back seat after genuflecting towards the main altar; all except James, who did not bend even his head; nor did he follow the others' example and kneel down, but sat with his arms folded across his chest and his cheek-bones making tight the skin of his face with their pressure.

Presently an altar-boy, trying hard to cover his amusement, came with an order from the priest; and they rose and filed down the aisle to the altar-rails. They had barely reached them when Father O'Malley appeared on the other side, his face as stiff as his vestments. With a peremptory finger he motioned James and Bridget to kneel down. And so the service began.

The priest's voice was not even audible. There was a hurried guttural mumbling of words, the flicking over of leaves of the prayer-book, the passing from one hand to the other of a penny, then the flinging of the words at James, 'Will you have this woman to be your lawful wedded wife?'

James flung the responses back in a voice that made the priest start in spite of his grim control; but so low was Bridget's 'I will' that the priest accepted it without having actually heard it.

It was over, and Cavan and Kathie followed the couple to the vestry. Cavan's face was the colour of chalk and Kathie's so red as to appear on the verge of apoplexy.

Once the register was signed it was as if Father O'Malley couldn't get rid of them quickly enough. Scrambling up the aisle ahead of them, he led the way to the church door, and without a word watched them file past him into the street, his eyes, like rapier-points, piercing each one of them in turn. James was the last to leave, and the door was allowed to swing behind him, almost catching his heels.

'Of all the rotten holy Joes in this world, he's one!' Kathie could contain herself no longer. 'I hope he finds himself dead in his bed one of these mornings, and God forgive me for sayin' such a thing; but that's me curse.'

'Shut up!' Cavan's voice was deep and angry. He was hurt to the very soul with the indignities his daughter had brought upon herself. 'We've reached rock-bottom when you curse the priest; we've had enough bad luck; hold your tongue!'

'I'll not hold me tongue; one of these days I'll tell him me opinion of him to his face, and chance Hell's flames for it, ye'll see.' Kathie talked at her husband all the way to the fifteen streets; but she did not laugh; nor did she address her daughter or son-in-law; she allowed them to walk well on in front until they reached their own street, where they stopped and waited for her. Then all she said was 'I'll see ye later.' Her laughter had failed her.

Bridget and James entered their house in silence, and as Bridget made to go upstairs James pulled her to him and stared at her fixedly; and Bridget was hurt by the look on the usually laughing face of her husband. Compassion for his bewilderment overcame her, and she laid her hand on his cheek. 'I'm sorry, James; it had to be done. Perhaps you'll understand later when you've had instructions.'

His face softened, and she was surprised at the relief she experienced with the sound of his voice; but for his answers at the altar-rails he had said no word to her since leaving the house; it was as if he were striving to keep the dignity he prized so much.

'Now you feel we married?'

She nodded dumbly.

'That's all right then.' He drew her into his arms and held her gently for a while in silence. Then holding her away from him, he smiled at her, saying, 'Now we can be happy; for two more days we can be happy. You sorry I'm sailing Monday, Rose?'

'Yes.'

'Truly?'

'Yes—yes.'

'You don't want me to leave you?'

'No.'

'You know I don't want leave you. I don't want leave you ever.' He sat down and drew her on to his knee and, taking off her hat, ran his hands over her hair. 'Most beautiful hair in the world. My Angela have hair like this.... Rose——' He buried his face between her breasts.

'Yes?'

'I want ask you something.... If German get my ship and I not come back, you not let her forget me ... you tell her about me?'

'Please, Jimmy, don't say that. Never fear, you'll be all right.'

She felt the strong conviction within herself that God would make her suffer all her life for her mistake, and that James would be immune from danger so that her punishment might be meted out to her. She repeated, 'Never fear.'

The broad sweep of his eyebrows lifted, showing more white to his eyes. 'Me?' I don't fear nothing or nobody—not for me I don't. But for you, yes. I won't tell no lies 'bout what I fear: two men I fear for you, 'cause they both make you afraid. One is that goddam priest, and the other is ...' He stopped; then went on slowly, '... your brother. He like me worse than the others. When I am here he can't touch you, for he knows I would break him like that.' He clenched his huge fist until the knuckles showed pink beneath the black skin. 'But when I'm gone, you very afraid of Matt.' The last was a statement.

'No—no I'm not—I won't be; he's all right.' She avoided his eyes and screwed nervously at the bottom of his waistcoat.

'No lie, Rose. Your brother mad because you marry black man—your brother like you very much. Me, I know. Your mother, da and others all right, but Matt ... he black inside. Me, I know men. From twelve years I work with men—all kinds of men—down stokehold. Eight years I been in same ship, and the Chief he say to me, "New bunch this trip, Jimmie. What you make of them?" The Chief, he think lot of me. I would have been his donkey-man many times over but for this.' He tapped the skin of his hand. 'Chief ask my opinion of men, not 'cause he don't know men. He big Geordie fellow. But he like talk with me, and he know I know men.... Oh! you no cry, Rose. Please you no cry.'

She leant against him and her sobs mounted; and he beseeched her, 'You no cry. Me, I am sorry, Rose; but I am full of fear for you—don't—don't. Why you cry so?'

She continued to sob and he swung her up into his arms; and as he rose to his feet with her she gasped out, 'Don't go, James; don't go away.'

'I got to go, honey, you know that.' He smiled down on her. 'But I mighty glad you don't want me go. And you no worry any more; I see that brother and I fix him 'fore I go. We go upstairs now, eh? And you put on pretty dress and new hat with feather, and we go out and make everybody look at my Rose, and fellas turn and say, "Him lucky fella ... him marry twice same girl." '

He smiled down on her; then opened the stair door with his foot and walked sideways up the stairs, hugging her closer to him.

CHAPTER THREE

MATT

James had been gone three days and Bridget was feeling strangely lonely. After the first flush of relief she began to miss him and his deep broken speech telling her how wonderful she was; she missed the feeling of strength and protection he gave her; she missed him at night, and this caused her to feel wicked. In the night she lay tossing and turning, fighting the feeling of wanting him; in the night she never thought of him as black, for the night made all colour one. It was in the daytime, going about the work of the house, that the barrier of his colour would loom up and terrify her. She knew that in marrying James she had committed a sort of outrage, and that this had lifted her in one sweep off the plane of her people; but it had not dropped her on to the plane of James's people; it left her in a no-man's-land where, as far as she could see, there was only herself.

As hour added to hour, she felt less inclined to leave her house, for she knew she was vulnerable to the hostile looks of the men and women of the fifteen streets, and for once she felt thankful and glad that the war was on, for in the excitement and sudden rush of prosperity they would, she thought, have less time to give to the scandal she had created; not that they would miss taking some action should the worst among them give tongue. So, for the time, she stayed within the precincts of her own four small rooms, and some part of her was rested with their sanctuary.

That she must soon face the people and even work among them she knew, for James's monthly half-pay note of two pounds fifteen shillings would scarcely keep her for four weeks and pay the rent, coals and light, which came to eight shillings a week. Then there were the instalments of five shillings per week to pay on the furniture. Although James had provided for this by leaving with her the remainder of his fortune, fifteen pounds, she had the desire not to touch a penny of what was to her a vast sum, but rather to add to it. She knew that he must have spent a great part of his earnings on women and drink, but the habit, started by the missionary, of saving a little of his earnings had stuck, and not a penny James had put into the Post Office in eighteen years had he withdrawn; until he met her. Thirty-five pounds he had saved, and the feeling of the growing wealth, Bridget felt, had in no small way added to the dignity he so greatly prized.

Only once during the past three days had Bridget visited her mother, for Matt was on night shift and she was afraid of encountering him without the shield of James. She sat now beneath the gas mantle that sported a pink porcelain shade, sewing at a minute flannel petticoat. Her expression was a mixture of tenderness and apprehension, and unconsciously her lips moved as she repeated the prayer that was never long out of her mind; and now it was almost audible; and as she murmured 'Please God, make it all right!' the knocker of the front door banged once, and after a moment's hesitation she rose slowly and laid the petticoat on the table; then stiffening her body she went through the front room and opened the door.

Her relief made her exclaim in an unnaturally high-pitched voice, 'Why, Tony! Come in ... I'd been wondering when you were coming.'

Tony limped over the step and into the dark room, and Bridget, her hand on his shoulder, guided him to the kitchen. 'Come and sit down; have you had your tea?' She pulled a highly varnished wooden chair towards the glowing fire.

'Yes.' He sat down without taking his eyes from her face.

She sat opposite to him and for a while they smiled at each other. Then she said awkwardly, 'It's funny me having a house, isn't it?'

He nodded, and the broken peak of his cap jerked further down his brow. He pushed it up and continued to stare at her.

'Do you like it?' She made a small motion with her hand around the room.

Reluctantly he took his eyes from her face, and screwed round on his chair to take it all in. 'Eeh, it's fine, Bridget.' Stretching out his hand he shyly touched the fringe of the green chenille cloth covering the table. 'It's lovely!'

'Come on, I'll light the gas and show you the front room.'

She ran from him, and he followed more slowly, his grey eyes wide with wonder, for she appeared to him now like the girl he saw when he first came to their house.

In the front room she pulled down the new cream paper blind, with its edging of imitation lace, and lit the gas. Tony looked from one piece to the other of the suite: four single chairs, two armchairs and a couch, each one defying comfort with its stiff back and red plush seat. He looked at the bouquets of flowers forming large diamonds on the linoleum; at the plant-stand before the window, holding a fuchsia which was actually in flower; then at the mantel border, an elaborate piece of black satin on which were pen-painted three large and unreal birds, and there was genuine admiration in his voice and in his eyes when he said, 'I've never seen anything like it, Bridget; it's beautiful.'

'Come on upstairs.' She was as eager as a child. 'Wait until you see the dressing-table.'

On the way upstairs he stopped and touched the corded stair-carpet with his hands; but his wonder was suddenly covered with embarrassment when he entered the bedroom. He had to walk close to the great iron and brass bedstead to get to the dressing-table, and as he did so he realised for the first time that Bridget was no longer the Bridget of the McQueens' laughter-filled kitchen; she was married ... she was a married woman, and she was married to a nigger.

'Look,' Bridget was saying, 'it has three mirrors, and the two side ones swing back and forward—like this. Have you ever seen anything like it?' And when he made no answer, Bridget turned to him and looked down on his lowered eyes, and his embarrassment reached her.

They went down the stairs in silence, and now Tony knew that in some way Bridget was aware of what he was thinking, and there was an agitation in him to reassure her. Bridget mustn't be hurt—she mustn't think he was like the others. He said suddenly, 'I like Jimmy—I like him better than anyone I know.'

She smiled sadly, and his heart twisted inside him as he saw the wet mist cover her eyes.

He began to talk with unusual rapidity. 'I've got a job, Bridget ... I'm starting at Crawley's grocer's shop the morrer—I'm going in the back first, weighing up spuds and flour. He's giving me five shillings a week, and I'll soon get a rise if I do all right, he says. I would have got more if I'd been able to go out with the orders, but it's me ... Anyway, I'll soon be serving in the shop. I'm glad the war's on; I wouldn't have got it if the war hadn't been on.'

'Oh, I'm glad for you, Tony—oh, I am!' Bridget was mashing the tea. 'We'll have a cup of tea ... you'd like a cup, wouldn't you?'

'Yes, Bridget. Yer ma's going to get me a pair of long trousers ... new ones ... as soon as I get a pay.'

'Oh, that'll be grand.'

'I'm dying to get into long trousers.... Bridget, you know in six years and ten months I'll be twenty-one; and you'll be twenty-six. You'll only be five years older than me then.'

She turned to him, puzzled and wondering at the odd turn of his thoughts. 'But I'm five years older than you now—I'll always be five years older than you.'

'Yes, yes, I know'—he wrung his cap between his hands —'but I'll be grown up then ... I'll be able to do things

39

... if people ...' He took his gaze from her, and his dark lashes cast a long shadow on to his thin, pale face, giving to it an almost girlish delicacy.

Bridget, looking at his bent head, read his unfinished words wrongly. 'Nobody will ever say anything about you, Tony—your limp isn't really noticeable, and you're growing now. Why, you are nearly as tall as me. And, you know, you're nice-looking—yes you are.'

As he gave an impatient shake with his body, saying, 'Oh, it wasn't that,' Bridget exclaimed, 'Hush a minute!' and they both stood listening to the rattling of the backyard door-latch.

'Is it locked? Will I go and open it?' he asked.

'No; drink your tea.'

He drank it, standing near the table, his eyes watching her listening as she moved about the kitchen. When the front door-knocker banged he put down his cup and asked, 'Will I go home, Bridget?'

She answered him on her way to the door, 'Yes, Tony, you'd better; but come again—come often.'

Matt stood on the pavement, the distant light of the street lamp emphasising the piercing blackness of his eyes. He did not even glance at Tony sidling past him, but stepped into the room and closed the door.

With the first sight of him Bridget had returned to the kitchen, where she now stood, staring down into the fire, her hands gripping the brass rod. She waited for him to speak until she could wait no longer, and she turned to where he stood just within the kitchen door, surveying her.

'You needn't think you're coming round here to frighten me, our Matt, because you're not.... James told you—I know he told you what would happen if you did anything.' Her voice trembled with the fear she denied, and she went on, throwing her words at him, 'You always wanted everything your own way—well, you can't run my life. I would never have left home if it hadn't been for you.' She had said all the things she had told herself she wouldn't say.

'Why did you do it?' Each word was thin and had a piercing quality that cut deep into her.

She shivered, but rapped out, 'That's my business.'

'You were drunk, weren't you?'

Her bust and shoulders lifted in an attempt at denial, but no words came. Their eyes fought each other's; then her head drooped and she flung round to the fire again.

'I warned you, didn't I, to keep off it ... I always told you it made you a sloppy, dribbling sot. You can't carry it ... I told you, you bloody young fool.' Every syllable dripped with his contempt of her.

'Well, you nor nobody else will have to pay for my mistake.' Her head was resting on the rod now, and her voice was flat and quiet.

'Won't we?' He took three rapid steps forward which brought him to the table. 'We're just the laughing-stock of the streets, that's all! Our street was raised yesterday, with Cissie Luck making that fat swine of hers stand aside to let her into her front door; he put his toe in her backside and she screamed up the street, "Now me next bairn'll be khaki."'

Bridget winced as if in physical pain; and Matt went on, 'And then Pat Skinner linked with his seedless piece when they were passing the corner, and the chaps nearly cracked their sides with laughing. They were yelling, "Give her the Paterson touch, lad" ... Nobody paying for your mistake!' He spat past her into the fire. 'By God! We're all paying for it, every damned one of us? And let me tell you this—we've only just started. As for you, you can thank your lucky stars there's a war on. If there hadn't been, they would have hounded you out of the place; and they'll likely do it yet. Some of the men in the Barium were throwing their quips at Terry yesterday; they were saying why should black swines have the houses when they've got to travel across the water each day.'

He was standing behind her now and the gusts of his breath were on her neck: 'Do you know what me ma heard that Dorrie Clark say? Do you?'

Bridget remained silent and still.

'She was spouting in the shop that you should be sent down to Holborn, among the Arabs. And do you know what the others said—that the Arabs wouldn't allow a dirty nigger among them.'

Bridget swung round on him, almost knocking him over. 'Shut up you, shut up! Don't you dare call him a dirty nigger. He's better than you or any of them around these doors—he's too good for me. Yes he is, yes he is.' She was screaming now. 'He knows how to treat a woman, that's more than the men here do. If they bring in their wages they think they're gods, and the women have to wait on them hand and foot from the day they marry them; and even when they are giving them bairns and wearing them out they are pawing at whoever will let them. They've got room to talk—they have, the men around here! And the women too, for that matter—dirty-mouthed lot.'

'At least they have white bairns.' As always when he had succeeded in arousing her anger, his own subsided. He spoke quietly now, but his mild barbed words had more effect on her than had his rage.

Bridget put her hand up to her throat and tore at it; and moved her head from side to side as if trying to free herself from some fearsome grip. Matt saw the colour drain from her face; and when she staggered and groped for a chair, he stood watching her, fighting the torrent of feeling that was pouring back into his veins now that they were together again, and as she slid from the chair on to the floor he sprang to catch her, crying, 'Bridget! ... here, Bridget! ... what's up?'

For a few minutes she lay lifeless on the mat, while he gripped her bloodless face, still entreating, 'Bridget; here, come on—what's up with you?'

It was strange, but never before had he seen a woman in a faint; women of his knowledge didn't faint, even when carrying bairns. So he kept calling to her, and when at last she opened her eyes his voice was soft with his anxiety. 'Brid, what's up? Are you all right? Can I get you something? Have you anything in the house—a drop of anything?'

The shake of her head was almost imperceivable.

'Come on, get up.' He lifted her into a chair and supported her with his arm, and she pointed weakly to the tea-pot, saying, 'Give me a drink.'

The tea did nothing to revive her, and he stood over her, his voice harsh again, yet threaded with his anxiety. 'You take the damn stuff when you shouldn't, yet when you need it you haven't got any. Will you be all right till I go and fetch you something?'

'I don't want anything.'

The weakness of her voice only strengthened his determination. 'You've got to have something to pull you round. I won't be a minute. Lie on the mat if you feel bad again.'

He was gone and she was left alone. The fear of him, too, was gone: it was ousted by the fear he had brought to the surface, the fear that she would have a black baby. Her mind was sick and her body shivering with the fear ... and all because she had got drunk.

She had known Matt knew how she had come to marry James and would make her admit it. The twice he had seen her drunk was at New Year parties. The first time, when she was seventeen, she only took two glasses of whisky, but those were enough to make her throw her arms around Len Bryant and kiss him in front of everyone. She could never remember doing it, as she disliked Len Bryant because he was always trying to touch her, and she wouldn't believe Matt; but she believed her father when he told her.

It was the following New Year's Eve before she again touched whisky ... her previous reaction to it having faded from her mind. She only knew that the smell of whisky held a fascination for her, and she liked the cutting taste, and in spite of—or perhaps because of—Matt's scowling eye she took a proffered glass. This time she lifted up her skirts and danced, and Frankie Flanagan, whose house the party was in, lifted her on to the table ... and his wife punched him in the face; and she herself had been slapped sober in the wash-house by Matt.

It was after this she swore to herself never to touch whisky again, for she knew she couldn't carry it. But looking back now she saw that the chain of circumstances that led to her next being drunk could not have been foreseen by even the most wary of individuals; for who would have thought getting friendly with another house-parlourmaid in London would have been the main link? This girl's sister had recently married a man who was managing a public house in Liverpool, and they had written asking her to work for them. Soon Bridget herself received a letter from her friend, with a glowing account of the highly paid jobs to be had in Liverpool; and it was no time at all until she found herself in such a daily post; and getting half as much money again as she had been receiving in London, but paying out much more than the half for an attic room above a stable attached to the public house; and it was the simplest thing in the world to grant the request of the sisters to help in the rush-time on a Saturday night; also the simplest thing to get merry in the back room afterwards with a few of the regular seafaring clients—the honour of being called into the back room being an inducement to the men to empty their pockets again at the end of the next trip. There she met James ... but she couldn't remember taking him to her room, she could only remember the horror of her awakening; and from then till now seemed but four hours instead of four months.

Her mind raked up again the humiliations that attended her marrying James; the scorn of her one-time friends; the order to get out by the supposedly outraged sister; the expressions on the faces of the many landladies; until she felt she could bear it no longer and that she must brave the shock that James would be to her people and go to them. She had imagined, too, that once inside the fifteen streets she would find a measure of peace and protection among her own kind; but when she thought this, the enormity of her crime in all its entirety had not been brought fully home to her ... it needed the return to her own class to do this.

'Here, drink this.'

She had not been aware of Matt's return. The smell of
the whisky from the glass held close to her face brought
her to herself, and she turned her head away, saying, 'I
don't want that.'

'Don't act the goat—here, get it down you!'

'I tell you I don't want it ... Matt, I don't want it!' She
gazed up at him pleadingly. 'I promised I wouldn't...'
She broke off and shook her head. 'I'll be all right; this'll
pass.'

Matt stood staring down at her, his lower lip pressed
out. Who had she promised? That dirty black swine? She
had promised him she wouldn't drink, had she! ... after
he had dropped her! Well, the nigger had got her
through drink; then, by God, it would be through drink
that he would lose her! He gripped the back of Bridget's
head; then, putting the glass to her lips, forced the whisky
between them.

CHAPTER FOUR

THE BIRTH

In such communities as that of the fifteen streets there is often found an outstanding personality, a personality that is respected for its self-sacrificing and good qualities, or one that is held in awe or fear for some power it is credited with possessing—mostly evil. Such a personality was Nellie Milligan. She was known as a fixer. Despairing women, realising that once again they had fallen, would immediately turn their thoughts to Nellie Milligan and wonder how the sovereign could be raised; but raise it they would, even to the extent of pawning every bit of bedding a pawnshop would accept, to enable them to pay for having the burden removed.

The days of the twelve or fifteen in a family were past; but to see up to half a dozen children with hungry eyes was more than enough for some of the women; so, ironically, many called God's blessing on Nellie Milligan, while here and there a woman, trailing out the remainder of her life only half alive, cursed the day she had seen her.

No one knew Nellie's age ... some of the old women said she was 'getting on' when they were young. She was known to possess various powers; she was a wart-charmer and she could also mix a concoction that would remove hair from the faces of women suffering 'the change'—that the new growth was stronger only called for a stronger potion; she was also known to possess powers which could overcome sterility; but these supposed powers she was chary of using. Apparently the most propitious time for using these powers was after she had fixed somebody; and

46

when, some years ago, Maisie Searle, who had never shown the sign of one during the ten years of her marriage, found she was carrying, and that after going to see Nellie who had just fixed Mrs. O'Leary of her ninth, Nellie's reputation was itself fixed, and both the priest and doctor were powerless against her.

Nellie never did anything straightforward ... all her jobs were surrounded by mystery. Even when she told the cards, it would be behind drawn blinds and before a coke fire, winter or summer; and all her fixing jobs were attended, at least on the patient's part, by drinking bottles of evil-smelling liquids. Most of the women did not mind this, as after drinking the prescribed doses they had little or no recollection of what followed.

It was rarely a woman went to Nellie with a first child; although sometimes a bride, finding herself flung into the maelstrom of life and seeing herself fast becoming like the child-weary women about her, would become fear-stricken; and she would pay Nellie a visit on the quiet.

Of all her jobs it was really only the first 'uns that brought Nellie any satisfaction; and nearly always she was cheated out of these. If it wasn't a young outraged husband threatening to strangle her for attempting to deprive him of the visible evidence of his manhood, it would be the older women themselves threatening to split on her if she did it. They would remain blind and dumb should she help one of them; but with a first, almost to a woman they would be against her. But none of them knew about Bridget Paterson. Nellie herself hadn't thought about it until a week ago, when she had been telling Kathie McQueen her cards ... and then with no intention of fixing it ... that had been Kathie's idea. Never before had she been called upon to do a job like this, not when the bairn was just on being born; and she wasn't quite easy in her mind about it.

She made her way now up and down various back lanes on her way to Dunstable Street. She was thankful that it was snowing, for other than a few stray children playing there was no one about ... but even if she were seen, who would dream she was going to fix a nine-months one. She reached Bridget's back door, and like a thin black shadow on the white snow she sidled up the yard and tapped on the kitchen door.

The door was opened with the utmost caution, and Kathie peered at the black-shawled figure standing in the yard. She held a warning finger to her lips before pulling the old woman over the threshold into the scullery.

'Not a sound above a whisper out of ye, for God's sake, Nellie.'

Nellie let the shawl fall from her head, to disclose an almost bald scalp, and she stared at Kathie with small, bird-like eyes, while her toothless jaws champed together as if she were munching something tough.

'Have ye got everything?'

The old woman nodded.

'Oh my God, I hope ye know what ye're doin'.'

The small figure bridled, and her jaws stopped their munching. 'Ye want it done? And anyway, is she the first I've tackled?'

'No; I know.'

'Are ye sure she's for havin' it away? She's late in the day in thinkin' about it.'

'Of course I am ... only she's too proud to say so. What do ye think she's been on the bottle these part months for? She's scared of the thing being black.'

'But I thought it wasn't due for two or three days yet?'

'So did I, but ye know what first ones are. I wouldn't have known she was even bad, but the boy Tony was here, and he came back and told me she had gone to bed. So I sent him straight to you.'

'Ye think it's near?'

'As near as makes no odds ... have ye got the stuff?'

'Aye.'

'But how'm I gonna get her to take it, all in a hurry an' all, like this?'

'I've bought a bit of horse-flesh.'

'Horse-flesh! What in the name of God for?'

48

'To burn ... there's nothing smells like burnt horse-flesh. Fry it in the frying pan till it burns and waff it up the stairs, then run up with the drink to her. She'll be so parched she'll gulp down anything. And by the way'—she knocked a drop off the end of her nose with the back of her hand—'it's a drink we'll be needing ourselves, to get through ... have you got owt?'

'I've got a wee drop of rum. But will the stuff knock her off?'

'Enough for me to do what I've got to do.'

'Ye won't use the crochet hook on her, Nellie? Ye won't hurt her?'

'I've told you before, there'll be no need ... it isn't an abortion you want.'

'And ye won't do owt to it, Nellie, if it's white, will ye?'

'No; but haven't I told ye? I saw it in your cards as plain as the nose on your face ... it's black it'll be, like night.'

'Aye.' Kathie rolled her head on her mountainous chins. 'Aye, ye did tell me, and I've never known a minute's rest since. And it won't look as if it had been ...?'

'Not a sign ... it'll be stillborn.'

'But if she knows it's you up there——' Kathie wrung the corner of her apron. 'She hasn't been near me since she saw us together a week past.'

'She'll not know a thing once she takes the stuff; and if she does, she'll think it's a doctor fiddling about with her.... Now come on and get me the pan.'

As Kathie watched Nellie bring a thick collop of horse-flesh from under her shawl she shuddered. 'God protect us! Where d'ye get it?'

'Never ye mind ... it'll cost ye a shilling.... And, Kathie'—the beady eyes closed still farther—'it's a pound, mind, when the job's done!'

'If it's dead.'

'It'll be dead all right.'

'But mind, not if it's white, mind, Nellie ... don't touch it if the colour's all right.'

As Nellie was about to place the pan on the fire she turned to Kathie, saying, 'Look, before I start: ye're sure she hasn't sent for the doctor, or the nurse or somebody? I've me name to think of, and it's late in the day.'

'How could she? I was round here within five minutes of the boy telling me. And she hardly knows what it's all about, anyway ... it's her first, isn't it? No, she couldn't have sent for anybody; and she's never been one for making neighbours, thank God for that! She's kept herself to herself for months now.'

The horse-steak sizzled on the hot pan, and Nellie stood silently watching it. For a moment the terrible cold menace of the shrivelled old woman was borne home to Kathie, and she had the urge to fling her out of the door; but the dread of being a grannie to a black bairn was too strong. So she, too, stood silent and waiting, until the stench began to fill the kitchen, forcing her to go to the back door. As her hand went to the latch Nellie's fingers, like cold steel, gripped her arm, and without a word she was drawn back into the kitchen again, choking and spluttering. And Kathie's fear of Nellie increased when she saw that the choking fumes were having little or no effect upon the old woman.

'Here, take the pan up on the landing and waff it about while I get the stuff ready.'

Kathie, her eyes streaming and her apron held across her mouth, took the pan and groped blindly for the stair door. Never before in her life had she smelt anything like this, and she had smelt some smells. God, why had she got herself into this? She crept up the stairs, the pan held at arm's length, but before she reached the top Bridget's voice came to her.

'What's that smell, Ma? What are you doing? Oh, what's that smell?'

'A bit of steak ... it dropped in the fire.' She coughed and spluttered. 'It'll be all right in a minute, I'm gonna open the window.'

Not being able to stand any more herself, she went hurriedly down the stairs again, and as she burst into the kitchen she let out a squeal like a trapped rabbit, for standing in front of Nellie, like some threatening giant, was Dr. Davidson. The pan tipped in her hand and the charred steak fell on to the mat.

'So it's you, is it?' The doctor's eyes struck fire at Kathie. 'Giving her a hand, are you? ... My God! Now listen to what I am saying.' His finger stabbed her in the chest. 'If anything goes wrong with that child up there, I'll see you both behind bars.'

For a moment Kathie was unable to utter a word, and her head rolled as if it would drop off her shoulders; then, sick with fright, she began to bluster. 'Behind bars, is it? And what, may I ask, am I goin' behind bars for ... for burning a bit of meat?'

'Burning a bit of meat...!' The doctor turned his attention to Nellie again. She had not uttered a syllable, but her eyes, stretched to their small wideness, had never left his face.

'You ... you fiend of hell! I've wanted to catch you red-handed for years. And now I've got you ... with your'—he coughed—'damned incantations.'

Still Nellie said no word; but her eyes slid to the table; his followed, and he said, 'I'll relieve you of that.'

His hand reached out to the unstoppered bottle, but, as quick as lightning strikes, Nellie was there before him. She grabbed up the medicine bottle; and whether by accident or design, Kathie, stooping in front of him to retrieve the steak, blocked his way; and Nellie, minus her shawl, escaped through the front room.

The doctor bestowed a look on Kathie that should have shrivelled her, but with relief filling her she faced him boldly. 'What's got into ye, Doctor, may I ask ye? What's got into ye?'

Doctor Davidson took a deep breath and almost choked. 'As long as something hasn't got into your daughter you'll be safe, Mrs. McQueen ... this time! But I'll see to it that your friend has killed her last child around these parts.'

He was forced to stop and cough into his handkerchief,

and Kathie, regaining her confidence and belligerence, broke in, 'What do you know about it all? ... You with your belly well fed. Nellie Milligan has saved many a poor soul from destruction around these doors. You and the priest between you are the ruination ... the priests keep on tellin' yer, ye must do yer duty as a wife, and ye do it, from sixteen to sixty; and yer belly's full of bairns every year. And who's to feed and clothe them, and pay the doctor? ... Aye, pay the doctor, eh? Nellie Milligan has been a godsend. I tell ye, to many a poor soul. Ye like bringing bairns into the world, because, given half the chance, ye cut them up so as ye can see their insides and try to find out where ye went wrong with the last one ye knocked off.... Oh, I know all yer tricks.'

Dr. Davidson stood surveying Kathie for a moment after she had finished. Then, between short coughs, he said, 'Well, if you've had your say, Mrs. McQueen, I'll go upstairs; but for your information I'll tell you that your daughter wants this baby, black or white. Perhaps you didn't know that?'

He left Kathie, her mouth half open and her hands on her hips, staring after him.

So the girl had suspected her mother was up to something, and rightly, too, Dr. Davidson thought as he mounted the stairs. Sending that strange, urgent little note to him, which told him nothing in the actual lines, but volumes between.

As he entered the bedroom, Bridget, in her nightdress, rose from the side of the bed, one arm hugging her waist. She showed evident relief at the sight of him, and said, 'I've got the pains, Doctor.'

'And what do you expect to have, eh?' He laughed as he placed his bag on the wash-stand.

'What's that dreadful smell, Doctor?'

'Oh, that.... Your mother's been doing some fancy cooking and tipped a steak into the fire.'

'A steak? ... But why should she?'

'Come; get into bed.'

As she slowly got back into bed he picked up a bottle

from the wash-stand and looked at it curiously. It was a bottle of disinfectant, and next to it were two neatly folded hand towels, while on a chair nearby stood a number of sheets and clothes; and before the fire in the small grate was a towel-rail with baby clothes arranged upon it. She certainly had everything ready. And disinfectant, too. He was surprised and pleased. The nearest they ever got to antiseptic in the fifteen streets was carbolic soap; and even the old hands rarely had everything ready and neat like this. Marrying that Negro had seemingly done her little harm. But hadn't he heard something about her taking to drink? Must have been idle rumour, for the house didn't look that of a drunk.

'You've got everything ready, I see,' he said, smiling down on her. 'And a very nice little place you've got here, too ... haven't seen better.' He knew she was pleased, and he continued to talk to her as he examined her. 'You've sent for Nurse Snell?'

'No, Doctor.'

'Oh, but you should have done. And, you know, you should have come and seen me before.... Who's going to look after you?'

'My mother.' Her tone did not reveal her fears, but she made no protest when he said, 'I think we'd better have the nurse, just for the first few days, eh?' He patted her shoulder, saying, 'It won't be long ... it nearly got here before me. How long have you had the pains?'

'Since early this morning.'

'Oh, you're going to be lucky, it's coming quick.... When is your husband due back?'

'Tonight or tomorrow.'

'Good ... good. Here, pull on that....' He tied a piece of sheeting to the bed-rail and left her gripping it while he went downstairs again, where, without any preamble, he said to Kathie, 'You know where Nurse Snell lives? Go and tell her I would like her to come along here at once. If she isn't in, leave word to that effect. And don't give the wrong message.'

'Nurse Snell, is it?' cried Kathie. 'Look ye here, Doctor,

if I want a nurse I'll get Dorrie Clark. In any case, I can do as good as either of them; and I don't charge seven and six or fifteen bob! I can see to me own daughter.'

'Yes, you very nearly did see to her! Now get yourself away this minute; if you're not gone on that errand before I reach the top of the stairs, I'll inform your daughter what the smell is she's so anxious about, and what her mother and Mrs. Milligan were up to.... Now what do you say?'

'Blast ye for an interfering swine! That's what I say.' Kathie snatched her shawl off the door. 'Don't think you'll frighten me ... you! ... nor a battalion like you. You and Father O'Malley would make a fine pair.'

God forbid, thought Dr. Davidson, as the door banged behind Kathie.

When he again entered the bedroom it was to find Bridget crying. 'Oh, come now. Come now,' he laughed, 'you'll forget all about the pains once the little nipper's here.'

Bridget shook her head. She could not tell him it wasn't the pain that was making her cry, but the dread of its result. For days now the child had lain comparatively quiet within her, and she had soothed herself by thinking that if it was black it would be full of vigour and life, and be making itself felt. Then despair would seize her, and she would imagine the baby's stillness was because it was black and content and good-tempered like James. But whatever she imagined its quiet movements to mean, she did not imagine the baby to be dying. Not for a moment did she want the movements to stop altogether and signify her release ... no, she wanted this child, as something that James might have for his own. But oh, Jesus, Jesus, she didn't want it to be black!

Soon the pains, gathering on themselves, formed a mountain that she must climb, and in the climbing there was no place for worry about colour. She was aware, as time went on, that the nurse was with the doctor, and when the child left her body all anxiety and worry flowed out with it. It was over. Whatever colour it was could not

54

be altered; she should have realised that from the very beginning. She had been silly to worry.

When she heard the doctor chuckling, a deep rounded chuckle, she thought, He's laughing because it's quaint; all black babies are quaint.

The baby was twenty-four hours old when James got in. He came in like a wind, a hot driving wind. Kathie cast startled eyes on him when he flung open the kitchen door, then turned her back to him; but Cavan rose from his seat by the fire and there was understanding and sympathy in his look. James, his eyes holding a depth of emotion and anxiety, uttered one deep-belled word, 'Well?'

'It's what you was wantin'.'

Before Cavan finished speaking, James pulled open the stair-door. He took the stairs in three leaps, but pulled up for an instant on the landing. It might be what he wanted, but was it what Rose wanted?

Bridget's eyes were closed when he neared the bed; he did not know whether she was asleep or not. Although his attention was riveted on the blanket-wrapped bundle lying on the far side of her, he stopped before going round the bed, and stooping, gently laid his face against hers. Because she made no movement whatever, he knew she was awake, but he said nothing, and going round to the other side he reverently picked up the bundle.

Through half-closed, sleepy lids, two brown eyes looked up at him, so like his own that a leaping, choking happiness that was almost an agony tore through him; but it was nothing to the ecstasy when the wonder was borne in on him that his child was white, with skin the colour of thick cream, and hair that was straight; it was as black as his own, but it was straight. The lids widened and the child gazed at him in fixed concentration, as if, he thought, she knew him. And when her hand wavered from the folds of the blanket and plucked at his finger his joy mounted, passing out of him and flying in thanksgiving to the God he was aware of, and to others dimly sensed. He raised his eyes to the ceiling and struggled to find words adequate to this feeling, but only one word came to his mind. He had first heard it outside the bars around the Liverpool docks, when, rain or shine, abused and laughed at, the Salvation Army had beaten its drums and tinkled its triangles in praise of God. He threw back his head and his voice resounded through the house, startling all but the child as he cried, 'Alleluia! Alleluia! Alleluia!'

PART TWO

CHAPTER FIVE

A MUCH-RESPECTED MAN

The fog-horn, blasting from a tug, seemed to carry its force through the grey drifts of mist right into the fore-castle without losing any of its strength. James, pulling the cord of his white sailor-bag tight, unconsciously screwed up his face in protest. There were few things he hated about the sea, but he hated the sound of the fog-horn; its melancholy note seemed to search out an answering chord within himself.

'You're not losing much time, Jimmy?' An old fireman, lying in his bunk, rolled on to his side and stared at the great black head level with his own.

'Not much time to lose.'

'Lucky for you we came to the Tyne to load this trip.'

'Yes, lucky for me.' James thumped his kit-bag on the floor to give him a better hold of the top, pulled his cap firmly down on his head, turned up the collar of his blue reefer jacket, then, thrusting the bag up the companion-way, climbed on to the deck with the voice of the old man shouting after him, 'Don't forget me, Jimmy, when your wife's givin' out that new bread, mind.'

The deck was abustle, the hatches were off, and the men, working by the light of naked gas jets run by piping from the jetty to the holds, were grabbing at the tubs from the swinging cranes and tipping the coal into the hatches as if the devil was after them.

The voice of the chief engineer spoke from out of the mist, 'Just off, Jimmy?'

'Yes, Chief.'

'Dirty night.'

'Yes, 'tis, Chief.' Jimmy turned towards the wavering outline of the engineer. 'If old man changes his mind, you let me know, Chief?'

'I will, Jimmy; but you know as well as me that it's no good. I told you what he said; and we are off as soon as she's loaded; he's been at the gaffer to stir those dock tykes up.'

'She out of breath with running, she catch her barnacles on the bottom one of these days. Good night, Chief.'

'Good night, Jimmy. Make good use of your time, and remember me to the nipper.'

Jimmy's smile wasn't evident to the engineer, but he could feel it in the voice as it came to him. 'I will. Sure I will, Chief. She always talks of the engineer-man; she never forgotten you bought her that doll, Chief ... and that near two years ago. Yes, I tell her 'bout you.'

The massive bulk of Jimmy was lost in the fog before he reached the gangway, but the chief continued to gaze in the direction he had taken. He felt uneasy in his mind about the man; he had done so for a long time now. At one time, Jimmy used to talk to him, especially about his white wife. At first, this association with a white woman had sickened him, but then he had asked himself why should it; Jimmy was a better man than some of the whites on the ship. Of course he was an exception, for most niggers made him sorry the old overseer's whip was out of fashion; but Jimmy was a good type, and there was no need to feel sorry for his wife. In any case, Jimmy was likely a damn sight too good for the type of woman who would marry a black man; any pity that was to be thrown about should go to him. Something had been wrong this long while, and it had to do with the wife, for he rarely spoke of her now; all his talk was about his child, his Rose Angela ... highfalutin name, that. She was an unusually bonny child. A pity, though, there was evidence of the tarbrush in her. The Chief stood for a moment longer looking in the direction James had taken; then, shaking his head, he turned towards his cabin to take comfort in his bottle. What could you expect, anyway? The sins of the fathers left their mark ... or was it the mother in this case? ...

As James passed the dock-policeman's little stone office by the side of the main gates the policeman on duty peered at him. 'Oh, hullo there, Jimmy. Why couldn't you bring better weather with you? In for long?'

'All the weather they would give me, boss,' James laughed. 'No, it tip, fill and run trip ... same as ever.'

'Good night, Jimmy.'

'Good night, boss.' He squeezed sideways through the small door in the gate and sprang across the road to the Jarrow tram and threw his bag on to the platform just as the tram moved off. He pushed the bag under the stairs and stood on the platform until the conductor said, 'Inside; there's a seat there.'

James took the seat—the corner one next to the door.

He gave a greeting to an old woman sitting opposite, who smiled at him, saying, 'You got back again then, Jimmy?' And he was about to answer her when the evident recoil of a young woman at his side froze his reply. He became still inside as he realised she was withdrawing her skirt from contact with him by tucking it under her hip. Slowly he turned and looked at her, but her eyes were staring straight ahead.

The old woman again spoke, her voice, loud and strident, filling the tram. 'Ye've just missed the Victory teas, Jimmy ... they've had 'em in nearly all the fifteen streets. Eeh! they've had some do's ... tables the length of the street, and the stuff to eat you wouldn't believe. And sports for the bairns; an' dancin'.' She rattled on, but James was not listening to her; he was conscious only of the inch of brown wooden lathe that separated his clothes from the girl's. It was many years since an incident like this had happened to him. He liked to think that the war had wiped all this feeling away, in England anyway, and he wanted to turn to the girl and say, 'I'm a steady, sober man, miss. I've worked to be respected, and I am respected. The people hereabouts know me and like me ...

59

you should have heard how dock pollis spoke to me, same as white man. And on my ship they call me Lucky Jim. I have a wife and a child, and money in bank. I do nothing bad ... I keep my dignity ... I'm much respected man.'

But he said nothing to the girl, he just sat staring, like her, ahead, reassuring himself that he was a ... much-respected man, and a very lucky man. Any man who had a daughter like his Rose Angela was a lucky man, wasn't he? And Rose, wasn't he lucky to have Rose? He refused to answer himself this question, but instead asked, 'How she be this time, I wonder? Will she be in temper or crying fit to burst?'

The thought of his wife overshadowed for the time the hurt he was feeling, and as the tram jogged along he sat brooding, as always now when his thoughts touched on Bridget. What was wrong with his Rose? What had come over her? It started right back before the child was born. His home-comings then found her irritable, but he excused that because the child was heavy on her. But after it was born she became worse; and once, looking at her unusually puffed face, he said seriously, 'Rose, you drinking!' Her fury had silenced further accusation, and for a time he believed his guess was wrong, until his reason told him he had seen the results of drink on too many women not to know that she was drinking, and drinking heavily. But what he could not make out was why she never took it when he was home. The longest he had been home during the past four years was a fortnight, and he remembered it as a period of stress. He also remembered her passionate crying when he was leaving, her begging him not to go—to get a shore job. But he needed the sea, and, what was more, the war was on, and the sea needed him. But now the war was over, and, big as the wrench would be, he was going to look for a shore job. He had tried to tell the chief during this trip, yet somehow he had been unable to bring himself to it; but next trip would be his last, he had made up his mind. This docking for only twenty-four hours had decided him; he'd thought they'd be in for at least a week, as the old tub needed her bottom scraping.

At the corner of the fifteen streets he rose from his seat, and he looked once more at the girl. And this time she returned his look, and the hostility in her eyes hurt him. She would have a separate tram-car for coloured people, he thought, as they did in some countries. And he wondered, as he had often done before, why one adverse look could outweigh, even totally obliterate for a time, the acceptance of the majority.

The old woman, lumbering off the tram, called, 'You'll be glad of something inside you a night like this, comin' off the water an' all ... Bridget'll have the old broth pan goin', I bet.'

'She don't know me coming; but all the same she have broth pan going. Good night.'

'Good night, Jimmy.'

He strode along the main road towards his own street, his mind heavy with the feeling of uncertainty now that he was nearing home. How would she look at him? If only that soft light of old would be in her eyes. She was sorry she had married him ... he knew that ... and yet she wanted him ... he knew that too. Life could be heaven, and life could be hell; but it had been mostly hell lately. He shifted his bag from one shoulder to the other, stiffening his back in the process.

He was nearing his door when the thick silence of the street was split by laughter, loud, high laughter that checked his step. It was Rose's laugh, but he had only once before heard her laugh in such a way—that night in the back room of the bar in Liverpool. He did not knock on the door, but stood listening, and he knew she was drunk again and that she wasn't alone. He became still; no anger filled him, only a questioning, and he began to reason with himself quietly, Now you find out ... now you know what it all about ... take things quietly ... go round back: she not drinking alone. This thing happen before to other men ... why you think it not happen to you? Into the stillness within him bored a pain, twisting the muscles of his chest. Not Rose ... she not bad. He

61

wiped the moisture from his face with his hand. You go find out. You don't be fool. You soft you know in some way ... you been clarts where Rose concerned, she got you on a string, she know it. No ... you no knock—it was as if something stayed his hand—you go clear this thing up. Gone on long enough it has. You don't know what matter with her half the time. You not coward 'bout other things, don't be coward 'bout this.

When he left the door, Rose's laugh followed him; it seemed to add weight to his legs, slowing his steps as he went round the bottom corner and up the back lane. Gently he tried the latch of the back door and found it locked, so, placing his hands on the top of the wall, he drew himself up and over, and, softly withdrawing the bolt, lifted his bag into the yard; then he re-bolted the door again.

Now, inside the yard and only a few feet from Rose and whoever was with her, the reasoning stillness was deserting him, and his muscles were knotting themselves. For a moment he hated Rose for being the cause of this undignified creeping up his own back yard.

When he reached the kitchen window her voice came to him, thick and fuddled, 'We'll have a tune—Sister Susie —eh?'

James bent down and put his head level with the bottom of the blind. He could see nothing, but the slow wail of a man's voice came to him:

> 'Pad-dy wrote a letter
> To his Irish Molly-oh,
> Saying if you don't receive
> Please write and let me know.'

Into the wailing broke a voice which brought James upright; it was saying, 'That's Tipperary, you fool! It's on the other side. Wind the damn thing up, and empty that glass.'

Before the last word died away James had thrust open the door and was in the kitchen. Bridget, her mouth open and moving in a vain effort to voice her surprise, was leaning back against the dresser, and the glass half full of whisky she held in her hand was spilling in a steady trickle to the floor. Matt, who had been in the act of pouring some beer from a tin can, placed the can on the table with an abruptness that caused the froth to shoot up in a spray and cover his waistcoat.

In one sweeping glance James took in every detail of the kitchen: the untidy hearth with the ashes filling the pan, the dirty dishes on the table, Rose Angela's clothes lying in a heap by the side of the fireplace, and the order of drinking. There was one beer glass and one whisky glass, and Matt had the beer glass. A hot fury swept through James, opening his pores and bringing the sweat in large greasy beads on to his face! Here was the answer to all his bewilderment ... Matt! Matt, who had always hated him for marrying his sister. Here was the explanation for the mirthless sneer in Matt's eyes.

Matt and he met seldom, but when they did the sneer was there, not only in his eyes but in the curl of his lip. Never had James encountered Matt in the house before, all their previous meetings having taken place in the McQueens' kitchen; but here was a man, James saw, who was very much at home, so much so that he himself was the intruder.

Matt, kicking his chair to one side, backed towards the little dresser, and his eyes, black with hate, never left James's face. James, throwing up his head, sniffed loudly in an unconscious primitive gesture, then, tearing off his coat, he cried, 'You not try get away; we settle this in yard. You pay for this, you dirty louse!'

'Jimmy, no! ... look, I'll tell you.' Bridget thrust out a wavering arm to him, but it was knocked to one side as Matt's hand flung back to grab at a knife lying on the dresser top.

'Who's trying to get away?' As Matt brought the knife forward Bridget screamed, and James, with a lightning stroke, swung up the flat iron that was standing on the pan hob and whirled it across the narrow space, just missing Matt's hand but striking the blade of the knife and sending it spinning into the air. Bridget screamed again; and she clasped her hands over her face as the knife scattered dishes to the floor. With a shove of his hand James thrust the table aside, and Matt and he were facing each other.

Matt's mouth was square, and his venom was ground from beneath his clenched teeth. 'You black swab! Why couldn't you stick to your own breed? You took her when she was drunk; well, you can have her now. She's so whisky-mad that you nor nobody else can stop her. So come on!'

James's fist almost covered Matt's face as it struck him, sending him crashing back against the dresser. His strength could have finished off any ordinary man with a single blow, but Matt was no ordinary man. He was possessed of a hate for the black man that gave him the tearing power of a lion. With a shake of his head he recovered from the blow and bore right into James, bringing both his fists and feet into play.

The gramophone and the little table on which it stood were whipped into the hearth, sending the pan off the hob in their flight. The soup spluttered into the fire and a shower of ash and steam filled the kitchen, and Bridget's screaming mingled with the hissing. She wrenched open the kitchen door and yelled, 'Help! ... My God! Help, somebody ... help!' She turned, still screaming, and saw Matt and James locked together as if in a passionate embrace: then she saw James free himself with a heave from Matt's entwined arms, and with one hand thrust him away and with the other deliver a blow under the chin that lifted him from the floor and sent him crashing on to the fender.

Bridget's world became very still; in the kitchen, in the yard, and all beyond there was no movement; the only sound was James's heavy breathing. She stared from the doorway in petrified horror at the still, limp figure of Matt, with the long gash in his cheek and the blood gushing from his temple. She lifted her eyes to James. His face seemed no longer black, but grey, and he was standing motionless, staring down at Matt. She moved slowly towards him and stood by his side. 'My God! What've you done? ... Oh, Holy Mary!'

He said nothing; and she stooped and touched Matt's wrist, and, with her hand still holding her brother's, turned her face up to her husband and whispered a terrified whisper.

She dropped Matt's hand; and as she stood looking at James with a startled look as if she had never seen him before, the stair-door opened and a voice whimpered, 'Ma.' She did not look at her child, but spoke her thoughts as they came to her. 'They'll hang him ... it was my fault, but they'll hang him ... Oh my God, what have I done?'

James did not move or answer her, but he screwed his head slowly round and looked at his daughter. She was crying and biting her knuckles, and, as a tiny smile for him broke through her tears, a fear never before experienced swept over him ... If Matt was dead, then he, too, would soon be dead, and never again would he see his Rose Angela, nor she him.

As a curl of fog came into the kitchen, seeming to bear on its grey tendrils the enquiring cries from the back lane, James shook himself, first his head and then his shoulders ... they'd hang him for sure ... no black man could hope to get off after killing a white; he'd seen the result of that more than once. It would be no use telling them he hadn't meant to kill Matt, that he didn't kill him, it was the corner of the steel fender that had done it ... it would be no use talking at all; there was one justice for the white and one for the black. He was no fool, he told himself; all his steady living would be forgotten in the face of the crime he would have to answer for. But he didn't want to die. He lifted his head, listening now to the yelling from the back lane:

'Are you all right, Bridget? What's up? Open the door there. Come on there, open up!'

If they once got hold of him there'd be no escape, he'd

die all right. But he wasn't going to die, he'd get away. If he could reach the ship he'd be all right—yes, that was the way out. He must get to the ship and see the chief. He wouldn't be the first the chief had got across the water. The chief held his own ideas on justice. The thumping on the back door told him that the time he had to accomplish this was very limited. He grabbed up his coat from the floor, but stopped in the act of thrusting his arms into it; if he went now there would be no return, he would never see his Rose Angela again. He looked from her to Rose, and at this moment there was in him no feeling but bitterness for his wife. She had brought him to this, to running away, to hiding for the rest of his life, and to separating him from his daughter. Even if he lived he might never see his child again. Suddenly he knew that this would be unbearable. He could suffer anything but to be separated for ever from his child. Where he went, the child must go, for she was all his; Rose did not need her as he did. Intuitively he knew that Rose resented the knowledge that their child held more of him than her, despite its looks to the contrary.

Bridget, shocked into soberness, watched her husband stoop towards Rose Angela. She knew that his intention was to escape, and she thought he was about to embrace the child. Even when he swung her up and into the shelter of his coat she did not for one moment imagine he would attempt to take her with him. Only when, clutching Rose Angela to him, he ran through the front room did it dawn on her, and then she screamed louder than she had done before, 'No, James! ... Jimmy! Jimmy! No! Don't ... leave her be.'

When she reached the front door there was no sign of James, and she stood on the road with the fog swirling round her, crying like a child herself. 'Jimmy, come back ... bring her back ... bring her back.'

Once clear of the streets and running along the main road, James's mind began to work, planning out a way to evade the pursuers he knew would soon be following him.

In between his planning he soothed the child, saying, 'You no cry, you with your da; you all right.' He would make straight for the ship, for they wouldn't expect him to be mad enough to go back to her. But he couldn't get to her through the dock gates, so he would have to enter the docks by way of the river. This would be no easy task in the fog, but if there was a sculler lying at the slipway, he'd chance it. If there wasn't, he'd climb the sawmill wall and thread his way to the jetty where his ship lay. Of the two ways, he preferred taking the sculler and running the risk of being rammed, for if he went by the wall he might be spotted by someone inside the docks.

Rose Angela was crying again, her cries jerking out of her with his running, and as he spoke to her a voice shouted through the fog, 'Why, Jimmy, is that you? Is that you, Jimmy? What's up?'

Although he recognised the voice, he did not stop, not even when he heard the uneven hop of Tony's run following him. But coming to the slipway, he paused and listened. There was no sound other than his own harsh breathing and the quiet whimpering of the child, so he judged that Tony had gone back to the fifteen streets; and as he ran down the narrow path leading to the water he felt a regret that he had not given Tony some last word, for he knew that the lad's liking for him was sincere.

There was no sculler tied to the wall at either side of the narrow slipway. He splashed frantically through the rim of the tide, feeling for one, but his hand encountered only the iron ring in the wall, and he cursed. There was nothing for it now but to climb the sawmill wall. Running up the path to the road again, he went more carefully, keeping to the grass verge to deaden his steps. Rose Angela was quiet now, as if asleep, and as he left the lane and came into the main road again the pale blur of the gas lamp showed him the slight figure of Tony. He knew it was him before he heard the voice asking again, 'Is that you, Jimmy?'

'Yes, it's me?'

'What on earth's up?'

Between deep gulps of air James answered, 'I row with Matt. He dead. I got to get away, Tony.'

'Matt dead? My God!'

'I no mean to do it, Tony.'

'But, Jimmy, why've you got the bairn with you?'

'I take her with me ... she mine.'

'You can't do that, man.'

'Yes, she go with me ... she all mine.'

'But, Jimmy, what about Bridget?'

'Sh!'

They both stood silent, listening. The sound of pounding feet and shouting came through the fog, and James started to run again, with Tony hopping unevenly by his side.

'I get over sawmill wall to my ship.'

'You're mad, man, you'll never be able to get over that wall with the bairn. They'll be on you before you can do it.'

'You hand her to me ... yes, you do that.'

'Listen, man, can't you hear them?'

James could hear them, and the voices were almost paralysing his legs. His body was wet with sweat, yet he was cold with the fear that penetrated to the core of him. He had seen black men collared before by angry whites.

'Jimmy, for God's sake don't get caught! If you keep running, they'll get you—if not here, at the docks. Look, I can't keep up ... Jimmy, look, it's your last chance.' Tony grabbed at his arm. 'Drop down here beside the slack bank and let them get by, then you can make your way to the sawmill wall keeping under cover of the bank.'

Whether it was Tony's reasoning or his own fear that made him follow the boy's advice James didn't know, but he dropped down the bank and lay on his side, pressed close to the wet seaweed-tangled grass, with Tony lying alongside him and the child lying as still as death between them. James pressed Rose Angela's face close to his own, but she made no sound, seeming to know that his life depended on her silence.

The men were passing them now, calling to each other as they ran:

'The dock pollis will nab him.'

'The trams and roads'll be watched.'

'They'll get him. The bairn will be the finish of him, anyway, the black swine!'

The black swine.... James stared into the chilling darkness. It didn't take long for a black man to jump from a damn good sort to a black swine ... you were given no benefit of the doubt if you were a black man.

'You see? You can't go on the road, Jimmy. There'll likely be more coming as it gets round the streets. You'll have to keep under cover of the bank and get into the sawmill yard from the gut side; and you'll have to plodge into the mud and water for a way.'

James made no answer. He knew that Tony was right, and that that was the only means of escape now. But he could only get that way on his own; it would be impossible to take the child. He pressed her closer to him, and Tony, guessing his thoughts, whispered urgently, 'Jimmy, man, you can't take her. And anyway, you could never keep her on the ship, can't you see? Get away while the going's good. Go on, man, for God's sake don't let them catch you! Matt's not worth swinging for ... he's bad, right through. I've been wanting to tell you for some time what he was doin', but I couldn't.'

After a space, during which only the lapping of the water could be heard, James's strangled whisper came through the grass to Tony. 'No comin' back, Tony—if I go without her, she forget me.'

'No she won't, Jimmy ... I won't let her. I promise you, man. I'll tell her what a fine fellow you are. I promise on my oath, Jimmy. And when she's older perhaps there'll be some way of her comin' to you.... I won't let her forget you, Jimmy, I won't, only for God's sake get away.'

As fresh footsteps passed above them Tony felt the quivering of James's body. He put his arms about the child and drew her from James's clinging hands. 'She'll be all right, Jimmy, as God's my honour. I'll see to her.'

'I come back, Tony ... some time I come back.'

'All right, Jimmy, only go on now ... hurry, man.'

As James's hand moved over his child's head Tony knew he was crying, and as he felt the Negro's hand pressing for a moment on his cap he turned his face into the grass to stifle his own emotion.

It was Rose Angela's whimpering, 'Da! I want me da,' that brought Tony up the bank and on to the road.

Not wishing to encounter anyone from the fifteen streets, he walked on the pathless side of the road, and in this way he brought Rose Angela home without being stopped.

There was a crowd around Bridget's door, silent, weird, misshapen bulks, all so intent on watching the stretcher being carried from the house to the vehicle standing in the road that they took no notice of Tony and the child. The sight of the workhouse ambulance puzzled him ... why were they taking Matt away? Would they bring the ambulance just to take him to his mother's to be laid out? He felt not the slightest touch of sorrow for Matt being dead. In fact, as he made his way to the back door, he knew a great surge of relief that Matt would no longer be Bridget's evil genie.

When he entered the yard Kathie's shouting came to him. 'He'll swing, what's left of him when Sam Luck and the lads get hold of him; they'll leave the print of their hobnails on his face, God speed them, the murderin' swine!'

Tony pushed the open door wide and entered the kitchen. It was crowded with the McQueens, and Eva was crying noisily. Only Bridget was seated, and Tony noticed that the last vestige of the girl was gone. Drunk or sober, he would never see the girl Bridget again. She was a woman with the stamp of sorrow on her. She became blotted from his gaze as the family surged round him. 'In the name of God where'd ye find her? Have they got the swine?'

'Have they got him?'

In Mr. McQueen's moderate tone Tony seemed to detect an odd anxiety, and as he pushed his way through them all to Bridget he answered, 'No, he was well on the road to Newcastle the last I saw of him.'

'Have you told the pollis?' screamed Kathie.

'No.'

'Then somebody off and tell them. The Newcastle road, go and tell them!' Kathie threw her order from one to the other, but no one obeyed her ... they were looking at Tony as he faced Bridget, who was standing now, leaning heavily on the table with one hand. The child was still clinging to him, and he said to Bridget, 'I promised Jimmy I'd look after her.'

'You what? Christ! Listen to him!' cried Kathie.

'Shut up yer mouth!' said Cavan.

Tony stared steadily at Bridget. He, too, in the past hour, seemed to have left his youth behind and become a man, so much so that he voiced his first and only criticism of Bridget. 'You can't blame Jimmy for this ... you asked for it.'

Bridget's head drooped, and for a space there was an uncomfortable, startled quiet in the kitchen. But it was soon shattered by a squeal from Kathie. 'Blame him be damned! If my Matt dies it'll be a rope's end for him. As it is, when they get him he'll get ten years for what he's done. Blame him, the ...!'

'What?' Tony swung round on her. 'He isn't dead, then?'

It was Mr. McQueen who answered. 'It's touch and go; he may not last the night. We've got to go down in an hour or so. Terry's gone in the van. It was Mr. Steel on his motor bike that got them here so quick. He brought the pollis back an' all.' Cavan stopped and looked about him with a helpless air. 'I'd better go and tell them we've got the bairn.'

Matt wasn't dead, then, and there was the chance he would go on living. Although Tony knew that Matt's survival had lifted the dread of hanging from Jimmy, at least for the present, a sense of disappointment enveloped him, and he experienced a feeling of shock that was not un-

71

mixed with horror when he realised that Mr. McQueen felt the same with regard to his son.

As Bridget took the child from his arms he wondered why, loving her as he did, he did not mind her being married to a black man, yet had always hated the fact that she spent a moment alone with her brother. If Matt didn't die and Jimmy couldn't come back, what would happen? There would only be him to stand between Bridget and Matt. And he would stand. He was eighteen and he was no longer a boy. Matt laughed at him because he was skinny and had a limp; they all either laughed at him or were sorry for him; well, he would show them. He struck Kathie speechless for a moment by saying, 'You want to get yourselves all away home and let Bridget and the bairn get some rest.'

Eva let out a laugh, then checked it abruptly and stood for a time looking somewhat shamefaced, until Cavan said, 'He's right; come on. Some of us must go down to the hospital, anyway.' Then she said, more to herself than anyone else, 'Well I never did. What next!'

Kathie took up Eva's words. 'What next! Aye, God Almighty, I wonder what next!' She stood behind Tony and her wavering forearm told of her desire to 'land him one'. But Cavan said authoritatively, 'Come on, the lot of you. . . . I'll see you later, lass.'

He went out, followed by Eva and her docile husband, but Kathie stood for a moment longer glaring at the uneven line of Tony's shoulder. Cavan's voice calling, 'D'ye hear, you?' broke the concentration of her gaze, and she swung up her coat from the chair and flung it about her, saying, 'Some people are getting too big for their boots, and they'd better watch out.' Her voice broke as she remembered her trouble, and she went on, 'As if I hadn't enough to put up with, me lad bein' battered to death an' all, without ye trying to be cock o' the midden.' She went out, shouting warningly, 'I'll see ye later, me lad!'

As the door banged Bridget sat down again, holding the child tightly to her. She looked vacant, as if her mind was emptied of thought, and when Tony said gently, 'Put

72

her to bed, Bridget, and go yourself, and I'll bring you up a cup of tea and clear up here,' she looked up at him, saying, 'If they catch him before the pollis they'll beat him up.'

He took her elbow and raised her to her feet. 'Don't you worry, they won't catch him.'

As he led her to the stairs, she said, 'I can't go to bed, Tony, I'll get her to sleep and come down. And Tony'— the tears flooded her swollen eyes again—'will you stay with me until I know?'

'As long as you want me, Bridget.'

He watched her going up the stairs, lifting one foot slowly after the other as if they were weighted, and he knew a queer feeling of possession. So surprising was it that it caused him to flush, and he turned sharply and started to clear the kitchen.

The McQueens had made no effort to straighten the upturned articles of furniture; even the broken crockery had been kicked under the dresser to make room for their feet. The fireplace was still a shambles, and for a moment Tony looked around helplessly, not knowing where to start. Then abruptly he took off his coat and hung it behind the door. The act of doing this made him pause, and his hand rested for a moment on the nail ... his coat hanging behind Bridget's door! It held a significance.

In his wideawake dreams of the night he imagined wild, wild things, such as something happening to make Bridget lean on him. Lean on him! That was laughable and fantastic. He knew this in the daytime, but in the night it was feasible. He had even pictured himself doing just what he had done this minute ... hang his coat up ... for when a man hung his coat up in a house....

What was he thinking, when there was poor Jimmy running for his life! If they caught him he'd be gaoled; if they didn't catch him he would come back some day, as he said. So wasn't Bridget still married? Slowly he dropped on to his knees and started to clear the fireplace.

CHAPTER SIX

ROSE ANGELA

All the children in the class knew that Miss Flynn
didn't like Rose Angela Paterson; and when Miss Flynn
got at Rosie, all their attention would be riveted on
Rosie's face. They would screw round from their various
positions to watch her, and they would wonder if her eyes
could possibly become any larger, and how long she could
stare at Miss Flynn without blinking. A day seldom
passed without their being entertained in some way; but
today Miss Flynn had been at Rosie twice ... this morning because she hadn't danced the way they all did, and
this afternoon because one of her long jet-black plaits had
come undone.

As Rosie stared at her teacher she knew that she must
remain silent, for it was no use trying to answer the question of how she lost her ribbon; if she said, 'Ribbons
won't stay on my hair,' Miss Flynn would say she was
insolent. She had long since learned that silence was the
best defence, although she knew she would be punished
for this too.

'Come out here!' Miss Flynn's voice was as thin as her
body; the combination of her prominent boned face and
thinly-covered scalp had justifiably earned her the name
of 'Scrag-end' among the children.

Even the motion of Rose Angela's walk was enough to
arouse a deep feeling of resentment in Miss Flynn. As she
watched the child thread her way among the desks towards her she wanted to dash at her and shake that quiet,
maddening poise out of her. She did not question herself
as to her reason for hating this child; consciously she told

74

herself that the child was the outcome of a sinful union; she was a half-caste, and looked it, with that thick olive skin and those great eyes. She didn't need to have thick lips and a pug nose for anyone to see that her father was a black man. That's what came of sinning. All men were sinful. She was glad, oh God, she was glad, that never once in her life had she done anything wrong or impure; she had never been out with a man and she never wanted to go. She stared down on Rosie and wet her lips, one over the other, as she arched the cane back and forward between her two hands . . . she'd knock some of the sin out of her.

'Hold your hand out!'

Rose Angela held out her hand, trying not to think that when the cane lashed her palm her heart would leap. She kept her eyes on the piece of cabbage fixed firmly between Miss Flynn's front teeth, but when the cane descended for the third time she closed her eyes tightly.

'Now perhaps you'll keep your hair plaited. No one wants to see the length of your hair. If I had my way I'd cut the lot off and relieve you of your vanity.'

If a pair of scissors had been at hand at that moment, Miss Flynn would not have been accountable for her actions. Of all the things she disliked about the child she disliked her hair most of all. She also resented the fact that this half-caste, with a runaway bully of a Negro for a father and a mother who was a daily servant, should be cleaner and better dressed than the other children. But of course there was that other man—that cripple. He was, she understood, the mother's fancy piece. That's where the money came from to dress the child like this . . . oh, the sins of some people!

'Get yourself to confession tonight and ask God to forgive you for your pride, for the proud can never enter into the Kingdom of Heaven,' she threw at Rose Angela's unsteadily retreating figure; and she added, 'Your road to Heaven, in any case, is going to be long and thorny . . . if you ever get there.'

After this outburst Miss Flynn felt curiously better, and

for the rest of the afternoon peace reigned; but the children's minds, as porous as sponges, absorbed the feeling Miss Flynn had given out, and when school was over four of the girls who were usually Rose Angela's travelling companions to and from the fifteen streets dashed away and left her.

Walking alone out of the school yard, the sadness that this wholesale desertion always created settled on her. Although she knew that tomorrow they would be pally with her again, she could never understand why Florrie Tyler, her best friend, should leave her and go with the others, when they hadn't quarrelled in any way. This had happened before. She found she was either with them all or she was standing alone, facing something that she could feel but as yet could not fathom.

Turning the corner of the school wall, she came face to face with her schoolmates. They had formed a blockade across the pavement, faces strained to keep from laughing, eyes wide and hands joined.

Janie Wilson, who lived next door to the McQueens, was the spokesman. 'We ain't goin' to let you play with us any more, are we?'

The other three shook their heads vigorously.

'An' we don't want a loan of your schoolbag. An' you can keep your Saturday penny and stick it, can't she?'

Again there was vigorous nodding of heads. Then in silence they waited for some response.

The quietness with which it came left them at a loss, and aggravated them more than any shouting would have done. 'All right, it doesn't matter.'

Rose Angela watched them as they formed a ring and whispered together; then, with one accord, they broke from each other and ran some way along the road before turning and shouting, 'Rosie Paterson, you'll never go to Heaven. Even if you get up there they won't let you in, 'cause you ain't white.'

The startled expression on Rosie's face amply repaid them for her previous lack of response, and Janie Wilson's voice came above the others. 'Miss Flynn's got it in for yer

... you ain't white and you can go to confession, but you'll not get to Heaven. I asked me ma, and she said yer da was a blackie, and you'd never get into our Heaven. You'll go down'—she pointed her thumb violently towards the pavement—'and be pitched into the fire.'

For a long time now it had seemed to Rose Angela that she had been gathering to herself different kinds of fear. There was the fear of going home and finding her ma crying, sometimes with her head on her arms on the kitchen table, sometimes lying across the bed upstairs. At these times the fear would paralyse her limbs and she would want to be sick. The fear would disappear if, as sometimes happened, her mother put her arms blindly about her and there was no smell of whisky from her.

Then there was the fear that Uncle Tony might die ... that he would fall under a tram, or that on a dark night he would slip into the water of the slacks, for if anything happened to Uncle Tony who would she have to talk to? or, what was more important, listen to? What would happen if a Sunday should pass and he didn't take her for a walk and sit or stand at the same spot on the slack bank, and tell her what a grand man her da was and that she must never be ashamed of him, for one day he was coming back? She knew why they stood at the same spot, for when she stood there a voice, deep and thick and melodious, echoed through her mind, murmuring words that were only intelligible by the feeling of warmth they created in her.

Then there was that other fear, the fear that caused her to wake up, trembling and sweating, in the night, and cry for her mother, but being aware as she cried that her mother could lift this fear from her did she so wish, that hers was the power to say to Uncle Matt, 'Don't come into this house any more!' In her Uncle Matt Rose Angela saw her idea of the devil; the jet-black eyes in the white face, with one end of the long scar on his cheek pulling down the corner of his eye while the other end pulled up one side of his mouth, were terrifying to her. When her Uncle Matt stood looking at her without blinking she wanted to scream. She had done so once, and her mother turned on Matt, saying, 'Get out!' But he didn't go, he just stood with his head bent, muttering, 'That's it ... you turn on me too. The lasses go in their back doors when they see me comin'. And who's to blame, eh? I didn't start this.' Matt's voice sounded to Rose Angela as if he were crying, but his eyes remained dry and hard. Her mother had sat down and beaten her fists slowly on the corner of the table ... that had been terrifying too.

So because of her Uncle Matt Rose Angela had a great desire to qualify for Heaven, for in the other place there'd be a man like him. And now here was Janie Wilson saying that she wouldn't go to Heaven.

She stood still, watching the girls hitching and skipping into the distance, and, try as she might, she could not stop her tears. As they rained down her cheeks she reassured herself: she would get to Heaven—she'd be good and she would go to Heaven. She wouldn't miss Mass and she'd go to Communion every week. Jesus, Mary and Joseph, say she would get to Heaven.... Her tears threatened to choke her. Why was everyone so nasty? Miss Flynn and the girls and Uncle Matt, and even Granma. What had she done? ... She made her way with bowed head along the road. She'd go into church, it'd be quiet there and she would get over her crying. She couldn't go home like this.

In the empty church she knelt out of habit in her class pew, and endeavoured to pray. But as her thoughts, dwelling on Janie Wilson, would form no set prayer, she made a mental note that she must confess the sin of 'wilful distractions at prayers' when she next went to confession. She knelt until her knees ached and her head swam; but her tears had stopped, so she rose, genuflected towards the main altar where Christ stayed, and left the church.

She was standing in the porch blowing her nose when the door opened behind her, and Father Bailey came through. Startled, she looked at him, wondering where he had sprung from, for the church was empty. She dropped her head as he said, 'Hallo there, Rosie.'

'Hullo, Father.'

'Have you been paying a visit to the Blessed Sacrament?'

'Yes, Father.' She began to breathe more evenly; he hadn't heard her crying or he'd surely be saying something.

'That's a good girl. Always keep a devotion for the Blessed Sacrament and you won't go far wrong in life.' He placed his hand on her hair and felt its silkiness. 'By, it's beautiful hair that you have, Rosie; it has the sheen of the starling on it.'

Forgetting her tears, she gazed up into his round, red face and her heart swelled. It wasn't wrong to have nice hair, then. Here was the priest saying it was nice ... she wasn't sinful, then, as Miss Flynn made out, because she kept her hair nice. But what was the good of having nice hair if you were destined for Hell? Suddenly Rose Angela knew that she couldn't bear the indecision—to go on all tonight and all the morrow, and perhaps for ever, knowing she mightn't be going to Heaven was unbearable. But here, standing right before her, was Father Bailey, and if anyone could tell if she were going to Heaven he could ... he could even send her there if he liked, for he knew so much about it.

'Father, could I ask you something?'

The pleading in her eyes that always affected the priest brought him a step nearer to her, and he whispered jocularly, 'Anything you like, Rosie. But mind, I'll charge you tuppence for it.'

A smile appeared for a moment on her face, but was gone again as she asked tentatively, 'Father, will they let me into the white Heaven?'

'The white what?'

'The white Heaven, Father.'

'Are you getting mixed up? You don't mean Heaven, surely. Are you meaning the public on the Cornwallis Road, The White Heather? Now what would you be wanting to get in there for, might I ask?'

'I do mean Heaven, Father ... God's Heaven.'

The priest straightened his stubby figure and tugged at the bottom of his waistcoat with both hands. 'Now what makes you ask such a question? Of course you'll go to Heaven, providing you're a good girl.'

'But they said ...'

'Who said?' he asked sternly.

She hung her head again. 'The girls said, Father ... because me da was black I won't get into the ... proper Heaven.'

The priest remained silent, staring at the bowed head of this eight-year-old child who was already feeling the weight of 'man's inhumanity to man'. The tears in the church were the forerunner of many she would shed. God help her. Although he smiled at her there was an unsteadiness in his voice as he said, 'Look at me, Rosie, for I have something to tell you. You're a very ignorant child, you know.' He shook his head with a hopeless gesture. 'Has no one ever told you that God is colour-blind?'

'Colour-blind ...? No, Father.' Her eyes were stretched to their widest.

'Haven't they now? Are you quite sure?'

'Yes, Father ... is he?'

'He is so ... as blind as a bat where colour is concerned ... of course, mind, he can make out the flowers, but not people; he doesn't know a black from a white, nor a yellow from a red ... God help him.' Father Bailey threw back his head and laughed; and with a mixture of appreciation of his wit and profound relief Rosie joined him.

'Ah! Rosie'—Father Bailey wiped his eyes—'the good Lord appreciates a joke, even against himself. Now away home you go. Good night and God Bless you.'

'Good night, Father.' Rose Angela paused in her turning from him. 'And I'll get in, Father?'

He patted her head gently. 'You'll get in, Rosie. You of all people, I should say, will get in. And remember what I've told you about God being colour-blind, for it's the truth—one of the great truths.'

'I will, Father—I'll always remember.'

'That's it. Now let me see you smile—you don't smile

enough. Ah, that's better. Now off you go.' With a push he helped her on her way, and she ran the whole distance home, her feet just skimming the pavement, so light was her body with relief.

Arriving at the corner of the fifteen streets, she again met Janie Wilson, accompanied by a new crony this time. Janie had acquired a large slice of bread, and she almost choked herself in gulping a mouthful when Rose Angela, with a hitherto unheard of assurance, said, 'You were wrong, Janie Wilson, I will get in, Father Bailey said so ... so there!' And with a lift of her head she was about to walk on when a violent push landed her against the wall.

'Who're you settin' your old buck up to?' Janie's face was purple with indignation and the dry bread wedged in her gullet. 'Take that, you cheeky bitch. And that!'

Rose Angela took the smacks on the face, and instead of the blows, as usual, frightening her, they aroused a strange exhilarating feeling in her, the feeling of wanting to strike back. She knew she could never hope to stand up to Janie, so she used her schoolbag. With a swing of the long strap she brought the bag in contact with the side of Janie's head. The manoeuvre was very effective, for Janie screamed and kept on screaming. Rose Angela did not stop to enquire why she screamed, but ran off, thinking, I'm glad I hit her ... I'm glad ... I'm glad.

It was a strange feeling; never could she remember standing up to anyone before. She had always been aware that the other children made use of her, and imposed on her; somehow she knew that because her colour was not exactly like theirs she qualified for all the dirty work of their play. She always allowed them to make her the finder in 'Deady-one', and when broken bottles and jars and other glassware had to be smashed still further to provide the imaginary contents of sweetshops it was she who had to sit before a stone, with another in her hand, breaking the glass, often with bleeding fingers. They liked her when they could use her; and she hadn't minded being used, for it made them happy, and she wanted people to be happy and laughing. But now she was going to stick up for herself: she was as good as them. The priest had said so hadn't he? Well...he said she would get into the same heaven as them, and that was the same thing, wasn't it? But her mind refused to dwell on this point; it didn't matter, anyway. If anyone hit her again she would hit them back, and if Miss Flynn got at her she would say.... What she would say to Miss Flynn she never told herself, for as she reached her back-yard door she heard her grandmother's voice, shouting as usual. It slowed her running to a walk, and she entered the house unsmiling and serious.

Her mother and Uncle Tony and her grandmother all turned and looked towards her. Rose Angela's eyes came to rest on Tony. Why, she had forgotten it was Wednesday and his half day—fancy forgetting that!

'Go on, stare at him!' her grandmother rapped out at her. 'Go on, worship him. If ever there was a mean sod in this world it's your Uncle Tony. But go on, stare at him and put him to shame.'

Rose Angela looked swiftly from one to the other. Her mother was ironing at the table and didn't raise her head; her Uncle Tony was staring at her grandmother, and, as always when he was angry, his nose was twitching.

Kathie was sitting entirely obliterating a wooden arm-chair, and each movement of her body was creating still more bulges of flesh. Her eyes, nestling in two full pouches, fastened themselves on her grandchild, and she went on, 'What would ye say if I told ye yer Uncle Tony had come into a house and a fortune?'

'It's no fortune, I'm telling you, it's forty pounds.'

Kathie, dismissing Tony's protests with a wave of her hand, went on addressing herself to Rose Angela. 'What's forty pounds but a fortune in these times? And a house, mind, a grand house with six rooms. And an estate around it.'

'Oh my God!' Tony held his head. 'A bit of a garden ...look here...'

'An estate, I said, with trees and flowers and veget-ables—taties and cabbages an' everything an' all.' She thrust her finger into Rose Angela's chest. 'He could sell the house, and get God knows how much for it . . . but will he? Be God, no! And will he let us go there to live in it? Eh?' Her eyes rolled sideways to Tony, and he, using her full title as he had done from a child, cried, 'Look, Mrs. McQueen! I'm going to have no more of it . . . I've told you . . . and don't keep on.'

'There we are, five grown-ups stuck in two bug-ridden boxes, and never a sight of a big tree for miles, as ye well know yerself, child. And him that I brought up and treated as me own refusing to give us house-room. I could understand him not jumping at Terry's scheme to start a grocery business, but to refuse us house-room, packed as we are . . .!'

'Well, I'll soon alter that!' cut in Tony. 'I can make one less any day.'

'That's it, threaten to walk out on us.' She turned her attention from Rose Angela. 'The fix I'm in, with only Matt workin', and him on half time, and not knowing where the next bite's comin' from. That's gratitude for you.'

Although Kathie still shouted, her eyes were wide, and showing in them was anxiety. Tony saw it, and blamed himself, but, oh God, if she'd only give over! She would try the patience of a saint. Why, oh why, he asked himself, had he not moved at the end of the war when they were all working, and she had money to squander but never to save. He was heart-sick of sharing the same room with Matt and Terry and of eating with them all, for now there was Eva and her growing brood to share the table.

When he received the letter three weeks ago asking him to go to Denver's, the solicitor in King Street, and there being told that his mother's only sister, she who refused to have him as a boy, had died, leaving him the money and the house, his first thoughts were, I don't want anything of hers, the upstart; she would have let me go into the workhouse! On reflection, however, he saw that this could be an answer to his unspoken prayers. Hadn't he longed for enough money to buy a special boot? Time and again he had saved the few pounds that would be necessary, only to hand them to Kathie 'just as a loan' to pay the rent, or the coals, or the tally man, or, more recently, to buy food. When asking for fresh loans, Kathie's conscience never seemed to trouble her about the dozens of unpaid ones, and Tony had come to think that all his life he would have to pay for her past kindness to him. But with regard to the unexpected legacy he was standing firm. When he had bought his boot, and perhaps a suit of clothes, and rigged Rosie out, then he'd see to Mrs. McQueen, but he'd be damned if he was going to let her get her hands on the whole of the money. He knew what it would mean—a grand bust-up to show off to the neighbours, clothes for them all ... so that when the money was gone there'd be plenty to pawn!

Kathie was still talking, addressing her remarks once again to Rose Angela ... How wonderful it would be not to hear her voice ever again.... Well, the choice was his ... he had a house now, all his own, packed with good furniture and linen, and a little garden, the like he had not even dreamed of. He could go there and live, there was nothing to stop him. Of course it would be a long way to travel to the shop, right from High Jarrow to yon side of Harton village, but he would soon get used to that.

He stared at Bridget's hands moving the iron back and forward, back and forward, into the gatherings of Rose Angela's dress.... What was he thinking about? Why was he playing games with himself? He could no more leave the vicinity of Bridget than he could walk without limping. There was only one way he could live in that house, and that dream was as impossible as.... He was recalled sharply to Kathie again.

'Yer Uncle Tony thinks the world of ye. Then why don't he let ye and yer ma rent his fine house; and then she can let us have this un.'

Bridget, putting her iron quietly down, looked at her mother. 'I've told you before, Ma, I'm not leaving this house.'

'No.' Kathie jumped up with surprising agility. 'Ye're

84

as mean a swine as he is. Four rooms for ye and the bairn ... ye could let us share this and we'd all have lived as happy as larks. But no. What ye keeping it for, may I ask? Hopin' for yer black man to come back? Well, God speed him to ye! And it's meself that'll escort him to clink, and make sure that he gets ten years for making my lad look like a beast. . . . As for you'—Kathie turned her venom on Tony—'standing there like a weakly bull gaping at a cow—whatever ye're keeping yer house for, remember ... what God has joined together let no man put asunder ... she's married till she knows the nigger's dead!' The door banged and she was gone.

After a moment of surprised silence Tony hopped for the door, crying, 'She's not getting off with that!'

But Bridget checked him, her voice quiet and even. 'It's no use, Tony, the less said the better.'

He turned to her, his face scarlet, and Bridget, picking a fresh iron from the heart of the fire, spoke to Rose Angela, 'Go upstairs and change your pinny and wash yourself up there ... there's water in the jug in my room. And your tea'll be ready in a minute or so.'

Without a word Rose Angela went upstairs; and Bridget, testing the iron by holding it near her face, said, 'Don't worry, Tony; you know my mother doesn't mean half what she says ... she never stops to think.'

He stood watching her across the table. He was as tall as her if he supported himself on the toe of his short leg, and now he wanted every centimetre of his height. He squared his shoulders to give him breadth. In the next few minutes she must see him as other men. He said slowly, 'She did mean it, she's not blind. . . . I suppose nobody is blind enough not to notice how I feel about you, Bridget.'

There, it was out; and with the voicing of what seemed to him the feelings of a thousand lifetimes his courage grew. 'She was right. Your mother's no fool; she knows that the only one who'll get that house will be you and the bairn.'

'Tony!' Bridget stopped moving the iron. Her calmness was probed and her face now showed her concern.

'Don't be silly; you're no longer a boy!'

'I'm glad you've noticed that, anyway.'

She flicked her head impatiently. 'Well, act like a man, and have some sense.... Look, Tony; use that house, and use it now. It's a gift from God. Don't sell it.' She leant across the table towards him. 'Tony, there's Molly Cullen; she's a nice girl and she dotes on you. Now here's your chance. Be sensible, and get away from here. Molly's a cut above the rest; she'll live up to Harton, given the chance, and ...'

He waved his hand at her. 'Bridget, save your breath, there'll be no Molly Cullen nor anybody else for me, and you know it.'

'And you know nothing can come of this'—her voice was harsh—'so why do you keep on? If you think I'll go and live with you in your house...'

'Who asked you? There'll be plenty of time to refuse me when I ask you. I'm offering you the house, with no tags to it.'

As they stared at each other, the look in her eyes and the excited churning of his stomach told him that at least she regarded him as a man.

Bridget resumed her ironing again. 'Have you forgotten Jimmy?' she asked quietly.

'No.'

'And you still believe what you've told her for years?' She indicated the stairs with a nod.

There was a slight pause before he answered, 'I used to; but now I don't know.... Bridget, look at me.... If there wasn't Jimmy, would you have me?'

She remained silent, her eyes fixed on his.

'Answer me.'

'I don't know ... I've never looked at it that way, because ... Anyway, I'm so much older than you. Oh, it's all so mad. Don't let's start any of that talk. All I want is peace and quiet; I've had enough.' She turned abruptly away from him and the table.

'Listen here!' His voice compelled her to stop. 'You've got to look at it that way! Jimmy might come back the morrow, and he mightn't come back for years ... or never; but one way or the other I've got to know how you feel. Do you want Jimmy to come back?'

The direct question startled her, and she stood gripping the rod and staring at the maker's name on the iron front of the fireplace: Greave & Gillespie, Jarrow-on-Tyne. Over the years the blackleaded words had formed a focus point for her thinking. Did she want James to come back? At times, yes. At times she longed for him, and had she known where he was she would have gone to him. But when these times passed she knew that the longing had been mainly of the body; most of the time her mind was filled with recrimination of herself for the trouble her folly had wrought. Father O'Malley foretold that retribution would fall on her for making such a marriage. It had fallen, and was still falling. Each day she paid. At first it was the stigma of the colour; but when James removed that with his flight he saddled her for life with Matt, with his twisted face and mind.

The first sight of Matt's face and the knowledge that his hold on her was greater than ever had made her resort again to the refuge of the bottle. But half a dozen glasses of whisky were not enough to shut out all her trials and to give her a brief feeling of gaiety; whereas before, two had done so. Rather, the effect of the whisky was to accentuate her troubles. But even though she knew its numbing effect was gone, she still retained the desire to drink. The habit was strong, and it needed an independent fight to conquer it. And only during the past few months had she known any real respite. She had never blamed Matt for making her drink, for it was her belief that no one could make you do anything you didn't want to do. And because of this opinion, she had also pointed out to herself time and again that some part of her must have wanted James enough to have married him. The only question she had been unable to answer was: would she have done so if she hadn't been afraid of having a baby? ... And likely as not in the workhouse, for she would never have come home.

And now Tony was asking did she want James back. If it would mean living quietly, as they had done during the first few months of their marriage, yes—even if it meant bearing the stigma of his colour again. But should he come back, her mother and Matt would see that his liberty was short; and knowing he was in jail would be worse than not knowing where he was.... But she must not go on thinking of James, she must answer Tony. If she said she wanted James back, would Tony go away? She turned quickly and looked at him, as if to assure herself that he was still there, and in a revealing moment she knew that life without him would become unbearable. Up till now she had not known how much she relied on him, on his kindness and his patient devotion and stead-fastness; and on the buffer he made of himself and placed between her and Matt. And in this moment, too, she realised that the feeling he bore her was no ordinary one; it had stood the iron test of witnessing her maudlin drunk. Her head drooped at the thought. Not once had he seen her drunk but many times, and yet here he was offering her his house, and all he was asking in return was to know she cared for him. If need of him meant caring, then she realised he was her life. For the first time she saw him, not as Tony, the boy, but as a man who loved her. She looked at his deep-set eyes, at his mop of light-brown hair, which seemed too weighty for the delicacy of his face, at the uneven slope of his shoulders that did not mar his bearing but lent to it an air of nonchalance, and she wished from the depths of her being that they had been of the same age. Then, in spite of Matt, she might never have left home; for at this moment she knew it would have been an easy thing to love Tony. But now it must not come about, it was too late. She had made her bed and she must lie on it alone; she must not drag him into the mire of her life. He must get away from the fifteen streets and all that they stood for. If he could not see Molly Cullen now as a mate, perhaps he would later, or find someone else; but under no circumstances must he remain invisibly tied to her. At least she would do this

88

decent thing.

She watched the pain come into his eyes as she said harshly, 'Isn't it natural I should want him back? I married him, didn't I?'

She returned to the table and proceeded to force out the creases from her blouse with a partly cold iron, knowing that his eyes were on her.

'It's all right, Bridget, it makes no difference'—the quietness of his voice brought a smarting to her eyes—'the offer still stands. If you don't take the house, it'll stay there. I'm not selling it—nor living in it.' He turned towards the door. 'Tell Rosie I'll be round for her after tea.'

She could not restrain her tears as she watched him limping down the yard. She was filled with relief, while at the same time despising herself. He wasn't going ... he wouldn't go, no matter what she said. Oh, it was wrong, all wrong, but—oh God—she was thankful that he felt as he did. He was like an anchor to which she could tie herself to stop the drift towards drink and, she sometimes thought, towards madness.

Rose Angela came quietly into the kitchen. 'Has Uncle Tony gone?'

'He's coming back for you after tea ... I won't be a minute, I'll just finish this. The kettle's boiling.'

Rose Angela stood looking at her mother. She saw that Bridget had been crying; but it hadn't been the kind of crying that was caused by the whisky bottle, so she was filled not with fear and revulsion but with a feeling of blinding love, which caused her to go to Bridget and shyly put her arms about her waist. As she hid her face under her mother's breast Bridget slowly placed the iron on the flat tin lid. The feeling from her child seeped into her, and, putting her arm about Rose Angela, she said, gently, 'What is it, hinny?'

Rose Angela moved her face against her mother, and the action was so like that of James that Bridget took a deep breath to steady herself.

'It doesn't matter if we don't go and live in Uncle

Tony's house ... I love you ... I love you, Ma.'

Bridget pressed the child to her. Her emotion, a mixture of remorse for having withheld her love from this child and the tenderness now flooding her, was almost unbearable. She was searching in her tear-flooded mind for appropriate words to express this tenderness when a commotion in the back yard caused her to push Rose Angela from her.

From between the curtains she could see Sarah Wilson striding up the yard, dragging her Janie with her. She knew that Sarah Wilson was no friend of hers, and now her raucous voice, louder than usual, was proclaiming that something was wrong. But what, and why was she coming here?

Bridget did not move towards the door but hastily dried her eyes and stood waiting until Sarah, peering into the kitchen between the gap in the curtains, called, 'You there, Mrs. Paterson?'

Mrs. Paterson! Something was wrong ... only when you were in the black books did you receive your full title. Bridget opened the kitchen door, saying, 'What is it? What's wrong?'

'What's wrong? Ah, ye might well ask. Here'—she pulled the straining Janie towards her—'hev a look at this.' She tried to force Janie's hand, which was holding a bloodstained cloth, away from her face, but Janie cried, 'Aw, don't, Ma ... don't; it'll bleed again.'

'Take yer blasted hand away and let her see!'

'Don't shout like that, Mrs. Wilson!' Now Bridget was on her dignity. 'Come inside if it's got anything to do with me.'

'Don't shout!' cried Sarah, pushing Janie into the kitchen. 'Don't shout! Wouldn't you shout if yer bairn's eye was nearly put out?'

'But how...?' began Bridget in perplexity.

'Aye, how? By that 'un there.' She pointed to Rose Angela, whose face was almost comical in its amazement.

'Rosie?'

'Aye—Ro-see.' There was definite mimicry in Sarah's

tone. 'Let her see.' She tore her daughter's hand down, and Bridget saw an ugly cut about half an inch long to the side of Janie's cheek-bone.

She looked from Janie to Rose Angela. The child was staring in horror at Janie's face. 'Did you do that?'

Rose Angela shook her head slowly, and Janie cried, 'Yes you did. You did it with your schoolbag.'

'Aye, with her schoolbag,' added her mother. 'She can't fight with her hands, like other bairns.'

As Bridget stared in amazement at Rose Angela, whose meekness was sometimes a source of irritation to her, she was conscious of the back door opening, but she didn't turn round. The whole incident so bewildered her that she just stood staring at her daughter and listening to Sarah.

'She used the buckle side deliberately, didn't she?'

Janie nodded at her mother. 'And what's going to be done about it? That's what I want to know. Marked for life, my bairn'll be, all through that one's wickedness ... through her not having proper control. Spoilt, that's what she is, decked up to the nines....'

'That's got nothing to do with you, Mrs. Wilson.'

'Ain't it? Ain't it though? If she wasn't spoilt, this wouldn't have happened. Wild she is, and dangerous, like him that was her da was.'

'You never said a truer word.'

Bridget swung round to find Matt surveying them from the doorway.

'Aye, you've had some of it. Look at my bairn's face, Matt.' Janie's face was turned up for Matt's inspection, and from it Matt's eyes travelled to Rose Angela, and their expression needed no translation. The hate was plain for all to see, so much so that Sarah said, 'Aye, well, it's enough to make anyone turn on their own kith and kin what you've had, lad. But it should be knocked out of her before it gets any worse. That's all I say, Matt, it should be knocked out of her.'

Matt, with his eyes still riveted upon Rose Angela, muttered, 'Aye, it should be knocked out of her.'

'If there's any chastising to do, I'll do it.' The sharpness of Bridget's tone brought Matt's gaze away from the shrinking child.

'Aye, you will, like hell,' he said. 'Soft as clarts you are with her, because she puts on her mealy-mouth to you—butter wouldn't melt in it, but I know her; I've watched her outside. This doesn't surprise me'—he pointed to Janie's face—'I've seen it coming.' His voice gathering deep in his throat, he went on, 'For two pins I'd take the buckle-end of me belt...' His hand moved as he spoke to his trousers.

'Just you try it and you'll see who'll get the belt,' cried Bridget, blocking Rose Angela from Matt's sight by standing in front of her. 'And now clear out, the lot of you. And Mrs. Wilson, if you take Janie to the doctor right away he'll put a stitch in it, and I'll pay—it'll heal all right if it's done now.'

'Aye, it'll heal ... like this.' Matt slapped his distorted cheek with his palm.

'Get out, I've told you!' Bridget's eyes blazed at her brother.

Mrs. Wilson went out, pushing Janie before her, crying, 'You haven't heard the last of it, by a long chalk.'

Matt, pausing at the door, spoke with chilling quietness, 'The buck nigger will never be dead as long as she's alive, and I hope she lives long enough to pay for this.' He again slapped his face. 'And she will pay, and with her physog too. I'll fix her one of these days so she won't mark anyone else.'

He was gone, and the kitchen was filled with dark premonition. It chilled Bridget, turning her faint and weak. She looked at Rose Angela. The child was leaning against the wall, and her face, pallid with stark terror, seemed more beautiful than ever before. She was too beautiful, Bridget thought—such looks brought nothing but trouble. And it was her face that enraged Matt—it always had—and given half a chance he would destroy it. My God! If he did anything to spoil the bairn's face! As if his intention was imminent, she pulled Rose Angela to her, and held her tightly, saying, 'It's all right, don't be frightened—your Uncle Matt won't do anything. Why did you hit Janie Wilson?'

She could feel the tenseness sinking out of Rose Angela's slight body while she waited for an answer. And when it came, it was in whispered gasps. 'Janie slapped my face, 'cause I told her I'd get to Heaven. She said I wouldn't, 'cause ... 'cause my da's a nigger. And I asked Father Bailey and he said I would ... 'cause God's colour-blind, he said.'

Bridget's arms became stiff, and her eyes, staring at James's fretwork pipe-rack on the wall, were fixed in their pity.

'I didn't mean to hurt her ... I just swung my bag at her ... Ma! ... Oh, Ma!'

'Sh! Sh! don't cry, hinny.'

'Ma, will Uncle Matt——' She was stiffening again.

'No, no.'

'But he said ...'

'Sh ... I'll not let him. Don't worry, don't cry.' As Bridget's arms tightened around the sobbing child she knew that only constant vigilance would save her from Matt's hands.

She had always known that there was something odd about Matt. When she was a girl she had been able to ignore it for long spells during which he was 'just like any of them', but when unintentionally she aroused his anger by laughing or joking with one of the lads she would be brought into painful awareness of the oddity. Even when, her own rage aroused, she was fighting him, she would be wondering all the time why he should be like this. She knew no other brother who treated his sister as he did her —sisters generally came in for scorn and derision.

She had expected her marriage to alienate him from her; but it hadn't, and the result was his twisted face. Nor did this, contrary to what she had imagined, direct his bitterness towards her. Instead, he used the disfigurement to bind her to him, to draw on the affection he could get in no other way. That he hadn't vented his venom and bitterness on her wasn't, she knew, because he didn't feel bitter; she was only too well aware that every fibre of his being was corroded with bitterness. It was towards the child that it was directed, and it always would be. Bridget, looking ahead down the succession of coming years, realised that she would always have to watch Matt in order to protect the bairn, just as her da and Tony watched him to protect her.

PART THREE

CHAPTER SEVEN

THE WORKLESS

The cancer of unemployment was eating the country, and the Tyneside in particular. It was eating into initiative and hope, and doubling despair. A man, becoming unemployed, went on the dole; and he would sign on each day before vainly doing the round of the shipyards. And in the evening he would stand at the corner with his pals, who were in the same predicament as himself, and they would hide their feelings in jokes. If he lay in bed at night and wondered what was to become of him and the wife and bairns once the dole was finished, he gave little sign of it during the day.

It is said that man can get used to any condition if he is in it long enough, and it would seem there was truth in this, for, as the years went on and the dole bred the Means Test, most of the men on the Tyne had forgotten how it felt to carry a bait tin—in fact they doubted whether there had ever been in time in their lives when they had worked. The younger men didn't have to wonder about this; those born just prior to or during the 1914 war never knew what it was to be employed. Even those apprenticed to the few small firms still in existence were stood off immediately they reached the age of nineteen.

It was strange, too, how stark poverty changed the flavour of the jokes from sex to food.

'Well, I'm off for me dinner.'

'What's it the day, lad?'

'Chicken.'

'Chicken agin?'

'Aye ... I'm so bloody full of chicken I've got the urge

to gan an' sit on a clutch of eggs.'

And so it went on. Here and there a man suddenly ended the struggle, and the effect on his mates, oddly enough, was such as to stiffen their fibre. 'It's no use taking things like that,' would be their attitude; 'things can't get any worse; the bloody Government will have to do something if they don't want trouble. Hang on a bit longer.'

There were protests, mass meetings, marches, but no perceptible change. In many houses the furniture was sold bit by bit, until only the table and mattresses remained. The sight of the bairns standing around the table to their meagre food hurt a man, but when the wife sat on the boards to feed the youngest, blazing anger would fill him; and so there would be more shouting at meetings, more protests. But even anger cannot be sustained on an empty stomach, and it would fade, except in the case of the few, in whom injustice burned as a fuel. These carried the fight in London—even to 10 Downing Street itself; but their sincere cries were lost in the noise of the rabble they gathered to themselves on the march.

The slump had long been with the McQueens—Cavan's last full week's work was in 1922, and his last work of all in 1926. Terence, too, had early joined the band of unemployed. Only Matt found work, odd days here and there. The McQueens seemed to think that Matt would always have work, however small ... for life owed him this. But latterly, even Matt had failed to achieve even a day a week; and now Tony was the only one to go out at a regular hour.

Although most shops sported a sign 'No more credit given' and the windows showed more and more empty cartons, Mr. Crawley's two shops still managed to keep their heads above water. Tony for some years now had been managing the second business, a small one-windowed shop in a side-street, and the fact that he was in the glorified position of manager and had never been out of work, added to which he was receiving the great sum of ten shillings per week rent for his house, surrounded him with an atmosphere of unwilling respect and thinly veiled resentment. If he had not been the asset that kept the wolf from the door, Kathie's spleen and Matt's venom, together with Terence's jealousy, would have been openly hurled at him. Only Cavan was grateful to him. It infuriated Kathie to know that for years now Tony had stayed in her house because, by doing so, he was helping Bridget.... He'd had the nerve to tell her he'd cut down the extra five shillings he had been giving her each week if she sponged on Bridget. Sometimes Kathie thought she hated Tony worse than she had the nigger ... for, give the devil his due, the nigger had been good for a few bob or so every trip, with no conditions attached.

And another infuriating thing was that her daughter Bridget, her that had been the apple of her eye, her who she had brought up like a lady, had withdrawn herself from them all during the years. Only Cavan seemed welcome in her house ... and, of course, her fancy man. It was the desire of Kathie's heart to hurl this latter accusation at Bridget, but fear of the consequences kept her tongue in her cheek. If Tony should go, God knew how she would manage. As it was, with such a lodger, she appeared to be in comfortable circumstances compared with those of her neighbours, and to shine in any way helped to make life bearable. It was good to be able to say to Jane Cullen, next door, 'It's a stone of flour I'm after bakin', and two dozen fresh herrin's I've got in the oven this minute. Oh, it's a tea they'll have the night,' for it gave her a queer sense of satisfaction to see Jane unconsciously moving her tongue over her blue lips whenever food was mentioned. On baking days she would open her back door and window wide to allow the smell to waft into the Cullens' hungry house.

The Cullens were meek, and Kathie despised them. Most of all did she despise Mollie, who had grown holloweyed and grey-faced waiting for Tony to take up with her. At this moment Kathie was thinking of the Cullens as she banged her oven door on a shelf of baking potatoes.... 'Gutless lot!' There were the scrap-ends of bacon Tony had brought home at dinner-time to be fried; she'd kick up such a stink of food that the smell would knock them all out.

Phew, it was hot! As she wiped the sweat from her neck with the oven rag Eva's youngest boy called through the open door, 'Grannie, Rosie's home. She's got her case an' all.'

'What?' Kathie swung round on the boy. 'When?'

'Just now.'

'My God, she's lost her job again.' Kathie turned abruptly to Cavan, who was sitting on the edge of the bed and peering over the top of a pair of wire rimmed spectacles at the boy.

He closed the book he was reading and asked quietly, 'Are you sure?'

'Aye, I am—she give me a ha'penny.'

Taking off the spectacles, Cavan placed them in an old black case, and put them in his waistcoat pocket.

As he slowly took his coat from the back of the door Kathie said, 'Three weeks she's been in that job ... my God!' and as he went out of the door she called after him, 'Mind, if she gives you owt, you stump up.'

Cavan threw an angry glance back at her, but said nothing. He turned into the back lane, dusting the front of his greasy coat as he went. What was it this time? It couldn't be the same thing again ... surely to God not. What was the lass going to do? If only she could get married or something. But there would be small chance round here—the fellows would be willing enough, God knew, but their mothers and sisters wouldn't be. It wasn't only the bit of colour in her that turned the women upon her, but something else—what, he didn't know—he couldn't lay a finger on it—it wouldn't go into words. Was it the proud way she walked that maddened them? or the quietness of her? or her voice, so like her father's, him that must be dead these many years? or was it her face? Aye, it was likely her face, for it did something to men, particularly married ones.

How many times had she been given a week's money in

advance and sent packing? He had lost count. And it was bad that she should be out of work at this time, too, with Bridget off an' all. He doubted whether he'd come in for anything at all the night. She was always liberal with her bit pocket-money—rarely did she see him without slipping a sixpence into his hand. And he always made the same protest, 'No ... no, lass, ye've got little enough'; but she would smile and say, 'Get yourself a bit baccy, Granda.' Aye, she was good; both her and Bridget—his pipe would have cracked many times during the past years had it not been for them. It was strange, he thought, that he felt no humiliation in taking from either of them, yet if Kathie threw him tuppence his stomach bridled.

Funny what life did to you; funny how people changed. Time and things that happened made you change. And many things had happened to him during the past ten years. But more so during the past two; for who would have thought the desire to work would go completely from him, that it would be sent packing by this other strange desire that filled him?

He walked slowly, taking the long way round to Dunstable Street.... He was sixty-two, and it was only during these last two years of abject poverty that he had become aware of living. It happened in an odd way, so odd that he trembled when he thought that but for a fight about St. Patrick's nationality, and being laughed into spending his last threepence on buying a hundred books that he didn't want, he would never have known this new world.

He remembered the night that Kathie bullied him into making a barrow out of a soap box and a couple of old bicycle wheels so that he should go to the tip and pick cinders. The barrow would hold twice as much as a sack, and he had been given the ultimatum of picking more cinders or going without food, for she couldn't buy both coal and food. His protest that the tip ripped the soles from his boots brought the retort from Kathie that he wrap old sacking about his feet and leave his boots at home. He had done this, but, like a great number of other men, not until it was dark.

99

Part of the tip burned continuously, and this saved many of the men from their death, for in the chill, often mist-ridden dawns they would huddle together as near the blazing parts as was safe. It was during one such dawn that the row began. A big Irishman was expounding, half in fun and whole in earnest, on the merits of being Irish, when a quiet voice from among a little group of men said, 'If it's such a grand country, why don't you go back there?'

'By me patron saint! Are ye meanin' to be insultin'?' the Irishman had demanded.

'Not necessarily,' went on the voice, 'but it's odd that you lot who are so bigoted about your country couldn't pick an Irishman for your saint.'

'What! In the name of God what is St. Patrick but the most Irish of the Irish?'

'English ... St. Patrick was English.'

That did it. The men had all their work cut out to keep the Irishman from throwing the man into the blazing tip. When the row subsided, Cavan, taking up his barrow, urged the young fellow to leave and come along with him.

Half-way home Cavan burst out laughing. 'It was funny the way you got him on the raw, joking about St. Patrick being English.'

'I wasn't joking—he is.'

'You're funning.'

'No, not a bit of it—he was English, all right.'

'How do you know?'

'Oh, I read it.'

'Well, you can't believe all you read. Was it in the paper?'

'No, of course not.'

They went on pushing their barrows; and Cavan looked through the drizzle of rain at this young fellow, tousle-haired, dirty and thin, as they all were, whose calm assurance was making even him have his doubts as to St. Patrick's nationality. But he felt he must warn the lad of making it an open statement, particularly around these quarters.

'I shouldn't repeat it too often, lad.'

'Why not?'

'Oh well, you know.'

'Aye, I know ... for the same reason that folk don't like to remember that Christ was a Jew. They like to think he was an Englishman, or God, which amounts to the same thing with some of the bloody church-going lot.'

Cavan was aghast. 'But why, man, he was God!'

'All right, if you think so. He may be to you, but he isn't to me; nor is he to two-thirds of the world. I think he was the greatest man who has yet lived, but I don't think he was God.'

Cavan stopped pushing his barrow.

'You serious, lad?'

'Yes, why shouldn't I be?'

The positive tone silenced further questioning. Cavan had never heard anyone talk like this.

It wasn't until Cavan was leaving him to continue his journey alone to Jarrow that the young fellow said, 'Do you read much?'

Cavan rubbed his sleeve across his face. 'Not in my line, lad. Although, mind'—he gave a superior nod—'I've got some books—stacks of them—nigh on fifty. There was nearly a hundred, but the wife stuffed some up the wash-house flue.'

The young fellow put the handles of his barrow down on to the road. 'What kind of books?'

'Oh, all kinds; some in foreign tongues; but some of the English ones are as bad—I can't make head or tail of them. Some are about science and some are about the Middle Ages. Some've got one pound marked on 'em. Fools and their money, I say. They all belonged to an old wife who died, by the name of Peggy Flaherty. The bums sold up the house to meet the back rent, and I went along 'cause I'd now't better to do, an' when they put the books up, just for a lark I said threepence ... and be hanged, I got them. Laugh—the place was razed. And there was me and all the bairns in the neighbourhood carrying the books home in a long procession, and Kathie raised Cain and made me dump them in the wash-house. Still, they've come in handy.'

'Can I see them?'

'Why, aye, lad.'

And that had been the beginning. Ted Grant saw the books and convinced Cavan of their value, not in money but in knowledge. He was absurdly grateful for the dozen that Cavan gave him, and he persuaded Cavan to take the rest into the house, which he did, and stacked them under the bed; and so impressed was he by Ted's praise of them that he threatened to annihilate Kathie if she stuffed any more of them up the flue.

Ted was a married man, with three children all under six. He was also an embittered man, because, having won a scholarship to the High School, his parents were forced by circumstances to take him away at fifteen. He was further embittered through having been so weak as to marry while on the dole, for he became dependent on his wife. He was still dependent on her, for she went out to work, leaving him to see to the house and the children. His trek to the tip was made mostly from choice, for it helped him to keep his self-respect—he was doing work of a sort, and among men.

Cavan's conversion to reading seemed to happen overnight. From Ted Grant, who was young enough to be his son, he learned, sitting half the night listening to him, being guided by him, step by step, until now he could read his own books with understanding. And there was rarely a day passed but he did not quote his tutor's words to the joking yet admiring men at the corner, 'They can starve your bellies, but only you can starve your mind.' So although there was little or no prospect of work for Cavan in the next few years, after which he would be really too old to bother, there were times now when the thought of sudden prosperity, returning life to its normal routine of the war years, was actually frightening to him. He wanted nothing to interfere with the orderliness of his days and nights—his sitting on the tip, except in very severe weather, from ten at night till five or six in the morning, his sleeping for six hours, and the rest of the day being taken up with his reading and keeping his eye on Matt. The only part of his present life which he resented was this trailing of his son—this casual shadowing of Matt whenever he thought he was making his way to Bridget, and his sitting in Bridget's kitchen in his endeavour to outstay Matt—wasting precious hours of his reading time in shielding Bridget from ... From what was he trying to shield Bridget? Cavan had never put it into words; but the feeling that he was preventing something happening never left him; and it was being strengthened as he watched his son's face becoming even more twisted, and his step losing its spring and beginning to slither, and his fingers plucking the front of his coat. This last habit was a recent addition to his queerness. Cavan noticed it first when Matt, Bridget and he were in the kitchen, and Rosie unexpectedly came in. Matt, his black, gimlet eyes fixed on the girl, who never looked at him if she could help it, began to pluck his coat like a woman plucking a hen.

Cavan began to dread the times when Rosie would be at home. It was one thing keeping his eye on Matt where Bridget was concerned, but he felt utterly inadequate to stand between Rosie, the girl, or the woman as she now was, and Matt. He had formed one point of the protective triangle in which she had stood as a child, the other points being Bridget and Tony; but as soon as she went into service the triangle became useless. And now here she was home again. He turned into Dunstable Street's back lane and into the house, and found Bridget alone in the kitchen.

'Well, lass?'

He took off his cap and hung it on the knob of the chair.

'She's back again.'

'Aye, I heard.'

'Somebody's been quick.' Bridget's tone was sharp.

'It was Johnnie.'

'It isn't her fault.'

'I never said it was, lass.'

Bridget doubled her fists and beat her knuckles together, betraying her worry. She stood gazing unseeingly out of the kitchen window, and as Cavan looked at her straight back he felt a stirring of pride that he, a little shrimp of a man, was father to such a fine, upstanding figure as Bridget. Here she was, on forty, with no grey hairs and a body as straight as a die. The only part of her showing the stamp of her trials was her face, which had a stiffness about it that at times he likened to enamel. He cleared his throat and spat into the fire.

'It's no use taking on, lass.'

'But this is the third place she's had in two months.' She swung round and faced him. 'Why in God's name can't they leave her alone?'

Cavan rasped his hand across his chin, and gazed down on his boots so covered with patches that there was no sign of the originals left.

'And she hasn't given her a reference.'

Cavan's head jerked up. 'That's bad ... what'll she do?' Bridget turned to the window again, saying, 'God knows ... where can she get without a reference?'

In the silence of the kitchen Cavan sat pulling his lower lip in and out between his finger and thumb; and when Bridget turned from the window and thumped the kettle on to the fire he said, 'Don't worry, lass, something'll turn up—she'll drop into a good place one of these days.'

'Where?' asked Bridget harshly. 'Oh, I could kill them all!' She ground the kettle into the cinders. . . .

Upstairs, Rose Angela, too, asked herself where she could go now—no decent mistress would take her without a reference. She sat on the side of the bed and looked at the reflection of her face in the little mirror of the dressing-table, and not for the first time she told herself how she hated that face—it had brought her nothing but misery. The brown of the eyes, in the depth of which lay the pain and mystery of her father's race, were deepened still further by the sweep of the long, black lashes, which shadowed the skin until it reached the cheek-bones, changing its colour from a creamy tint to that of deep olive.

It was this face which laid her open to men like Mr. Spalding—oh, Mr. Spalding and his hands—she shuddered and closed her eyes—waking her up in the night, moving over her in the dark. She had wanted to scream, but she knew it would bring his wife, so she had pleaded, 'Leave me alone ... please leave me alone.' But she did scream; even with his hand over her mouth she screamed. But apparently not even the scream convinced Mrs. Spalding that her husband was at fault—Rose Angela had enticed him, and would have to leave. But such was Mrs. Spalding's mentality that she said nothing the next morning, and allowed Rose Angela to continue with her usual routine of doing the washing; but when this was finished she handed her three days' wages and told her to go. Rose Angela did not even protest that she was entitled to a week's wages in lieu of notice; she packed her things and went, tired, and slightly dazed, and burning under the humiliation of yet once again losing her place and having to go home.

What was she to do? She saw her head shaking in the mirror. Should she try to get into some shop? But there were so many trying, and one stood little chance because of the married women, who pleaded a family to support. She could perhaps go into that working-man's café.... No! She stood up and began to unpack her case, stacking her uniform neatly in the drawers of the dressing-table, her morning pink prints and big white aprons, her black afternoon dress and little frilled caps. No! She would first try to get a place somewhere.

She began to move about the room, straightening things out of habit. Always on her return from the big houses her home seemed smaller and the fifteen streets more grim. She paused in her moving and looked down into the street. The children as usual were filling the pavement, more so immediately below the window. When they were chased from other doors they invariably settled outside twenty-eight, for Bridget never shooed them off. Rose Angela watched them with the yearning that had never left her. How often had she stood as she was doing now and watched their play. The longing to join them was past, but the hurt of being ostracised by them still remained.

This being cast out was not due entirely to the tint of her skin, but because, since the day she marked Janie Wilson, she had become suspect ... there were two people now in the fifteen streets scarred, and by a Paterson; and mothers warned their children, 'Keep clear of that Rosie Paterson, mind,' and the children, ever anxious to create bogies, fed their inherent cruelty on this ready-made one. The spark of courage Rose Angela had felt after hitting Janie Wilson had been crushed, and had never risen again. More and more she began to sit by the fire, sometimes thinking and wondering why her thoughts hurt her, sometimes listening to Bridget reading stories. But very seldom did she hear a story right through, for when her Uncle Matt came in Bridget would send her upstairs. There had been a period of stark fear, she remembered, after she hit Janie, when she was afraid even to go to school, and would walk with her head bowed and her arms ready to shield her face. Her fear, she knew, was not unwarranted, for her mother would often be at the school gate to meet her, and if this were impossible she would tell her to go along to her place and wait there. The years did little to lessen the fear.

Directly below her a group of children were taking turns at kicking the bottom of a broken bottle into chalked squares. They were doing this while standing on one foot and with their hands behind them. Rose Angela looked at the smallest among them, a child of five, Janie Wilson's child, and thought how like her mother she was. A boy was manipulating a piece of tin, through the centre of which were drawn two pieces of string. As he pulled the string the tin whirled, making a sawing noise, and he dashed among the girls, working it against their faces. There were screams and yells, and they scattered and ran, all except Janie's child, who stood fixed and screaming. Rosie was about to knock on the window when a big girl pounced on the boy, crying, in a very good imitation of her elders, 'Get out of it! Do you want her to be marked for life, like her mother?'

Rosie turned sharply from the window. Marked for life! The mark of the buckle had shrunk until now it wasn't a quarter of an inch in length. It had not spoiled Janie's looks, for she had none to spoil. Rosie had long suspected that this lay at the core of Janie sustaining the hate over the years. Oh, what did it all mean.... She sat down on her bed again. What did living amount to? Fear and hate, fear and hate, that's what her living amounted to. It always had and it looked as if it always would. She could count on one hand those who had never caused her to be afraid—her mother and Uncle Tony, her grandfather, Father Bailey and Mrs. Kent. If only Mrs. Kent hadn't died—she would still have been with her, and happy. Mrs. Kent had made her feel as if she was different; and not because she was a half-caste, either. She would come to the kitchen at nights and talk about her husband, who had been killed in the war. But more often she would talk about Rose Angela herself. Frequently during the two years they were together she had said, 'Don't you worry, my dear, you won't always be doing this. You'll see ... you'll marry, and marry well, and I'll live to see it.' But she was dead, and Rose Angela often thought that if those two comparatively happy years could have gone on she would have been content to let Mrs. Kent's prophecy of a happy marriage go forever unfulfilled.

Her mother's voice came to her from the foot of the stairs, 'Rosie, there's a cup of tea ... your granda's here.'

'I'll be there in a minute, Ma.' She straightened the coils of her shining black hair and smoothed down her grey print dress; then she went downstairs.

'Hallo, Granda.'

'Hallo, lass—how are you?'

'Oh, all right, Granda.' She smiled at him, and took a

cup of tea from her mother's hand, then sat down near him; and Cavan, returning her smile, thought, You can't blame the chaps, really. God in Heav'n, but she's bonny! While he was thinking this he felt that the description was not quite right, but how could anyone find words to fit the effect she had on a man? He could well see her driving a fellow crackers, and doing so unconsciously, because he knew she was unaware of her power. Her movements were so natural and unaffected, yet in them was the sensuousness that tore at a man's control ... God help and protect her! Where would she end?

'How's your reading going, Granda?' There was a faint twinkle in her eye.

'Oh, fine, lass.'

'And the professor?'

'Oh, Ted's still goin' strong.'

'Has he unravelled any more mysteries?'

'My God, yes.' He hitched his chair nearer. 'Do you know something, Rosie?' He stopped and pinched his lip and nodded to himself before going on. 'I'd like to be letting on to Father O'Malley about this—aye, well, I might an' all some day—— Well, do you know there's not a bit of truth in this Adam and Garden of Eden business —never has been.'

Rose lifted her eyebrows.

'Yes, it surprised me, but there's been books written about it ... do you know it's the belief—and that of men of great learning—that we come from...'

'Monkeys!' put in Bridget, endeavouring to forget her anxieties by joining in her father's pet pastime.

'Not a bit of it. Life in the first place was nothing but slime. Now can you take that in? Slime. And another thing; do you know why a snake's the length it is, eh?'

'No, Granda.'

'Well, because it wanted to be that long.'

Both Bridget and Rose Angela remained silent during his impressive pauses, knowing that it gave him great pleasure to expound the knowledge gathered from his books and Ted Grant.

'And do you know why a bull has horns?'

'No. Granda.' Rose Angela shook her head.

'Because it thought them up.'

Here Bridget and Rose Angela laughed.

'Ah, you can laugh, but it's a fact. It's all in a book by a fellow called Lemarck ... the bulls and cows and such had only their heads to fight with, and they wanted something hard there so much that it affected their glands and things, so horns started to grow out of the tops of their heads.'

'They weren't made by God, then?' The twinkle was evident in Rose Angela's eyes now. 'Where does he come in, then, Granda?'

'Ah, ye've asked me something there. Where does he, lass? It makes a fellow think. It made me think a bit, I can tell you, 'cause, as Ted says, he could've made the slime in the first place; but that does away with this business of making the world in seven days. But then again Ted says it was only them Romans who chopped time up into days. A day could've been the word that meant a million years, for all we know. And then, as Ted says again, who's to know how long he took over making it? That's if he did. He's never told anybody, for Ted says half them prophet fellows, if they were about the day, would be shut up as loonies. People believed them in bygone times 'cause they was always frightened of what they couldn't understand. Aye, and that's another point. Have you ever thought of how our lives are ruled by what other people say? They say God wants you to do this or that, but how does anybody know what God wants of them, other than what the good part of their hearts tells them, eh?'

'Don't you believe in God then, Granda?'

'I don't know, lass; I just don't know.' He stroked the bare part of his scalp with two fingers. Then, looking from one to the other, he laughed. 'Be damned, it's funny, but I just don't know.'

Bridget, getting up to refill the cups said. 'Then I wouldn't let on to Father O'Malley about it.'

And while they were all laughing together Rose Angela

thought, This is nice, just the three of us here. If only there could be more times like this. She listened to her Granda with only half her mind—she was thinking how strange it was that he should have become so altered by the reading of a few books, and him an old man. Perhaps when she was old she would get to love books, too; but now she only wanted to look at things, and listen. If only she could go to far-away places, where there was colour—lots of colour—earth colours and water colours and sky colours. And if only she could sit and listen to music. Oh, if only she had a wireless, a wireless all her own, so she could listen to music—any kind of music, for any music was better than none.

'Do you believe in God, Rosie? Do you believe Jesus Christ was God?'

'Of course, Granda.'

'That's right, then, that's right. Stick to your belief. But I wonder, would you still believe if I was to lend you some of my books? Now there's one by that fellow called Darwin—a right stink that fellow kicked up at one time. . . .'

Cavan's voice went on, getting more excited, and Bridget rose and cleared the cups away, and Rose Angela, her eyes intent on her grandfather, followed her own thinking. She would always believe in God—life would be unbearable without this belief. How often, when a child, had Father Bailey's words 'God is colour-blind' soothed and comforted her. And how often now did she turn to that saying for comfort. Should she lose her belief in God, then she would be lost indeed, for she had come to know that he alone in all the world was . . . colour-blind. Even her mother, whom she loved with a deep, unshakable love . . . she wasn't colour-blind. Rose Angela knew that when Bridget stared at her without seeing her she was seeing her husband. She looked at Bridget now, and not for the first time realised just how lonely her mother's life was. She had been alone for years. Even loving Uncle Tony hadn't filled her life.

Rose Angela could look back to the day when she first

discovered that her mother loved Uncle Tony. It was a Sunday, and Uncle Tony came to take her for the usual walk. As they were leaving Bridget said, 'Don't tell her that any more.' And she had watched her mother and Uncle Tony stare at each other; and when they were outside Tony looked happy, and suddenly he laughed. But from that day he never again told her that her father would come back. Was her father dead? Sometimes she thought he was. At other times she was strongly convinced he wasn't. Now and again she experienced an odd feeling that he was speaking to her, in a sort of pleading way, as if he were asking her not to forget him. There was no fear of her ever forgetting him—he was too much a part of her, too deeply buried in her being, to ever throw him off, even if she desired to. And never once had that been the case. Even as a child, realising he was black, she did not want him to be other than he was; for it was the man himself she loved, not in the way she loved her mother, but in a protective way. The term seemed silly to apply to the great black man she could still remember with astonishing clearness ... but would she know him now if she saw him?

She was recalled to what her grandfather was saying by him tapping her knee. 'And did you know there is a fly that flutters about in a horse's stomach and drives him mad? Did you know that?'

'No, Granda.'

'Well, there is. And can you explain this? When the horse sees that fly buzzing around him, trying to find a sore patch to lay his eggs on, he nearly goes mad and no one can hold him. Off his dashes, hell for leather. Now how does the horse recognise that fly? And how does he know what it will do to him? 'Cause if he'd already had a dose of him, he'd be dead.... Now can you explain that?'

'No, Granda.'

'No, nor nobody else.... And here's another thing that'll surprise you....' What the other thing was Cavan didn't explain, for the kitchen door opened and Matt entered. And the harmony of the kitchen was immediately shattered. Cavan spat into the grate and said, 'I'm sorry, lass, I've marked yer hob.'

'That's all right.' Bridget took up a paper, and, folding it, began to swat flies vigorously.

Rose Angela, after one startled look at Matt as the door opened, remained still. It was difficult to sit still with Matt's eyes on her, but lately she had told herself she must run no more—she must show him by her stillness that he could scare her no longer. If only she could make a pretence of not being afraid it would be something, for inside of her, always and forever, she knew she would fear Matt and what he might do. Her voice sounded a little cracked as she said, 'You were telling me about the horse, Granda.'

'Aye, aye, I was.' Cavan, now slowly and laboriously, went on talking, while Bridget banged the paper against the walls, on the table and against the window pane.

No one spoke to Matt, nor he to them. He had moved into the kitchen and was standing leaning against the cupboard door, picking his teeth with a broken matchstick. The years had brought a stoop to his thin figure, and his face had grown two different kinds of skin—the puckered side was faintly blue, with the scars showing silver, like a winding river seen from a great height, while on the other side the skin was of a deadly whiteness and unrelieved by a trace of colour. His hair was sparse over his pointed head, and his eyes seemed to have narrowed to slits, from which jets of red light darted. For a time his gaze followed Bridget and her banging; then it again became focused on Rose Angela. The match-stick worked up and down the crevices of his teeth as his eyes swept their menacing light over her. They came to rest at length on her face, and forced her eyes to meet his. And when, despite her efforts, he saw the fear in their brown depths, his lip curled and he said, 'Been at your whoring again, eh? And got the...?'

Before he could finish speaking the newspaper struck him across the mouth. 'I've warned you, haven't I?' Bridget's face was livid.

Matt made no answer, but stood looking at his sister. The red light from his pupils seemed to have diffused itself into his skin, for the top part of his face was pink-hued. Dead flies from the swatter were sticking to the stubble of his chin; and their squashed bodies, adding to the terribleness of his face, together with his accusation, were too much for Rose Angela. Pressing her hands over her mouth she fled upstairs.

Cavan, too, felt a great sickness rising in him as he looked at his son, and not for the first time he wished with all his heart that the nigger had done the job properly, for he knew that Bridget's blow had been in the nature of a caress to him—Matt did not mind what Bridget did as long as she noticed him. Why should this be? Cavan asked himself. Why should he have bred a man with this un-natural feeling? He could find no answer within himself, nor would his books be able to provide him with the reason, as they did for so many things; and it wasn't a question he could ask of anyone, so he would never know the answer.

CHAPTER EIGHT

THE JOB

The night had been exceptionally close, and Rose Angela lay waiting for the light to break. She had slept hardly at all. The heat of the past few days had made the houses like ovens, and the nights were not long enough to allow them to cool before another day dawned and their bricks were re-baked. As she lay listening to a baby crying in a house across the street she knew that she should be everlastingly grateful for having a room to herself, when all around her four to a room was privacy. Yet she could feel nothing but a great anxiety—what was to become of her? For three weeks now she had walked the streets of the towns on both sides of the river, but when there were girls with good references what chance had she? To every place she went she had to admit that her last mistress wouldn't be likely to give her a reference. When asked why, she could only say, 'We had words.' She would offer the name of her previous mistress, but with the women practically lining up for jobs why should a mistress bother herself about this person, who dared to 'have words', and who was undoubtedly a half-caste—it would be inviting trouble. Rose Angela could read the thoughts of prospective mistresses as their calculating eyes surveyed her. Now, after weeks of tramping, her mind and body were tired and a despair was settling on her. It would have to be that café—he said he would always set her on—the manager with his big red hands, and his fat body which seemed to have been poured into his greasy suit. And there wouldn't be him alone, but the riff-raff of the waterside, with whom, in comparison, the men of the fifteen streets were gentlemen. But she must have work of some kind, things were getting desperate. Her mother had only been able to secure two half-days a week for some time now, and so she was afraid the necessity might arise when her Uncle Tony would stop the extra he now gave to her grandma to give to them. And this would mean more bickering, more rows, with her grandma yelling for all the world to hear. Oh, what would it be like to really live in one of the houses in which she had worked, where you couldn't hear what the people in the next house were saying? ... Or in Uncle Tony's house, that little red house all by itself? Why had he never gone to live there? Was it because of her mother? If only he had taken them away from the fifteen streets years ago when he had first come by it. In that quiet, sheltered house she would have been free from her Uncle Matt's eyes, and the fear of him would have died. Why had her mother stayed on here? Was she waiting for her father to come back? He would never come back now after all this time. Anyway, what would she do about Uncle Tony if he did come back?

She turned restlessly over and lay on her stomach, and one long black plait hung down by the bedside and brushed the floor. The light through the blind began to change, and she lay waiting to hear the sound of the barrows as the men passed the street corner. This was usually her time-signal, a signal without pain now, for the men would be dry and warm. But in the winter the creaking of the barrow wheels filled her with pity and despair ... there they were now, the wheels on the bricks. She could hear a man singing ... 'Oft in the Stilly Night' ... the song of reflection,

> The eyes that shone,
> Now dimmed and gone,
> The cheerful heart's now broken.

Oh, why must they sing? And that song with the heart-breaking words. She thrust her fingers into her ears, shutting out the unquenchable spirit of man, but almost instantly she released them as the unusual sound of the front door-knocker being banged came to her. Who on earth could it be at this hour of the morning?

She was on the landing pulling a coat round her when Bridget, opening her door, said, 'Wait, I'll go.' She had forgotten it might be her Uncle Matt. So she stood aside and let her mother go downstairs; but when Cavan's voice came to her from the kitchen she ran downstairs and asked, 'What's wrong, Granda?'

'Wrong? Nothing, lass.' He wiped the dust and sweat from his face with a piece of rag. 'I've just been telling your mother if you're lucky you'll be getting a job this mornin'.'

'A job?'

'Aye, lass. You know Ted's wife was in a good place in Shields? Well, she's ricked her foot.' He tried to cover his excitement and to appear sympathetic. 'Bad job altogether. Poor Ted's proper cut up about it, and he doesn't know what's going to be done now.'

He wiped his face again and sat down, while Bridget and Rose Angela watched him, waiting for him to go on.

'It'll likely be weeks before she can go back there again, for it takes a young 'un to climb over them sleepers and such like to get to the house; and then there's the stairs; and with him a bit cranky—he has the house cleaned every day.'

'What you talking about, Da?' asked Bridget impatiently. 'I thought you said it was a good place.'

'It is.'

'Well, what's this about getting over sleepers? ... And who's the mistress?'

'Where is it, Granda?' asked Rose Angela. 'I don't mind how much work there is.'

'Off Holborn, hinny.' Cavan rubbed the back of his hand sheepishly under his nose.

'Holborn!' Both Bridget and Rose Angela spoke the name together.

'Off, I said. Look, give me a chance to tell you. Do you

know Cassy's Wharf? No, you don't. Well, it's by a cut off the Mill Dam bank afore you get to Holborn proper. It's never been used for years as a wharf, but long ago—God knows how long—somebody built a house there. By all accounts the builder must have been as cranky as the chap who lives there now—great windows it has. Anyway, there was once a field all round the house. That was God knows how long ago, too, but it was gradually surrounded by sidings. Then the field became the graveyard for all the old bogies and wagons. But the house still stands there, and this painter fellow has it done out white twice a year, and everything's to be cleaned every day. And he hardly ever sees it, 'cause he's always up top painting. Ted says Bessie used to get tired going up trying to get him to come to a meal. When he's the mood on him, he'll paint night and day, then sleep for days and get up roaring for something to eat and go for her if it isn't ready.'

'But, Granda'—Rose Angela's voice was quiet—'there isn't a woman there? He's not married?'

'No, lass, that's what I was going to tell you. You see'—he looked apologetically from her to Bridget and back to her again—'you see, you won't need to fear him—Ted's Bessie says he dislikes women. He never paints owt but men and boats, and they've both got to be on their last legs afore he'll do either.'

'Is he mental?' asked Bridget.

'No, he's just cranky. But cranky or not, he makes money; and he must spend it, 'cause he gave Bessie a free hand. And she makes quite a bit, so Ted says, out of the housekeeping. So, lass, if you get a place like that...'

'If she gets a place like that, we won't depend on anything out of the housekeeping,' said Bridget, stiffly.

'Well, I was only saying, lass,' said Cavan, getting up; 'I was trying to do me best.'

'Look, Granda,' Rose Angela said soothingly, 'sit down a minute and I'll make you a cup of tea. And go on, tell me more about it. When did this happen to Mrs. Grant, and what's the man's name?'

'Just last night, hinny. She tripped over a sleeper, and a

117

bloke found her and went for the painter chap; and he put her in a taxi-cab and sent her home. Ted says all you've got to say is you've come in Mrs. Grant's place until she's better. But mind, hinny'—he nodded cautiously at her—'you'll have to give it up when she's better. Ted was clear about that.'

'Oh yes, Granda, I understand—that's only fair. But what's the man's name?'

'Stanhope. It's easy to remember ... like Stanhope Road in Shields. Mr. Michael Stanhope. And there's another bloke; but he's away most of the time. He's in Austria now, in a place called Teeroll or some-such. He's another painter. Although he's madder by a week than this one, Bessie says, you can have a laugh with him, where you can't with the Stanhope bloke. I think Bessie's just a bit scared of him.'

'Are you sure he's not mental?' asked Bridget again.

'Not as far as I can make out, lass.'

'I'll soon find out when I get there, Ma.' Hope had almost made Rose Angela gay. 'And I don't care if he is a bit mental, I'll look after him.'

'You'll have nothing to do with the place if he's not all there; you'll go and get yourself——' Bridget was about to say 'murdered', but she feared the word, so she substituted 'in trouble'.

'There's always been trouble down there,' she went on. 'Look at that Saturday a few years back, when the Arabs rioted around the shipping office and stabbed them three policemen.'

'You couldn't only blame the Arabs for that,' Cavan put in sharply; 'it were our blokes agitating them not to sign the P.C.5 form that did that, together with those bloody Arab boarding-house masters who bleed them dry. Look what them masters did a while back ... sent the Arabs in droves up to the workhouse. Blackmail it was, just to compel the town to give them outdoor relief, so as the poor skinny scabs could tip up their dibs to them again. It was the white agitators and the black masters who caused that shipping trouble, I'm telling you....

Anyway'—he turned towards Rose Angela—'you won't be near them. As I've told you, Cassy's Wharf cuts away from Holborn.'

'What time did Mrs. Grant start, Granda?'

'Eight, hinny.'

'All right, I'll be there at eight.' She touched his stubbly cheek. 'Thanks, Granda. You know, it's a good job for me that you read.'

'How do you make that out, hinny?'

'Well, if you hadn't got interested in books you wouldn't have had Ted Grant for a friend, and he would likely have given someone else the chance to fill his wife's place.'

The deduction pleased Cavan, and he laughed. 'Aye, there's that in it.' And when Rose Angela handed him his cup of tea he raised the cup to her, saying, 'Here's to Bessie's slow recovery. Not that I'm wishing her any harm, mind you, but——' He chuckled and winked at her. 'Good luck, lass.'

Rose Angela took the seven o'clock workmen's tram into Shields. The appellation was a mere courtesy title—now only a sprinkling of miners and odd workmen occupied it. She alighted by the slaughterhouse, where the piteous bellowings of the beasts were already to be heard. She had left the tram earlier than was necessary in order that she might ask the way of some 'white person', for beyond the Mill Dam lay Holborn, and Arabs. And strange though it appeared, her dislike of Arabs exceeded that held by most white people. When on one or two occasions an Arab had spoken to her, his very approach had seemed an insult. Yet it was this feeling of revulsion which gave her the insight into how the Negro was viewed by a white, and helped her to understand a little the white man's deep dislike of the Negro who was penetrating his preserves. But her understanding did not make her situation easier to bear, even though the touch of colour in herself, at least outwardly, was slight.

She reached the top of the Mill Dam bank without meeting any women, so she stopped an old man and enquired of him the whereabouts of Cassy's Wharf.

'Cassy's Wharf? Aye, I know where that is, but it's a job to get at. Why d'ya want to get there?'

'I'm after a job.'

'Funny place for a job—a lot of queer characters around this quarter, you know, lass—although it isn't as bad as it used to be in my young days, except for the bloody Arabs. They're swarming like flies here. But now let me see, which is your best way.' He ruminated for a moment. 'Aye, look. Go down that street there—it's the only street you need touch if you follow where I tell you. At the end of it you'll see a narrow cut between two warehouses. Go down there, it'll bring you to the river bank; then turn right and keep straight on ... well, you won't be able to keep straight on, for you'll have to dodge between trucks and things, but keep as near the river as you can and you can't miss the wharf. They tell me there's still a house along there. Is that where you're going?'

Rose Angela said it was, and, after thanking him warmly, followed his directions. All the doors in the street were closed; the blinds of the windows were still drawn, and the bright morning sun intensified the blackness of the passageways separating every other house. The place seemed entirely dead; the only live thing was herself, and the only noise the heels of her shoes on the pavement. She came to the cut between the warehouses, and this was as dark as the passageways, for the towering buildings seemed to meet above the narrow slit. She couldn't see the end of the cut, only where it curved in the dim distance. But as she rounded the curve she saw coming towards her a man with lowered head. He was walking slowly and was merged in the duskiness of the passage. It was well he wasn't fat, she thought, for the breadth of the cut was hardly wide enough to allow two people to pass. It was with an inward shrinking she realised that the approaching man was an Arab. She could see him peering at her across the narrowing distance. He stopped, and, standing with his back to the wall, waited for her to pass. She did not look at him or alter her pace, but as she passed him her coat brushed him and her heart thumped in agitation. He did not speak, but she knew his eyes were fixed on her, and as she walked on she was conscious of his gaze on her back. She wrinkled her nose in distaste—that sweet-scented smell peculiar to most Arabs hung in the air. When as a child sitting in a tram she had first smelt this heavy aroma she had wondered if her father too had that kind of smell, only to dismiss it as impossible.

Immediately beyond the passage she came to the river, and turned right; but as the old man said, she was unable to keep straight on for long—the banks seemed a grave-yard for old trucks, some wheelless, some on their sides. An old railway carriage, also without wheels, and sunk in coarse sea grass, attracted her attention, and she glanced through a window, only to hurry quickly on again, for two men fully dressed were lying in huddled positions on its floor.

Climbing over piles of stacked rails, walking in and out of the maze of wagons, she felt she was entering a sort of waking nightmare, and this feeling leapt into certainty when she saw the house. The jumble of debris stopped suddenly, and there ahead of her was a clear space of about thirty feet, with a narrow red-brick house at the end of it, the windows and door shining startlingly white. She stopped, and for no accountable reason a surge of happiness welled in her. She knew she had never seen this house before, yet it was familiar. It was as if she had known it, and through knowing it had been happy. She entered the clearing and began to walk slowly towards the house.... Would he be up? It wasn't yet eight. She had better find the back door.

As she turned round the side of the house the river, too, turned, seeming to follow the line of the bright golden beach pathway; and when she came to the back she stopped again in pleased surprise. There lay the wharf not eight yards from the house, with the sun thick and warm on the fawn-coloured planks of the landing and lining the black water-marked piles of the jetty with silver streaks. A vivid splash of blue moving gently on the sparkling water drew her to the jetty edge, and she looked down almost tenderly on a little boat with a white furled mast lying down at its centre ... how lovely! If only the man himself turned out to be all right and she could work here.

'Well, and what do you want?' The deep grunt of the voice, and the unexpectedness with which it came, nearly caused her to topple into the water. She gripped the jetty post, and, turning, looked towards the house. Her first jumbled impression was that the whole back of the house was made of three huge panes of glass, the widest being the top one, out of which was thrust the wildest looking head she had ever seen. She opened her mouth to explain her presence, but his next words halted her, and she experienced a faint tingling of pleasure at them.

'I don't want a model—I have more than I can cope with.'

She looked at his eyes sweeping over her, but felt not the slightest embarrassment. She could not name the expression they held; she only knew they were without that look she had come to fear in the eyes of man.

'I don't do women, anyway.'

'I am not a model, Mr. Stanhope—I came to take Mrs. Grant's place until she's better ... that's if I'll be suitable.'

He blinked down on her as if recalling who Mrs. Grant was.

'Oh yes, the blasted woman hurt her foot. Well, come in.'

Breathing quickly, she moved towards the door, set back in a little porch, and entered the house. If only he would take to her! Oh, Holy Mother, let me get this place.

She stood waiting for him in the most beautiful kitchen she had ever seen. The woodwork, she noticed, wasn't white, but of the palest blue. There were cupboards all along one side of the room and the little fireplace was blue-tiled, and never made for cooking, she thought. She turned to the window. The wharf and a large stretch of the river was framed in it like a picture. She had never imagined the Tyne looking like this ... and the sight of a boat moving swiftly, with the grace of a dancer, across the middle of the pane intensified her prayer; Dear, dear God, let me get this place.

'What's the matter with your legs?' The bellow, coming from somewhere inside the house, startled her.

Was he shouting at her? Who else, if he lived here alone? She moved towards the half-open door and stepped into the hall, which for all its whiteness appeared dark after the sun-filled kitchen. Before her was the side of the staircase, and she looked up, but could see no one, so she asked softly, 'Were you calling for me, sir?'

'Yes. Are you deaf?'

Quickly she mounted the stairs, her steps making no sound on the thick dark-blue carpet, but when she came to the landing it was empty. She looked at the four closed doors, then at the second flight of stairs, and went hurriedly up these; and there he was, standing in the doorway of a room, seeming to fill it not with height so much as with breadth. He was not much taller than she, but his solidness made him appear like a giant to her. Her eyes went to his hair, which looked like a tangled matting of coarse rope. She couldn't tell what colour it was, for the light behind him made it a mixture of red and brown, while the piece hanging over his brow appeared black.

'There's nothing the matter with your legs, is there?' He looked at them with close scrutiny, but his gaze did not offend her.

She shook her head slightly; and he turned into the room, saying, 'All the women I had before Bessie had legs—bad legs, swollen legs, stiff legs. They had a job to get here, and when they did the stairs were too much for them. Are stairs too much for you?' His voice was staccato and his eyes held an angry look, as if he was indulging in a row.

'No, I'm used to stairs.'

She was now in the room, and the scene bewildered her. From floor to ceiling the walls were covered with paintings. The sun, pouring through the great window, merged them into one rainbow whole, but apart from the window-seat there was not another fixture or article of furniture in the room—not even an easel stood on the bare floor. He walked to the window and turned there, his back to the light; and she stood in the centre of the room, facing him. The sun was dazzling her eyes and he became indistinct, only the vivid blue of his eyes remaining clear.

'How long is Bessie likely to be? Can you cook?'

'I don't really know—yes, yes, I can do ...'

'Don't say it!' He held out a hand, short-fingered and square, in protest. 'Plain cooking! Floating cabbage and fries!'

She smiled, in no way offended. 'They tell me I'm a good cook.'

'What wage do you want?'

She was nonplussed at the question—to be asked what wage she wanted! She'd be sleeping out, so dared she ask for ... twenty-five shillings? No, she'd better make it a pound. But then he might come down.

'Could I ask a pound?'

'A pound!' His face was wrinkled in the light.

Now she had done it. She began, 'Well, I...' when he cut in, 'Bessie got thirty-five shillings; you'll have the same if you suit.'

Thirty-five shillings! She could only swallow and say, 'Yes, sir.'

'What's your name?'

'Rose Angela Paterson—I'm called Rosie.'

'Well, all right.' Half turning, he blinked into the sun, and stifled a yawn. 'I'm hungry and I want a meal. But listen'—he swung round on her again, his manner more aggressive than before—'I don't want my breakfast at nine, and dinner at one, and tea at six. If you don't think you'll like that arrangement, say so now. And I knock down when I want a meal—I don't have bells, I don't like them. And when I say I don't want to be disturbed I mean it. When I want you I knock, you understand?'

Still she said nothing, knowing he wasn't finished.

'And I want the rooms dusted every day, not with a

duster but with a wash-leather. Why do I want unused rooms done every day? Because I hate dirt and muddle. Get rid of the idea that any old thing or condition does for an artist. Another thing—I don't mind being robbed, but I don't want it overdone.' He paused, waiting for some response; and when none came he went on, 'Why don't you bridle and say that you're an honest woman and don't touch anything that doesn't belong to you?'

She regarded him steadily, and said, 'Because I know it's done.'

'Oh, you do?' He nodded his great head at her. 'Well, you're honest about it, anyway, that's more than most of them are. Where were you last?'

Dear Lord, here it came!

'At Mrs. Spalding's in Paddington Road. But that was three weeks ago—I haven't been well.' Would he ask for her card? If he did she would tell him the truth and chance it.

But he didn't ask for the card.

He said, 'We'll try it a week and see how it goes. And now I want a meal—a big meal, a dinner. And strong coffee. You'll find plenty of stuff downstairs. I'll have it in the drawing-room.'

'Yes, sir.'

She turned quickly away, only to be pulled up by his next words, 'And take that frightened look off your face, there's nothing to be afraid of here.'

She wanted to say, 'I'm not afraid of you,' but after a pause she went on her way without saying anything. Her body was feeling inflated and light with relief. She had got the place, and he was nice. Her mind questioned how anyone so abrupt and who said such unorthodox things could be nice, but he was, and she knew she would like working for him in this lovely, quaint house.

She ran down the last flight of stairs to the kitchen. He wanted a dinner. What would she make him? Something tasty and quick. She tore off her coat and opened one door after another. The cupboards in the kitchen were well stocked, and in the larder was a half chicken and a piece of cooked fresh salmon—a salad, yes—but something hot before—soup. Lentils, an onion and a little curry powder. After searching at frantic speed she found all that she required.

The soup was simmering and the fruit pie baking, and she was standing at the table by the window arranging the salad when her hands became still and her eyes widened ... her master, for she thought of him as that already, was walking, practically naked, towards the end of the wharf, his body looking even broader without clothes. His hair was still on end, and as she watched him she had a great desire to laugh. When he dived he became lost to her view, and she resumed her hurried preparations. But when the squat lumbering line of a tug ploughing up the centre of the river caught her eye, she stopped again, for in line with it she saw the shining lift of an arm cutting the water with regular precision. A figure leaning over the side of the tug waved, and a hand from the water answered the salute, and a faint call that could have been a greeting came to her. The atmosphere was homely, and she felt a warmth growing inside her ... he must swim often, the tugmen knew him. And he'd be hungry....If only he liked the dinner....

Half an hour later she was standing dropping little squares of bread into boiling fat, to serve with his soup, when she heard his footsteps in the hall. Oh, if only he didn't bang or call for a minute, and then everything would be ready.

There was neither bang nor call, and when she took the soup in to him her knees were trembling so much that she felt her body was about to fold up, the consequences of which would be disastrous.

He was lying fully dressed on a divan; his eyes were closed, and as she said quietly, 'Your dinner, sir,' he opened one eye and looked at her.

'Dinner?'

For one moment she thought that his order had been a joke, for his tone was full of surprise, so that when he got up at once and went to the table her sigh of relief was almost audible. But if she expected any word of praise for her quickness or the quality of the meal she was disappointed.

She left him with his coffee and prepared herself a cup of tea, for she could eat nothing—excitement being her food at this moment.

She had barely finished the tea when his voice came to her, not from the drawing-room but from the upstairs window. Was he calling her? She sprang up, but stopped on her way to the open door, for there, in the middle of the wharf, looking upwards, were two men, one tall and thin and the other a dwarf, whose head was sunk deep into his shoulders and whose features were so strong and shapely as to give the impression of a sculptor's cast.

'I told you I didn't want you till three o'clock!'

'Yes, guv'nor.' It was the tall man who spoke.

'Well, what the hell're you nosing round for?'

'Just takin' a walk, guv'nor.'

'Walk be damned! Then walk some place else—this is my back yard, or front yard. It's private, and you know it.'

'We were just thinkin', guv'nor ... we were just wondering——' The man broke off. He was still looking up, and the stretched sinews of his neck cast their own deep shadows. The silence continued until the man raised his hand and grabbed at the coin flashing through the sunlight. He touched his brow with his finger, saying, 'Thanks, guv'nor—we'll be here at three.'

There was no response from the upper window, and Rose Angela watched the men shambling off, ludicrous in their different heights, and pitiable in their crumpled threadbare clothes. Why hadn't they come and asked for a bite or something? She guessed these were the two men who had been lying in the railway carriage.

As she returned to her cup of tea her master's voice again startled her.

'Pete! You, Pete!'

The dwarf reappeared from the side of the house. He did not speak but stared up at the window.

'Seen anything of that fellow yet?'

'I asked him. He won't come.' The dwarf's voice was guttural and the words strangely clipped.

'Why not?'

'He says he don't want to be painted.'

'Did you tell him I'd give him two shillings an hour?'

'Yes.'

'Where does he live?'

There was a slight puuse before the dwarf answered, 'I dunno.'

'You're a liar—you do.'

The dwarf remained silent, gazing upwards.

'Murphy!'

As if being produced from a gigantic hat, the tall man sprang round the corner. 'Yes, guv'nor?'

'Where does that fellow live?'

Murphy dropped his gaze from the top window to the dwarf's face, then he lifted it again. 'I dunno, guv'nor.'

'You're a liar, too.'

'Yes, guv'nor.'

'Look, I'll give you a pound if you get him here.'

'A quid!' Again Murphy dropped his eyes to the dwarf, but whatever he saw there wasn't reassuring. 'I'll try, guv'nor, but I ain't promising owt.'

'I'll make it two.'

They both stared upwards in silence, then turned slowly away; and once again it was quiet on the wharf.

Offering them two pounds just to get a man to come and sit for him! He must be made of money. Rose Angela went into the drawing-room to clear the table, and as she looked about the room she thought again, He must be made of money.

In her various places she had come to recognise good furniture from shoddy imitations, and although her knowledge of antiques was limited she knew that every piece in this room had been specially picked, for here, with the air of age and elegance, was comfort. The main tone of the room was brown, a deep patina brown, relieved in the upholstery by a shade of green that was almost blue. The window of this room, which ran the whole length of the house, looked out on to a white trellis, constructed to shut off the jumble of debris beyond. She would have liked to linger and examine the room further, but the desire was checked when she remembered what still had to be done with the wash-leather.

By mid-day she had finished the ground floor and the four rooms on the first floor. One of these had taken very little doing, as it was another studio belonging to the 'other one', whom her grandfather had referred to as being 'madder by a week' than her master. In contrast, the bedroom adjoining this studio was, to Rose Angela's mind, more like an overcrowded sitting-room, and unlike her master's, which was practically bare, without even a carpet on the floor, a large orange rug being the only covering on the bare polished boards.

She did not venture to the top of the house, and as the afternoon wore on she began to await anxiously the summons for another meal. It was close on three o'clock when it came ... a dull thumping from above. With fast-beating heart she mounted the stairs and knocked on the studio door, and entered, only to find it empty. Staring along its length, she saw a crumpled rug lying on the boards by the window. Had he been sleeping on the floor?

Her conjecturing was interrupted by his voice coming through a partly-opened door to the right of her. 'Rosie!'

It was as familiar-sounding as if he had used her name every day for years. There was none of the harshness of the morning in his tone.

'Yes, sir.' She went into the room and saw him standing at a table, stretching some canvas over a frame. He did not lift his eyes from his work, nor speak further, until he had taken some tacks from his mouth and hammered them home.

'I'll have a pot of tea. Make it strong. Nothing to eat; but you can make me a meal about six. You needn't stay to clear—do that in the morning.'

'Is there anything particular you would like, sir?'

He walked to an easel, with a full-length empty canvas set on its pegs, and moved it to the side of a dais which ran the breadth of the room.

'No—as long as it's nothing hashed up, it'll do ... I like fresh food.'

'Yes, sir. About the ordering, sir—do I do that?'

'Yes, yes, of course. Bessie always did. But mind'—he swung round and faced her, and his tone took on the edge that she associated with him as natural—'sixteen pounds a month's my limit—not a penny more.'

'Sixteen pounds a month for food!' Her expression carried further the surprise of her voice.

'Yes, for food.' His eyes narrowed and their blueness became intensified. 'What do you think? It's not enough?'

Sixteen pounds a month to keep one man and a daily maid in food. Was he a fool? No, she dismissed the idea. Had Bessie been charging him all that? If so, it was absolutely robbery. It was understandable her wanting to make a bit extra, with the family to feed, but four pounds a week for food! ... Yet Bessie would be coming back, she must be careful what she said.

His narrowed, concentrated gaze remained fixed on her, and she met it. 'It will be more than enough, sir.'

'I'm glad of that.'

He turned to his easel again and she went out. Was there a touch of sarcasm in his voice? One couldn't blame him if there was—as he had said that morning, he knew he was being robbed. But four pounds a week!

She had just reached the bottom of the stairs when his voice came again. 'Rosie! Tell those two men to wait for a quarter of an hour or so. I'll shout when I want them.'

'Yes, sir.'

As she reached the kitchen there was a tap on the open door, and there stood Murphy and Pete ... she thought of them immediately by their names. On closer inspection they looked more disreputable than they had looked on the wharf.

'You can come in and sit down. Mr. Stanhope will knock when he wants you.'

'Thank you, miss. You're new, aren't you? What's happened to the other one?' It was Murphy who did the talking.

'She's hurt her foot.'

She made the tea, conscious of the men's eyes gravely watching her movements, and as she went out of the room with the tray she said, 'I'll make you a cup when I come back.'

But when she returned to the kitchen Murphy spoke again, hesitantly and sadly. 'I'd better tell you, miss—he doesn't like it, the guv'nor don't. He don't like us getting anything.'

'Has he said so?'

'Aye; at least he told Mrs. Grant we weren't to come begging here or he'd stop us sitting.'

'Has he ever said anything to you himself?'

'No.'

Would a man who knew he was being robbed by his servants begrudge a bite and a cup of tea to these half-starved men? If Bessie wouldn't give them anything, it would be for reasons of her own.

'He hasn't said anything to me, so until he does you can have what's over—he doesn't like things hashed up.' And with a feeling of one in authority Rose Angela went to the pantry, and Murphy's long furrowed face gazed down on Pete with an almost angelic smile. But Pete did not return the smile. His eyes were riveted on the door, waiting for Rose Angela's return; and when she motioned them to the table his gaze did not flicker from her.

As hungry men will sometimes do, they began to eat the food in small bites, with a seeming finickiness—it was the habit of making a little go a long way; and they were only half-way through their plates of food when a hail from above brought them to their feet.

'Look, miss, we are much obliged. Could we put it in a bit paper and take it with us?'

'Yes, go on, I'll see to it.'

Murphy went into the hall rubbing his mouth vigorously, but Pete, standing in front of Rose Angela, asked abruptly, 'What's your name?'

'Rosie.'

'Your other name—full name?'

'Rose Angela Paterson—why?'

The dwarf did not answer, but hurried after Murphy; and about a minute later, when passing through the hall, Rose Angela was amazed to see them still standing half-way up the stairs. They both looked silently down on her and she up at them.

'What the hell you doing down there, Murphy?'

At the bellow from the upper landing they turned and sprang up the remaining stairs, and Rose Angela went on her way to the drawing-room, wondering if she had been wise, after all, to break Bessie's rule. For what were they up to, she wondered, looking at her like that and whispering on the stairs?

CHAPTER NINE

THE AWAKENING

It was eighteen days since Rose Angela came to Wharf House, and she knew now that one of the main things she wanted from life was the opportunity to manage a house; not just to work in one, but to control it—to be able to say, as she was doing now, 'I'll order this today,' or 'I'll make that for dinner the morrow.' Never could she remember being so happy; yet the eighteen days had not been without their worry.

She disliked fighting or arguing of any kind, and, on such occasions, had always found herself strangely backward with her tongue; yet the way she had stood up to the grocer had been gratifying, even if the meeting with Mrs. Grant had still to be faced.

The barefacedness of the twisting that Mrs. Grant and the grocer's man worked incensed her—four pounds' worth of groceries, fowl, meat and fish were certainly bought, but only half the amount was delivered to the house. The rest was divided between the two of them. She had wanted to change to another shop, but was afraid of doing so in case this particular shop had been the master's choice; but she was firm in her ordering, and with ham at sixpence a pound and streaky at threepence, and eggs a penny each, while cooking ones were twenty-four a shilling, not to overlook the fact that one pound of steak with a rabbit thrown in was little more than a shilling, a great deal of food could be bought for two pounds. She knew her refusal to co-operate with the man would make it awkward when she met Mrs. Grant, but she could feel no regret. In any case, Mrs. Grant would likely return to her own system, for it was doubtful whether the master would notice any difference, since so far she had given only one order of her own and perhaps she would not give another, for only yesterday Cavan had regretfully told her that Mrs. Grant's ankle was considerably better.

Slowly she crumpled the pastry in the bowl as she looked out of the window towards the wharf. The sun had gone in and the river was lead-coloured and choppy, but it was still beautiful. Soon she would no longer be able to look at it, in either sunshine or shadow. As she was staring at the water the blue boat ran alongside the wharf, and for the moment Mrs. Grant and her impending return were put aside. The scones would be done—perhaps he'd like one with his coffee; it would have been cold on the water.

As he entered the kitchen she trembled a little, as always when in his presence; yet she wasn't afraid of him.

'There are some scones just out of the oven, sir. Would you like one with your coffee?' She turned her head towards him, her hands still rubbing the pastry.

'Yes ... yes, I would—nice smell.'

He sniffed the air, and she said, 'I won't be a minute, sir, I'll bring it up.'

She was clapping the flour from her hands over the bowl when he said, 'I'll have it here.'

He pulled a chair to the table and sat down, and so great was her surprise that she stood with her palms pressed together and stared at him.

'You don't mind?'

'Oh no, sir—no.'

'Cold on the water.'

'Yes, sir.'

In spite of his abruptness, she knew he was trying to be pleasant, and a little whirl of happiness went through her.

'How old are you, Rosie?' The question was brusquely put, as were all his enquiries.

She turned, and for a flash of time looked directly into

134

the blue eyes surveying her before answering, 'Twenty, sir.'

'You look older.'

'Yes, I know I do, sir.'

He pulled off his top boots and placed them by the side of the hearth, asking as he did so, 'What have you done all your life? This kind of work?'

'Yes.'

'What have you wanted to do?'

'Just this, sir—look after a house.'

'My God! Nothing more?' He twisted round and looked up at her incredulously.

'It isn't everyone who's lucky enough to do even that these days.'

Her voice was serious, and he answered more curtly still, 'Yes, I know all about that; but you ... haven't you wanted something different—to be a dancer or get on the films? or be a mannequin, or an artist's model? ... you'd make a good model, you know—not that I want to do you.' He raised his hand as if pressing her away. 'No, no; but there are plenty who would.'

She waited until she returned from the scullery with the coffee before saying, 'I can't see myself getting such work around the Tyne, sir.' And she smiled ruefully as she placed his coffee on the table.

'The Tyne! You don't want to stick around here all your days, do you? Get up to London and you'll be snapped up.'

'You think so, sir?' Her voice held no belief, but her smile broadened and she gazed for a moment on his bent head as he stirred his coffee briskly. London, and mannequins, and artists' models! Who would want such things if they could work in a house like this, with the river flowing by and him up there painting away and thumping occasionally on the floor, and the peace that prevailed even when he was bellowing down the stairs. And now him sitting here talking to her! She experienced a feeling of satisfaction as she watched him bite into one of her scones—his mouth was full-lipped, and wide, like the rest of him; his hair still bore its numerous partings, and even without the sun's misleading light was of different colours. She often tried to guess how old he was, for on different days he looked a different age. Today he looked youngish, about thirty. Tomorrow, painting like mad, his hair standing up on end, he would look anything up to forty-five. She couldn't tell what his age was.

A knock on the kitchen door checked something further he was about to say, and Rose Angela, opening it, found Murphy there.

'Can I see the guv'nor, miss?'

'What do you want?' Stanhope called.

Murphy sidled into the kitchen, cap in hand and his long body swaying.

'Well? What you after?'

'I've got him, guv'nor.'

'The fellow?' Stanhope rose to his feet, his excitement evident.

'He'll come the morrow.'

'Why not today?'

'Well ... ye see ... he's been bad.'

'Bad!—— Pah! You're just stalling to push me up a bit, like you've done all along ... I'm not rising, Murphy.'

'No, guv'nor, honest to God! Just when he said he would come, he took bad—week afore last he was took bad.'

'Well, I'm giving you nothing on account this time ... I want to see the fellow first.'

'Yes, guv'nor.' There was disappointment in Murphy's voice.

Stanhope sat down again and looked at Murphy, at the long, shambling length of him—— By God, he had got him on to that canvas—every undernourished pore. And the little fellow too. It should shake them up, there ... but he wouldn't send it until this other fellow was done.... Now he should make a picture, especially if he could get him to look as he had done that day when he first saw him gazing across the river. He'd get him all right; he'd work on him night and day.

His attention was drawn to Murphy's working mouth and the saliva at the corners of it. 'I suppose you could squeeze a cup of coffee into that fat carcass of yours, eh? Well, you'd better get round Rosie—she makes quite good coffee ... or perhaps you know that?' His eyes were crinkled at the corners and he threw a quick glance towards Rose Angela, and as a tinge of colour mounted her cheeks he laughed and scraped his chair back from the table, but his rising was checked by the abrupt opening of the door. He turned, with Rose Angela and Murphy, and stared at the young woman surveying them. The door in her hand, she looked from one to the other before coming into the kitchen; then she advanced with such a proprietary air that even Stanhope for the moment seemed in a subordinate position.

Rose Angela, strangely enough, had never met Bessie Grant, but the faintness in the pit of her stomach told her who this plump, fair woman was. She wasn't much older than herself, but she had all the assurance in the world.

'Good morning, sir.'

'Oh, hallo, Bessie. You're better then, I see.'

'Yes ... yes, I'm better.' The look she threw towards Murphy said plainly 'and not before time'.

Stanhope rose and walked towards the hall, saying, 'Come upstairs a minute, Bessie, will you?' His voice had lost the harsh note usual to it—it was now soft, and even pleasant. Perhaps he was glad to have her back, Rose Angela thought, with an accompanying pang.

Bessie, in the act of unbuttoning her coat, stopped. She looked at Rose Angela, and Rose Angela managed to smile at her and say, 'I'm glad you're better, Mrs. Grant.'

To this pleasantry Bessie made no rejoinder, but with the same air of being in command she followed Stanhope.

Rose Angela turned to the window. She was finished, then. She hadn't thought it would be like this, like a bolt from the blue—she had imagined there would be a little warning, such as her granda saying, 'Bessie's better. I think she intends starting next week, lass.' But this suddenness, and coming at a time when everything was so wonderful ... him sitting there drinking his coffee at the kitchen table, much the same as her Uncle Tony or her granda would have done ... and poor Murphy and Pete—there'd be no more bits and pieces for them ... and herself—there would be the round again—the humiliations, the despair. He said she could get a job as a model any day in London. Should she try? She knew it was a stupid question to ask herself, for she had not the courage to leave the small security of her home, and Bridget, Tony and her granda, for a life she thought would be just as hostile towards her as this one was, together with added dangers.

'I'm sorry, miss.'

She turned towards Murphy. 'Well, I was only temporary, you know, Murphy.'

'You'll be goin' right away, then, this mornin'?'

'Yes.'

'We'll miss yer, miss.'

'I'll miss you, too, Murphy, and Pete ... I'll miss everything.' She turned blindly towards the window again. It would have been better if she'd never got the job ... oh, a thousand times better.

'Look, miss'—Murphy came up behind her—'could ye pop this way the morrer? Round about eightish.' He was whispering now. 'Pete and me—we've got something for ye—a surprise, like. If ye could come just to the carriage, round about eight, miss—could you?'

'Oh, I don't think so, Murphy ... it's very kind of you ... but——' She turned to him and her refusal was checked by the look of utter disappointment on his face. 'All right,' she added listlessly, 'I'll come.'

It would be a chance to see the house again, even if only from the outside, and she'd have to be out early going the rounds, anyway.

As Murphy, turning to go, muttered, 'I'm dead sorry you're going, miss,' she remembered the drink she had been about to get him, and she said, 'I forgot your coffee, Murphy. Just a minute; I'll get it.' But as she went into the scullery the sound of a door closing overhead reached them, and Murphy whispered, 'Never bother, miss. Thanks all the same, but I'd best be off.'

'No—wait.' If it was the last drink Murphy was to have here, he should have it, in spite of Bessie.

Suddenly Rose Angela found she heartily disliked Bessie. She had disliked her before she met her, because of her blatant robbery and her meanness towards these half-starved men.

She listened to the quick, soft padding on the stairs, and as she handed the cup to Murphy her eyes turned towards the kitchen door, awaiting Bessie's entry. But it didn't come. Instead, the front door banged with such violence that the window panes rattled, and Murphy almost dropped the cup.

Rose Angela and he stared at each other; then Murphy, putting down his cup, went quickly out of the house. He was back again in a minute, his body jangling with excitement and his enlarged Adam's apple jerking inside the loose skin of his neck.

'She's gone, miss ... in a tear too—like the divil was after her. What d'ye make of it?'

What could she make of it? She shook her head and watched Murphy gulping the coffee, his face crinkled and happy—she dared not think of what she could make of it.

Murphy, wiping his mouth with the back of his hand, beamed on her. 'It looks as if ye might be set, miss.'

He left her, and from the window she watched his shank-like legs running across the wharf. . . . Her being set would mean a lot to Murphy and Pete, but what would it mean to her?

She worked on in a daze, awaiting a summons upstairs, but none came. His dinner was ordered for two o'clock, and when she took it into the drawing-room he was there waiting. But he did not speak until she was leaving the room; then, quite briefly, he said, 'Bessie isn't coming back. Would you like to stay on?'

After a moment of silence, during which he turned his head and looked at her, she said quietly, 'Yes, sir, thank you.'

That was all; but as usual after any nervous strain she wanted to be sick, and she stood in the closed scullery, retching and asking herself what had happened. What could have happened? Surely Bessie hadn't come to give her notice in. She dismissed the idea—when Bessie came through that door it was into 'her kitchen'. Every particle of her declared it. Whatever had happened, she would likely have to wait until Ted told her granda before she knew.

At half-past six she closed the kitchen door—her kitchen door now—and went home. She had never felt so gay in her life before, nor so free. She had a job that she could see stretching on for ever; she could look ahead and say, 'I'll save up and buy things ... I'll save up for Christmas and buy things for me ma and granda, and Uncle Tony. And perhaps some day I'll be able to buy a fur.... Oh to have a fur!' She'd always wanted a fur—a long one.... As she hurried over the sleepers and around the wagons she kept her mind from the man who had made this possible. Later tonight she would think of him and the events of the day, but now to get home and tell Bridget, and talk of the things she'd buy in the future.

Coming out on to the piece of clear ground before she entered the passage, she saw the Arab. He was standing as usual leaning against the broken wall surmounting the river bank, and as usual on her approach he took a step or two from the wall and awaited her coming. She had ceased being actively afraid of him; and now she wondered curiously if he was dumb, for since their first meeting in the passage she had encountered him both morning and evening, rain or shine, and always in the same place —against the broken wall. And never had he spoken, but tonight, adding to the events of the day, he said, 'Good evening.'

Her present happiness held down her fear of him, and she answered, 'Good evening,' but quickened her step as she did so.

'Excuse me ... please don't be afraid. Can I walk with you?'

His hand came out to check her flight, but she swerved aside, saying, 'No—no thank you.'

'It's all right.'

The words reached her as she entered the passage. He was making no attempt to follow her, and she breathed more easily. She could even smile to herself about it. It was like something one read in a book—'Good evening—may I walk with you?' Not ... 'Goin' my road?' or 'Who's tyekin' ye hyem?' His precise English was surprising, for the Arabs one heard talking in the trams jabbered, and he looked so different from any of the others in his tight blue suit, except perhaps a bit taller. All Arabs looked the same to her, of medium height and extreme thinness.

But if, at any time, he should attempt to walk with her, what would she do? There was plenty of time to meet that when he tried it. Anyway, all she'd have to do would be to tell Mr. Stanhope. Yes, she'd tell Mr. Stanhope, for he didn't like the Arabs, and one bellow from him would scare a dozen Arabs. She laughed to herself—it was like a child saying, 'I'll tell me ma, mind!', or 'I'll tell me da, mind'—only she had never said the latter.

The journey to Jarrow seemed interminable, and when she alighted at the fifteen streets the sight of Matt standing with a group of men at her Grannie's street corner did not, as usual, stiffen her with apprehension. She would be afraid of nothing or no one today ... she was happy ... she had a permanent job, and what a job! The sound of someone spitting followed her. She knew it was Matt, and that it was meant for her, but what did it matter? She walked on, her head high, her step free and swinging, and her face alight, but the moment she entered the kitchen the light was quenched, for there, sitting facing her, was Bessie Grant. On the other side of the hearth sat her Uncle Tony, it being Wednesday, and her mother sat by the table. They were all three quiet, but it was a quietness that any moment could have snapped with extreme tension.

Bridget rose and said, 'I suppose you know why Mrs. Grant's here?'

'Oh, she knows, all right.' Bessie uncrossed and re-crossed her thick legs.

'Wait a minute.' Bridget put out a gently suppressing hand towards Bessie. 'One story's good till another one's told. We'll take one thing at a time. Rosie—did you tell Mr. Stanhope about the—the grocer? ... You know ... about Mr. Pillin?'

'No, not a word. He knows nothing about it. I only cut down one week, and he hasn't seen the bill.'

'Hasn't seen the bill!' repeated Bessie, with utter scorn.

'He hasn't,' said Rose Angela heatedly, 'for it's in my bag. I've kept it here all the time.'

'Sh!' said Bridget, silencing them both. 'Then how was it, Rosie, that Mr. Stanhope could tell Mrs. Grant that she had been ... well ... getting a bit too much stuff?'

'Not through me. I tell you I've never said a word to him, and he couldn't have heard what I said to Mr. Pillin because he was out. He was up the river at the time.'

'Then,' said Bessie, emphasising each word with a nod of her head, 'it's merely a damned excuse, as I said it was.'

'You'd better be careful what you're saying, Mrs. Grant.' Tony rose to his feet. 'You can be made to pay for such statements.'

'Made to pay!' Bessie rounded on him. 'What with, eh? When she's even taken the bread out of me bairns' mouths because she's low enough to supply Mr. bloody Stanhope with something that I wouldn't! I might have known—but that's what you get for helping people.'

At this moment Bessie was cursing her husband for persuading her, as she liked to think, to let her job to old McQueen's girl, who had been up against it. She was for-getting that at the time she thought it was a good idea, for had she asked any of her friends to take over, they would have known a little too much of her business—and Mr. Pillin's, and she didn't want that. But she had considered McQueen's grand-daughter would be so grateful she'd keep her mouth shut. Yet what had happened? Yes, what had happened? It was as plain as a pikestaff—she knew now why this young bitch couldn't keep a job with a mistress. It had been easy going for her with no mistress at Wharf House. The Stanhope bloke was supposed not to like women, but he was a man, and that type of bitch would soon let him know how much of a man he was.

She looked at Rose Angela, and said with insinuating quietness, 'I wouldn't do what you're doing, not for thirty-five bob a week, I wouldn't. But perhaps you've come to some arrangement, eh? You can call the piper now. The lot of you here'll be decked out soon, and be moving, for he's rotten with money.'

Bridget, with set, white face, moved towards the door. 'You'd better be going, Mrs. Grant.'

'Aye, I'll go ... but mark you, don't think she's heard the last of this. Oh no, I'm not taking this lying down— I'll see me day with her, if it's the last thing I do.' She nodded, emphasising her threat as she passed Bridget.

The door closed, and Bridget turned towards Rose Angela, saying quietly, 'Now let's hear what you've got to say.'

'You don't believe her—do you?' Rose Angela stood supporting herself against the table edge.

'I don't know what to believe.'

'Ma!'

'Well, why has he kept you on when she's been with him over a year, if he knew nothing about her doing him? She's known to be a good, clean worker.'

'He didn't know from me.'

After a moment, during which Bridget's eyes bored into her daughter's, she turned to the fire, and took up her attitude of staring at the grate, her hands moving slowly back and forth along the rod. Her voice sounded muffled as she murmured, 'Mrs. Grant said she found him in the kitchen with you this morning—you were having coffee together, and laughing; and all the time she was there she never came into the kitchen half a dozen times—he always used the front door.'

Through the righteous anger that was rising in her

143

against Bessie Grant and her mother, and anyone who should think this of her, streaked a feeling of pleasurable surprise that he should have altered even slightly his habits since she had come to live in the house. But the pleasure vanished as quickly as it was born, for here was her mother half-believing Bessie Grant's implications. If Bridget believed this, what could be expected of others?

'I'd rather you left there,' said Bridget softly, 'rather than get yourself a bad name.'

Leave the house, and the river ... and ... and him ... leave such a job, all because of Bessie Grant's spite. 'I'll not leave the job ... I'll not leave there until he sacks me. As for what people believe—who's going to stop them if I leave tomorrow, when you believe what she said.'

Bridget turned in surprise at Rose Angela's tone. 'I don't want to believe it; but can't you see yourself it looks fishy? Why has he kept you on?'

'I don't know ... I only know I've found a job I like, and I'm going to stick to it. And you can all think and say what you like.'

So finishing the most forcible words of her life, Rose Angela swung round and went upstairs, leaving Tony and Bridget staring after her.

Nothing could have confirmed her guilt so much in Bridget's eyes as this bold stand ... her shy, timid Rosie to speak out like that! She could have come to such courage, Bridget reasoned, through one thing only—she was no longer a girl, she had been with that man. Bessie Grant had been right. The Rosie upstairs now was a different Rosie from the one who had returned so often from other places. A great sadness settled on Bridget ... it wouldn't even be her own case over again, for such a man as the artist was, with money an' all, he wouldn't marry her. And if there was a bairn ... Bridget was unaware of wringing her hands together until she felt Tony's hands gently unloosing her fingers. Impatiently she pulled them away from him. Here she was blaming her girl for what, all things considered, it was a wonder she hadn't done years ago, for even as a child she must have been aware of what was going on in the house between Tony and herself. Bridget dropped into a chair and bowed her head, saying dully, 'I'm to blame for this.'

Tony looked down on the beloved head and his face fell into lines of sadness. 'You mean, because of us, Bridget!' She did not answer the appeal in his voice, nor raise her eyes to his, and he went on, 'She could have been brought up a thousand times worse. You have nothing to blame yourself for—any blame there is rests on me; I badgered you into it. But I'd do it again and again if need be.... Bridget, look at me.'

When she did not raise her head he took her face gently between his hands and lifted it to his. 'Don't worry, love' —he smiled down on her the gentle, comforting smile that had warmed her heart for years—'she's your girl— she'll be all right. Do you know'—his smile broadened— 'looking at her just now I had the feeling she's coming into her own, somehow—she's been awakened.'

His artless words had other than the desired effect— Bridget groaned. 'Aye, she's been awakened all right!' she said.

CHAPTER TEN

THE RETURN

There was a wind blowing from the river, a cold, damp wind. It seemed to fill the cut with a solidness that had to be forced apart. Rose Angela pressed against it, head bent, and her coat hugged tightly to her. She was so cold that she felt she would never be warm again. All night she had been cold—the only warmth that was in her life had been wrenched out last night, not by Bessie Grant's accusations but by her mother believing it so rapidly. How could she? was the question she kept asking herself. Hadn't she left place after place to avoid that very thing? Her name now, she knew, would be so much dirt in the fifteen streets, not because she was suspect of being 'thick' with her boss so much as of having done Bessie Grant out of her job by it. What if the rumour should reach her master's ears? She shivered, imagining the violence of his reaction. Thank God the fifteen streets were miles away. To her knowledge he had never been there, nor was he ever likely to go.

Why was life like this? No little joy or happiness lasted; only the fears and hurts lasted, and the feeling of inferiority. And now the old tormenting questioning was upon her again: why, being a half-caste, were you credited with inheriting the lowest traits of both parents? The injustice had been hard to bear before, but now, since her mother, of all people, was holding her suspect, life looked black and hopeless. She could, of course, prove to her mother that she was wrong by giving up the job; but that would be madness—it was the best place she'd had since Mrs. Kent's, and she knew, anyway, that now the job was hers she would never leave it until he sacked her.

After passing through the cut she again saw the Arab standing, sheltering from the wind, close against the wall. He made no move towards her, but said, with a strangely pleasant smile, 'Good morning; the wind is cold.'

Here was a coloured man in a foreign land who likely felt very much as she did. It should be natural to feel in sympathy with him, but all she felt was revulsion, yet so courteous was his greeting that she could not but answer him civilly, 'Yes, it is cold.'

'Can I speak with you a moment?'

'No, I'm late.'

'I won't keep you a minute. Don't be afraid—I mean you no harm.' He moved from the wall. 'Won't you let me talk to you?'

'No!' she shouted back at him, her walk on the verge of becoming a run.

Talk to an Arab! She had only to be seen doing that and ... Once your name was coupled with an Arab you were ... taboo. The word was associated in her mind with two girls she knew of who had 'taken up with' Arabs. One had married an Arab and gone to live in Holborn, the other wasn't married but just lived there—they were both taboo. Having heard the word connected with the disgrace of going with an Arab from her childhood, she now put no other construction on it; and she had plenty of fears in her life, she told herself, without a taboo being realised. To be accused of have a 'fancy man' was bad enough, but it was an entirely separate and pure thing compared with having your name coupled with that of an Arab. For a moment she thought of her mother, and, knowing the temper of the fifteen streets, she wondered at her ever being allowed to stay there with a black man. And she had been married.

Pete was outside the railway carriage, protecting a fire built in a hollow scooped out of the earth—he was kneeling, his back to the wind, holding the sides of his coat about it. He glanced up at her, but gave her no greeting, nor did the sombre expression on his face alter. Yet she knew he was very much aware of her, and had been before he glanced up. If, like Murphy, he was pleased she was being kept on he certainly didn't show it. He was a strange man, she thought, for only once had he spoken to her—the time he asked what her name was.

She wished that Murphy was about, for she felt that if she told him about the Arab he would walk with her to the Mill Dam each night, especially as the nights were cutting in. She remembered now he has asked her to be here at eight o'clock; yet he wasn't here. But when she reached the wharf she saw him talking to the guv'nor. They both turned at her approach and she shuddered at the dripping nakedness of 'the master'—he had just come out of the river and was pressing the water out of his hair with both hands. And once again she had the impression of immense strength. Her eyes barely touched him, yet in their flicking she was more acutely aware of Bessie Grant's accusation than she had been before.

His tone was unusually gay as he called to her, 'Breakfast, Rosie; and plenty of it.'

She surmised he was excited about this man coming, who must be even worse than Murphy and Pete to arouse his interest like this. Murphy had been strangely reticent about the new model when she questioned him shortly after her coming here, so she had not brought up the subject since. Doubtless she, too, would have been interested in the man's coming, but for last night—and her mother's reaction.

At nine o'clock the breakfast was over and the dishes washed, and the master was upstairs waiting for the man. She had orders not to leave the kitchen until he came. At quarter past nine he had not arrived, and Stanhope came into the kitchen, his good humour decidedly strained.

'Nine o'clock sharp he was to have been here. No sign of him, eh?' His laughter of yesterday was as if it had never been.

'No, sir.'

'I'll break that blasted Murphy's neck—he did this to me once before. It's my own damn fault—I shouldn't have given him a penny until I had the fellow here.'

Rose Angela made no comment, and he looked at her, his eyes narrowed and scrutinising. 'What's the matter? You all right?'

'Yes, sir.'

'Not bad or anything?'

'Oh no, sir.'

'Did you . . . have you come across Mrs. Grant?'

Rose Angela replaced three plates on the delf rack before answering, 'She came to my home last night.'

'Ah!' The sound was expressive. 'Well, don't let her worry you—her notice was coming to her anyway. I was only waiting. If it hadn't been you it would have been someone else.'

She could find nothing to say, and as he left the kitchen muttering to himself about Murphy she thought that even the knowledge that Mrs. Grant would have been dismissed in any case wasn't going to be much consolation to her now, for her mother wouldn't believe it.

Stanhope couldn't have reached the top of the stairs when a tap came on the back door. With hardly any interest, and with not the slightest emotion that could be indicative of a premonition, Rose Angela opened it.

The man confronting her was tall; he could at one time have been described as massive. He was still big, but it was merely the framework of bone. He was hatless and his frizzy black hair was greying to a whiteness about the temples. His neck, chin and the lower part of his cheeks were badly disfigured with deep pock marks; and one ear was distorted out of all semblance to an ear, and was twice its normal size. Rose Angela saw all these things at a glance—they were part of the dreadful and pathetic whole—yet her ready sympathy and pity was not touched by them, for she was filled with an incredible emotion. It had not come into her being at this moment at the sight of the man; it seemed to have been born when her body was born and to have lain waiting, to be touched into life on looking into this Negro's eyes. For the eyes resembled those she saw when she herself looked into a mirror.

149

She was conscious that her mouth was agape, and she felt dazed and stupid as if she had received a blow. She drew slowly aside and allowed him to step into the kitchen, and in his moving his eyes never left hers and hers became fixed in their amazement. She closed the door and stood with her back pressed to it and her hands gripping the sides of her apron. She was aware of the Negro's mouth working and his lips forming words that gave no sound. She saw his eyes glaze and a tremor pass down his body; then, outside herself, she heard the quick padding on the stairs again, and part of her mind shouted at her, 'Be careful!' But she still stood where she was, even when Stanhope entered the kitchen. He, however, did not notice her, for he was looking at the Negro, and when he spoke his voice was quiet, almost tender.

'There you are, then. So you got here.' Stanhope's eyes were devouring the Negro, moving over him with an ecstatic look such as a dealer would bestow on a rare gem.

'Yes, sah.'

The sound of the voice lifted Rose Angela immediately to the slack bank; the darkness was again around her, and she was smelling the rough smell of the jacket, a mixture of tar and mothballs and brine, and the voice that had lived in her mind only by the feeling of warmth its memory aroused was in her ears, speaking now, 'My Rose Angela—she mine.' She had never been able to remember one word from that night, but the simple 'Yes, sah' was the unlocking of the door, closed all these years, on the dim yet cherished memory. This was her da ... the eyes had told her, and the voice wiped all doubt away.

'Come this way.' Stanhope held an arm out as if to guide the Negro, and added, 'Have you had anything to eat?'

'Yes, sah, thank you.'

He did not look at Rose Angela again, but went into the hall, guided by Stanhope's hand, and Rose Angela leant against the door, repeating stupidly to herself, 'After all these years ... after all these years. It can't be.

150

And to come here!' She could think of nothing clearly, her thoughts were racing and tumbling about. Only one impression stood out in the jumble of her mind—she was shocked at the sight of this man. If he was her da, and she had no doubt about it, he could not look more unlike what she had imagined. Only his eyes remained true to her picture of him, the picture her Uncle Tony had kept bright for years by saying, 'Your eyes are the same as your da's.' Her Uncle Tony ... oh, her mother and Uncle Tony! What would her Uncle Tony do if her mother went back to her father? But would she go back? This wasn't the man she had married, not with all those pock marks and that ear. But the eyes must be the same as those her mother knew—gentle, with the gentleness lying deep in their warm brown.... He mightn't look the same, but he was the same. Somehow she knew this. She looked up to the ceiling—up there was that great battered man who was her da. A faintness overcoming her, she groped her way to a chair and sat down. Mr. Stanhope was painting him. What would he say if he knew? Would he look into his eyes and notice the resemblance? No, she doubted it. He would see the Negro as a whole ... she shuddered ... or what was left of the whole. The master was only interested in one thing, she thought—getting on to his canvas the last dregs of life. Yet Murphy had seen ... or was it Pete? Yes, Pete's eyes saw everything. But he must have had something to go on. What? She would likely know later. Was this Murphy's surprise? He had asked her to come back this morning. What must she do now? Her thoughts raced again. What would happen when her Uncle Matt got to know? There'd be murder, for her Uncle Matt would surely overpower this great shadow of a man.

She sat on, her hands stretched out before her on the table and joined as if in prayer, until she was startled by two simultaneous sounds—the hall clock striking ten and a thudding from above. As she mounted the stairs she had to hold on to the banisters for support, and after she had tapped on the studio door she was thankful for the pause before Stanhope's voice called, 'Here!'

She went in, telling herself not to look towards the dais, but immediately her eyes were drawn to it. There he was sitting on the platform, his legs slightly apart and his hands lying palm upwards, one on each thigh. His back was supported by a cunningly contrived rotten hulk of a boat, kept in place by packing-cases; and the double effect of decay was such as almost to make her cry out.

Stanhope was standing before a full-length canvas, and as he softly called her to him his hand, moving the charcoal in swift, broken lines, did not stop, nor did his eyes stray from their darting back and forth to the platform.

'Make some coffee, Rosie, and bring some brandy up. And about twelve o'clock make a meal—something good. I'll have it up here. Bring enough for two.'

His voice stopped and she moved away without emitting the usual, 'Yes, sir.' As she reached the door she knew the Negro's eyes were following her, yet he was apparently gazing straight ahead. It was like the picture of the nun she had in her bedroom—wherever you moved the eyes followed you.

In the kitchen the old feeling of sickness threatened to overcome her, and it took all her will-power to conquer it. When she took the coffee up, Stanhope stopped work, and, pouring a generous amount of brandy into the cup, handed it to the Negro, saying, 'Drink this and have a break. How're you feeling?'

'All right, sah.'

The sound of the voice sent a pain through Rose Angela, and she knew a sudden longing to be alone and to cry. She stumbled uncertainly downstairs, and in the kitchen she had to upbraid herself, saying, 'It's no use going on like this ... pull yourself together—he wants a dinner for twelve o'clock, and when he says twelve he means twelve; you know that.' But the upbraiding did little good and she commenced the preparations like a sleepwalker.

Once, going to the corner of the house where the dustbin was, she saw Murphy and Pete. They were standing looking speculatively towards the house from the edge of the clearing. She withdrew sharply from their gaze, for she wanted to talk to no one yet about this thing . . . not until she had first talked to him. How long would the master keep him? As long as he could sit or stand, she supposed.

She made three journeys in all when she took the dinner up, but never once did she allow herself to look towards the Negro; yet when he rose and slowly stretched himself she was conscious of his every movement. Nor did she look at the master, for part of her was daring to question his gay mood—did this man's presence call for gaiety and bantering jokes?

As the afternoon wore on she wondered when she would get a chance to speak to him—she shied from using the word da, even to herself. Would she manage it when he came downstairs?

But she did not speak to him when he came downstairs, for Stanhope was with him, shepherding him as if indeed he was a precious jewel. He even walked out to the wharf with him, solicitous to the last moment, saying, 'Now are you sure it hasn't been too long? We'll cut it down tomorrow if it has.'

His gentleness and consideration sounded strange, this manner being utterly unlike that which he showed to Murphy and Pete. The Negro seemed to have adopted the tone Stanhope had set, for his voice sounded quite gay as he replied, 'No, sah. No hard work 'bout that—jus' settin'.'

'Well, I'm glad you think so. You'll be here the same time tomorrow?'

'Yes sah, same time.'

Through the window Rose Angela watched him walking away until he disappeared round the corner of the house. Stanhope, too, watched him until he disappeared from sight; then he came slowly into the kitchen, rubbing the palms of his hands together as if savouring his day's work.

'Well, what do you think of him? Marvellous specimen, isn't he?'

She turned towards her master—that's all he was to him, a marvellous specimen. For a second she felt a strong feeling of resentment against this man who saw misery only as something to paint; then it was replaced by a feeling of dread which his next words evoked.

'Poor devil, he's not long for the top ... he'll be lucky if he sees the winter out.'

She put her hand up to her lips and closed her eyes, and his voice, for a moment, receded from her.

'What is it, Rosie? Are you ill? Come and sit down.' He placed a chair for her and she walked unsteadily towards it. His hand hovered uncertainly over her shoulder as if about to touch her. 'What's upset you today? Are you still thinking about Bessie?'

She gave a slight nod, and he went on, 'You're a silly girl. Look here, go and lie down on the couch in the drawing-room for a while, and go home as soon as you are feeling fit again.'

'I'm all right, sir.'

She rose to her feet, and he said harshly, 'You're not all right, but you'll do as you like, I suppose. You want to get this into your head—your life will be one long hell if you take notice of what the other fellow says—in this case the other woman.'

'Yes, sir.'

'Oh, for God's sake, don't agree with everything I say. And don't keep saying "Yes, sir".'

She marvelled at her own audacity when she asked quietly, 'What do you expect me to do—contradict you?'

His lips twisted into a smile that brought a boyishness to his face and his eyes twinkled at her. 'That would stagger me, wouldn't it?'

As he laughed she thought how she would have enjoyed this little exchange yesterday, or more probably the day before, but now she could think of nothing but what he had recently said. When she gave no reply to his bantering he went out abruptly, saying, 'Do what I tell you and get off home.'

He's not long for the top ... he's not long for the top ...

the phrase kept repeating itself. Her da was not long for the top. She had scarcely met him, yet already she knew he was marked for death by the words that had always created pity in her—old so-and-so's not long for the top. Now pity for this great, battered, grotesque man began to rise in her; it obliterated the disfigured face—all she could see were the eyes, looking at her with love and pleading in their depth, and all she wanted now was to meet him and confirm the certainty of the kinship.

At six o'clock, as usual, she gave a last look round, adjusted the cloth cover on the supper tray and went out, closing the kitchen door behind her. She tried not to hurry, and her step was unusually slow as she entered the chaotic jumble of wagons. She felt he would be waiting for her somewhere along here ... but where? She must not miss him.

He was sitting on the step of the railway carriage; and at the sight of her he rose, and she went towards him, still walking slowly. When within a few feet of him, she stopped, and they took their quiet fill of each other.

'You know me, Rose Angela?' The appeal in his voice brought a pain to her heart.

'Yes.' She wanted to say 'Da', but she felt shy of the word.

'Long time, Rose Angela.'

'Yes.'

'You remember me, way back?' His voice was deep, yet had a hollow ring.

She nodded.

'All the years I want to see you ... I think of you. But you more beautiful than I think.'

His voice cracked and the wet mist was in his eyes again, and she could bear no more. Her arms went out, and with a sound that was forced out of the suppressed depth of him he flung out his own, and they held each other. Their tears mingling, they stood pressed face to face, and as her lips touched his pock-marked cheek he let escape a cry as he had done on the day of her birth, but this time there were no words to it. After a time, during which neither of them spoke, she began to feel the shaking of his limbs as if the bones beneath his skin were jangling, and she said anxiously, 'Sit down.'

Like a child he obeyed her and sat down on the step again. 'You're cold,' she said, bending over him. 'Go inside.'

'No, I'm all right. Inside not very clean, but they not help it. Them good fellows ... good fellows,' he repeated. He put up his hand to her. 'Sit down here, close by me, and you talk. All years I wait to hear you talk, Rose Angela.' His voice slurred over her name, making it sound like a caress.

She sat below him on the block of wood that formed the step, but she could not talk. Her feelings could not be interpreted into speech, but she bowed her head and pressed it against his knee and held his hands tightly with her own; and slowly the feeling was born in her that although she looked like and loved her mother, she was not of her, she never had been ... she was of this man. Were he ten times as black, it would be the same.

He's not long for the top. As Stanhope's words came to her she sat up and looked into James's face. 'You're not well, you haven't been well—what's wrong?' she asked gently.

'Oh, that.' He shook his head and gave a laugh that was punctured by a little clicking sound in his throat that couldn't be called a cough. 'I was sick for time ... but now me get like fighting cock.'

'What were you sick with?' she asked with concern.

He pointed silently to the pock marks on his face; then said, ''Fore this I was big fine fellow, go round with fair and boxed twice a day—twenty rounds I could take. But you wait'—he held her face lovingly between his hands—'you wait. Now nothing stop me getting fit again.' So convincing was his tone that she believed him ... She would look after him and get him well; she would spend on him the ten shillings a week she had intended saving to buy Christmas presents and clothes; she would feed him and feed him.

She asked suddenly, 'How did Pete and Murphy know who I was?'

He said again, 'Them very good fellows—them best fellows.'

'But how did they know?'

He turned his head away and looked across the river. 'I been in lower part of town three months, but I been sick. I want to go to fifteen streets, but no know how land lie. Pete, he scout for me; he talk to men round docks.' James paused, then looked at his daughter again. 'Matt still bad ... still hate me ... I no want to go to jail before I see you little time.'

'Oh, Da!' the word escaped her.

'Long time I wait to hear that.' He stroked her cheek and went on, 'You no worry, I not go.' He touched the corner of her eyes with a gentle trembling finger. 'Pete, he say he knew you by your eyes—they like mine. When he think you my girl he ask your name, then Murphy, he make sure and follow you home. Me, I near mad 'cos I not come right away—I laid up with little cold.'

Not one word had he said about Bridget, and as Rose Angela gazed up into the eyes so like her own she knew why, and a hot flush covered her body. Murphy, in his scouting, would have heard more than just how her Uncle Matt felt—he would have heard, too, of the relationship that existed between Tony and her mother. That relationship would now have to end—her mother must be told. Her da couldn't return to the fifteen streets as long as Matt was there, but her mother could come to him here—he must want to see her so much. She forced herself to mention Bridget's name. Gently she said, 'My mother will get a shock, but she'll be glad.'

James looked away again to the river: 'No tell your mother, Rose Angela. She might come down here, and Matt, he guess. No tell anyone I here.'

For a moment she believed the reason he gave, and unwittingly said, 'But Uncle Tony ... I could tell Uncle Tony; he would be safe.'

By the stillness of him she knew she had made a mistake, and she murmured, 'I'm sorry.'

He turned quickly towards her, reassurance in his tone. 'You no worry; I have all I want now I have you. We not be parted again, eh?'

The question had a timorous sound; and he inhaled deeply and slowly when, shaking her head, she said, 'Never again.'

After a silence, during which they each seemed to be savouring the other, James went on, 'Tony always good boy ... him quite a man now.'

There was no bitterness in his tone, so she could say, 'He's always been very good to me.'

'Yes ... that's what he promise: Me, I look after your Rose Angela, he said. Me, I tell her what a fine fellow you are....' His smile took on a piteous twist.

'He did—every Sunday for years he took me to the slack bank and talked about you.'

'He did?' There was some amazement in James's voice.

'Yes, for years; until I think he thought I was too big.' She did not even admit to herself that the Sunday walks had stopped from the time she happened upon her mother and Tony in the front room in each other's arms.

Again a silence fell between them; until James said sorrowfully, 'Me, I never thought I'd come back to you like this; always I dream I have pots of money, and always I see myself decking you out ... I think I make so much money I even square Matt.'

As Rose Angela listened, her throat tight with tears, she knew that in a thousand lifetimes James could never have made enough money to placate Matt's hate—that was something beyond the bounds of bargaining or reasoning.

'You know I try and take you with me that night?'

He watched her nod.

'Yes, and I always mad I not do it. I could have got you away all right—not even old man know I was on board, and you were good child, quiet and making no trouble. You would have been all right in chief's cabin till ship got clear; then old man if he did find you not do nothing. Things been different perhaps if you with me.'

He shook his head musingly towards the river, and Rose Angela asked, 'What became of the chief?'

James straightened up on the step. 'Him die on next trip, when boilers bust. Sometime I tell you 'bout it ... not now. Now we just talk of us, eh? Rose Angela'—he bent above her—'will you take your hat off?' The request was humble, as if asking her to confer on him a great favour, but as Rose Angela's hands went readily to her head he stopped her with a warning movement of his hand, 'Sh! we got company; I hear somebody.'

Rose Angela had heard nothing, but, bending forward, she glanced between the wagons, and then saw the Arab.

'It's an Arab,' she said uneasily; 'he's always about here. He stands by the wall at the bottom of the passage nearly every day.'

James was in no way perturbed; in fact his expression showed pleasure. 'Oh, then, that be Hassan. He all right. Like me, he like river. Every day he come to river. He quite good sort, not like some.'

'Do you know him?'

'Yes—I work for him 'fore I was sick. He got eating-house ... he quite rich man. But him not like some ... him like the river and talk 'bout places and other peoples.'

She turned her head and watched the Arab coming into view, and she saw the blank look of astonishment appear on his face when he saw her and James together. James raised his hand to his forehead in salute, and after a moment, during which he stood stock still, the Arab, too, raised his hand; then came forward.

'You courtin' river again?' said James.

The Arab nodded and smiled, but his eyes rested on Rose Angela; and James, standing up, said with deep pride, 'This my daughter ... you never believe I had white daughter that time I tell you, did you?'

The Arab continued to smile, and shook his head slowly. Rose Angela did not return his smile, but as she looked at him she thought, Now he will speak to me; if I meet him in Shields he will speak to me, and people will see us, and that will be the end of any name I have left. But this thought did not fill her with the usual fear and apprehension, and she wondered at it. Instead, she felt a new strength flowing through her veins, bringing with it courage. She looked at James. She had a da, and she was going to look after him and keep him safe. She had a feeling of belonging, of moving out of the inbetween world in which she had lived her life into another, more steady, planet. In this moment she experienced a sense of exhilaration in which she feared nothing or nobody ... no—she made her mind gather the words together and present them to her—not even her Uncle Matt!

PART FOUR

CHAPTER ELEVEN

THE BOOKS

'Go ye down now and put yer spoke in and she'll do it.' Kathie leant across the table towards Cavan, who was sitting, his hands clenched on the arms of the chair, gazing stonily at her. 'She's got to do it. And why not for, I ask you? To let her brother sleep in her house a few nights. If it was her fancy man there wouldn't be two ways about it.'

Still Cavan said nothing, and Kathie went on, 'Christmas soon upon us an' all, an' ye know, none better, how we are fixed for coppers. It's worse I'm off since they put Terry on that job, with his tram fares and him eating like a ravenous loon, and wantin' pocket-money an' all ... and now this to happen—to bring Matt up for a means test! God in Heaven, don't ye see it's less than nothing he'll get when they know Terry's bringing a penny in, an' us havin' a lodger an' all? But if he says he's sleeping out, for there's no place to sleep five of us in these two rooms, then he'll likely stand a chance of getting his full seventeen shillings. Don't you see?'

'Aye, I see.' Cavan's voice rasped like a jangle of steel filings. 'And he's not sleeping there! He can get a bed anywhere around for five bob or so a week.' As he glared at his wife he wondered if she was being purposely blind to Matt's feelings for Bridget—or was she just a fool?

'Five bob or so a week! Will ye listen to him! Five bob or so—the Virgin stand by me side and guide me. We have so much, sure we have, that we can throw five bobs about! Listen to me, Cavan McQueen. My Matt's goin' into nobody's house while his sister sports two rooms with not a soul lying in them.'

Cavan stood up. 'If she had ten empty rooms, he's not going there.'

'An' who the hell are you to say he's not goin' there?'

'I'm the same bloke who used to give you a hammerin'. It's a long time since you had one, but you're asking for it now.'

'Go on, ye little bantam, ye try it on.' Kathie stepped back from the table and rolled up the sleeves of her blouse.

'Oh, away to hell!' Cavan waved her off with a deprecatory move of his hand. 'Don't tempt me... only listen to this! We've heard the last of Matt goin' to Bridget's—do you hear that?'

Kathie was almost black in the face with the torrent of mixed emotions filling her great bulk—her thoughts moved from Matt and the means test to a more personal trouble—more than anything at this moment she desired that Cavan should hit her; his refusal to do so was like an insult. She watched him move towards the door, and so great was her feeling that her usual flow of invective was checked, and she stammered and stuttered, 'You ... you ... sod! I'll get even with you. Ye won't lift a finger to help yer own kith and kin, but I'll get even with ye—by God, I'll get even with ye before many hours have passed over yer head.'

The door banged and she was left yelling at the walls. 'I'll see me day with ye. Like me fine daughter Bridget ye are, getting too big for yer boots—with her loose piece of a girl giving her twenty-five shillings a week. And I know where that un 'll end, too. And she's another mean sod, for not a penny has she given me since she started. But you'—she flung herself to the window and yelled fruitlessly—'yer Rosie gives you a backhander, don't she!' The sound of her voice echoed around the walls, and the words seemed to fall about her and hurt her. She turned into the room and beat the table in her rage. He hadn't lifted a finger to her, and she had gone at him like that! Years ago, when the bairns were young, he often landed her one, and then he was sorry and she cooked him a good feed after; but now ... now, nothing. Her head swung from side to side. Bridget and Matt were entirely forgotten, only her own failure confronted her. She could no longer rouse her man; nothing she did could touch him. How long was it since he last slapped her a wallop across the backside? Years; not since he had started that reading business. She no longer meant anything to him—she was just a fat hulk that he even turned from in bed at night. He wasn't always like that—by God, no! At one time she could say yes or nay, but not since he took to that reading. Her head stopped swinging.... It was them books that had made him different ... he wanted nothing but them books. Pity for herself turned to rage again. She looked towards the shelf that held eight books, all brown paper-backed and stacked according to their size. Cavan had made the shelf and hung it above the bed. As she stared, her fingers cupping one great breast began to twitch, and the fire dropping in the grate sent a glow into the darkening kitchen and showed up her mouth and eyes, stretching in their portraying of her thoughts. Who said she couldn't touch him? Didn't she say she'd get even with him? And what better way? She'd let him see she wasn't dead yet. Scorn her, would he? Sit there, hour after hour, reading and never a word out of him, never a laugh, never a joke? Well, she'd finish all that.

With three steps and a sweep of her hand the books were scattered over the bed and on the floor, and as she stooped to pick one up the enormity of her intention stilled her hand for the moment. Then with a growl which seemed to emerge from some dark depth, even beyond that of her enormous body, she gripped the pages and wrenched them out; and she threw them on the fire. But the dull glow of the cinders seemed to hesitate before sending even a small flame to lick their edges, and Kathie, taking a poker, scattered the pages, the more readily to catch the flame; and when they were alight she threw on the mutilated book cover. One book after the other followed until the fire was banked high with smouldering

163

cardboard and blackened paper. And when there was no more to tear she thought of the box under the bed—she'd make a clean job of it. Scorn her, would he? She'd make him sorry he had ever imagined he could live without her. Once his books were burnt he'd be finished, for he'd never have the face to go into Shields to the library; even if he had the nerve he'd never go because he wasn't decently put on. And whichever way he went—Jarrow or Shields—it meant walking miles there and back; and he hadn't the boots, anyway. No, she had him right enough. Like some unwieldy animal she went down on her knees and dragged the tin box from under the bed.

Still kneeling, she went on working in a frenzy, pulling and tearing at the books and telling herself that no one would slight her and get off with it; least of all that little rat who had chased her for months before she'd look at him. He'd thought nothing about reading in those days, nor did it matter a damn that she could neither read nor write.

That it was forty-five years ago Cavan had pursued her did not enter into her reasoning; nor had her illiteracy troubled her in the least until recently, when she imagined that part of Cavan's indifference was bred by scorn of her ignorance. She knew that the days of love-making were long past, and she herself was past wanting them renewed, but there had been little acts of endearment between them which, with the years, had taken the place of passion—such as him bringing her a wallop across the backside after being supplied with a good feed, or his feet searching and twining around hers in the night. But during the past two years even these had ceased.

Deaf to all sound but that of her rage, she did not notice the opening of the door; and so astonished was Eva's Johnnie at the sacrilege being perpetrated that he could not speak. For a time he remained still, watching his grannie; then silently closing the door, he ran off to tell his granda, whom he had just left standing at the corner of the street.

'Granda! Granda'—he flung himself against Cavan's legs—'me grannie's gone off her chump—she's throwing your books on the fire!'

Cavan had not run for years, but now his running had an arrow's swiftness to it that far outstripped Johnnie's youthful legs; nor did his speed slacken until he reached the kitchen door. Still in his stride, he flung it open and was brought up sharply by the sight of the fire piled high with his treasures. Kathie turned and confronted him, pieces of charred paper clinging to her hair and face, which, with her frantic exertion and the heat, was looking like a great red balloon. For perhaps a moment Cavan stared at her, his mouth and eyes stretched wide; then rushing forward, he plunged his hands into the smouldering mass, and flinging handful after handful on to the floor, began to stamp on it, seemingly unaware that they were no longer his books, but small pieces of paper, most of them charred.

Standing amid the smoke and the paper, Kathie taunted him as he thrust his hands again and again into the now flaming jumble; and when, as if at a given signal, he stopped his vain efforts, her voice faded away in her throat, and she stood slumped, watching him looking helplessly down at the debris. He lifted his head and stared at her through the smoke, and she saw how useless had been her effort. Not even this would make him lift his hand again to her, for in his eyes was only sorrow and pain. Her flesh seemed to shrink from her bones as she watched the tears gathering in his eyes—never had she known her man to cry. She watched him stumble to a chair and sit down, and spread his burned hands out before him on the table; and when he dropped his head between them and began to sob, she, too, groped for a chair and sat down; and the knowledge that Cavan was not made hers again by the loss of his books but gone from her for ever made her great body tremble. Entirely forgotten now was the cause of the row, and she began searching her mind for a reason, asking herself what had led her to do such a thing. A surge of emotion she was unable to understand and had no power to control rushed upon her. Like a penance, it filled her with sorrow and regret; feelings that were both new to her, so new that they made her fearful—of what, she didn't know. She only knew that she was sorry and she must cry ... she, who had laughed so much in her life, must cry as if for the first time. Slowly and painfully her sobs mingled with Cavan's; and the sound and the sight scared Johnnie, who was standing staring through the window; and since his mother wasn't in he ran to tell his Aunt Bridget.

Bridget was standing in her favourite position, hand gripping the brass rod and her eyes resting on the words 'Grieve and Gillespie, Jarrow-on-Tyne' on the stove. How many times during the years had she faced a problem standing thus, and mostly about the man behind her now? She stood listening to his voice, soft and whining, and she thought for the countless time, Oh, if he were only dead! and for the countless time she was shocked and grieved at her thoughts.

'Just for a little while ... I won't be in your way.'

'Matt'—her voice, too, was soft—'I've told you. You can't stay here.... Look, don't let's have any more rows over it—I've told you what I'll do—I'll give you a few shillings towards you getting a room for a week or two.'

'But why should I, when you've got two rooms doing nothing? And what'll folks say? They'll think it funny, I'll tell you, when me own sister won't take me in for a night or two.'

Bridget sighed. 'It's immaterial to me what people say.'

'Is it?' There was a challenge in his tone.

Bridget did not reply, and he went on, 'If your great managing director was to ask, he wouldn't be refused—he never has yet.'

'You know that's a lie!' She swung round on him. 'He's never stayed here at nights.'

'No, he gets what he wants before that.'

She raised her hand and dropped it helplessly. 'Matt— you're not staying here, and that's final.'

Bridget's rage was always more bearable to Matt than her indifference or her reasonableness. Now she was trying to be reasonable, to put him off with soft words, and it maddened him. Why was she trying to put him off? He knew why—because of that dirty half-caste. It was strange that although he hated Tony, the feeling was as nothing compared with that which even the thought of Rose Angela could rouse in him. Rose Angela still stood as a symbol of the thing that had taken his Bridget away from him; every part of her reminded him of the man whom he held responsible for his distorted face and the frustrations of his life.

Years ago he would have taken what he deemed his just revenge on Rose Angela's face, but for the knowledge that in doing so he would be cutting himself off for ever from Bridget. The hate of Rose Angela the child had been bearable because he knew that Bridget bore her no real love, but from the time he sensed the change in Bridget's affections his hate, when Rose Angela was present, often made it almost impossible for him to restrain his urge to destroy.

He would not admit to himself that the reason Bridget was refusing him was because she didn't want him in the house—he could not face the fact that his Bridget did not want him. She was, in his mind, the only one who did want him. And were it not for that 'un she would take him in like a shot; it was because of her he was being refused.

'I know why you won't have me here.' He addressed Bridget's back as she took a table cloth from the dresser drawer preparatory to laying the table. She did not answer him, and he went on, 'It's because of that 'un, isn't it?'

Still Bridget made no rejoinder.

'Well, it looks as if that reason will soon be moved.'

Bridget swung the cloth over the table.

'She's changed her fancy man. The funny thing is, the other bloke must be in the dark, as she's still working for him.'

'What badness are you concocting now?' Bridget's mouth was grim as she jerked round and faced him.

'I'm concocting nothing—it's the truth. She's picked up with one of her own kind.'

The muscles of Bridget's face sagged, and her voice shook as she said, 'Matt, be careful—I can only stand so much.'

'You'll have to stand this sooner or later; if not from me from somebody else.'

'Go on.'

'She's thick with an Arab.'

Bridget remained still.

'You don't believe me? Well, get on to Jack Rundall. He was with me the first time I saw them. She was standing talking to an Arab in the open near the ferry, as brazen as brass she was, and he eating her with his eyes.'

Matt was quiet now, both inside and out, for he had roused Bridget not to anger but to fear. Her face was stiff with it.

'No!' Her whisper was scarcely audible, but Matt heard it and said, 'It's true. And then there was last night, I watched her. The same Arab was waiting for her near the river, at the end of the cut that leads into Holborn. I saw them under the lamp. She gives him her hand and they start talking, then off they go, right into Holborn ... into a café affair; and you don't have to be told what those places are.' His voice had assumed an almost sympathetic tone.

Bridget whispered again to herself, 'No, oh no, Rosie.'

Last night she was late—it was nearly nine o'clock when she came in. She had been late other nights, too, because, she said, there were some people staying with Mr. Stanhope and she had to cook a late dinner. It sounded so feasible, and she had tried not to think there might be another reason for the lateness ... and all the time she was going with an Arab. Oh God! Bridget folded her arms about her waist and began to rock herself.... Not that, not an Arab. Yet could she be blamed? What example had she to follow? What had she thought all these years

168

about her mother marrying a black man, not to speak of what she knew of Tony? ... But an Arab! James had been handsome in his way, but the Arabs were like weeds. And then, what about her master?

Bridget had just said she cared nothing for people's gossip. For herself, she could bear it; but when it touched her daughter, it tore at her. Because of Bessie Grant, people had for months looked askance at Rose Angela, but now she would be stamped 'a real loose piece'; and she wasn't bad, somehow she wasn't bad. Lately when Bridget covertly watched her daughter's face she was forced to say to herself, 'If she's bad, then there's no good in heaven or earth.' No, she wouldn't believe it—Rose Angela would never go with an Arab, she had always been afraid of them. This was another of Matt's tricks. He was evil—she stopped her rocking—but strangely enough he wasn't a liar. This fact forced itself on her mind and she muttered to herself, 'Oh my god, there must be something in it, somehow.' And Matt said Jack Rundall had seen her and all. If that was so, then most of the fifteen streets knew about it by now. Suppose they did to Rose Angela what they did to Rene Batten a few years ago ... pelt her out of the streets. Oh Holy Mary, don't let this happen to my lass!

As Bridget sent up this fervent prayer Johnnie's voice came screaming up the yard, 'Aunt Bridget! Aunt Bridget!' And Bridget turned sharply as he burst into the kitchen, crying, 'Stop that yelling, you!'

'But Aunt Bridget'—he stood panting, the saliva running over his loose lower lip—'there's hell on at me grannie's; she's burnt all the books an' me granda kept putting his hands in the fire and he's crying.'

'What! What you talking about?'

'They've been fightin'. Me ma's not in ... oh, come on Aunt Bridget!' he pleaded. 'I tell you me granda's cryin'.'

Momentarily Bridget's personal worries were thrust on one side; but she looked suspiciously at her nephew, and, remembering his tendency to practical jokes, said, 'You're not having me on, Johnnie, are you, for I can't stand your games the day.'

'No, no, Aunt Bridget, strike me dead. They were rowin' and me granda went out and me grannie threw his books on the fire, and now she's cryin' an' all.'

Her ma crying! Bridget ran up the stairs for her coat, and when she returned to the kitchen Matt said, 'It'll be a damn good job if she has burnt the lot of them; he's been dotty since he got them books.'

If what Johnnie said was true, Bridget realised it would be nothing less than a catastrophe for her father, and as she hurried through the streets, Matt shuffling at her side, her own trouble was obliterated for the moment. If her da's books were gone, life would be finished for him. There were thousands of other books, she knew, but the motley assortment with their fund of varied topics were his books, even though sometimes she had been a little scornful in her own mind regarding his attitude towards them, thinking that he showed signs of senility in his treating them like children.

As they neared the back-yard door Matt exclaimed, 'By God, she must have done it ... smell that?'

The yard was full of the smell of burning and Bridget's uneasiness grew; and when she entered the kitchen she was appalled at the sight of her parents sitting one each side of the table in utter dejection amidst the chaos of the room, but more so was she shocked by the look of her father. His already small body seemed to have shrunk and he now looked a tiny old man; and her heart was wrung when, lifting his brimming eyes to her, he said with the simplicity of a child, 'She burned me books, Bridget; she's burned all me books, lass.' It was as if he had said, 'She has burned all I hold dear in life; I am finished; there is nothing more to live for.'

That his dejection should then cause a slight irritation to assail her surprised Bridget. She knew her mother had done wrong in taking her spite out on him by burning his books, but need he take it like this? It wasn't as if he'd been a great reader all his life, and she doubted whether he understood one quarter of what he read. He remembered interesting facts and outstanding episodes, and delighted to relate his knowledge, also to pass on that which he gleaned from Ted Grant. But then again Bridget recalled that he had been happier during the past few years than she had ever known him to be, and her irritation vanished—he'd be happy no more.

She looked at her mother, pitiable with age and slobbery fat. She hadn't laughed so much lately. Strangely, in contrast with Cavan, she had seemed less happy these past two years. Was this why she had destroyed the books, because they had brought him happiness? But she was old, and she shouldn't feel like this. Yet, as Bridget continued to stare at her mother, the thought came to her that age brought no respite—there still remained the worries, the fears and hurts ... the tearing of one human being to shreds by another. Life was ruled by emotion, and when emotion was frustrated this was the result—people died while they still breathed. And although, of the two, Bridget liked her father best, her sympathy at this moment went to her mother.

Rose Angela had been at Wharf House four months now. At times she could not believe this; it seemed like four years, or even fourteen, for the events before she came here were dim and dream-like in her mind, and no day up till today had been long enough for her. She wanted the hours to spread themselves so that she could savour the two great things that had come into her life— her father's return and their nightly meetings; and this other great thing, which she would not admit openly to herself but which made her days joyous and coloured her dreams at night with what might be if miracles could happen. But this latter had been thrust into the background and now only the thought of her father filled her mind. For last night she had left the house as usual at six o'clock and made her way to the spot where she always met James, near the railway carriage. But he was not there.

It was their custom, if it was dry, to walk along the river

bank, but if a gale was blowing they shared the shelter of the railway carriage with Murphy and Pete. The railway carriage had been turned into winter quarters, the windows being covered at night with pieces of sacking nailed on to frames to hide the light of the fire in the home-made stove, and more recently, the light of a little lamp supplied by Rose Angela. Into the company sometimes came the Arab, Ali Hassan; and the contrasts of the men gave Rose Angela food for thought as she sat, silent mostly, listening to their individual tales—the Arab, the Negro, the dwarf who was half-Russian, and Murphy, born of an English mother and father unknown and brought up in the workhouse. And she often marvelled that never once in all the talks she had sat through was a swear word used in her presence. The courtesy with which they each treated her often brought a lump to her throat. It was as if she were someone of note—even a queen, she sometimes thought, could not receive more respect than she did. And the many sore places in her heart were soothed.

But last night her father was not waiting for her, nor was there any sign of Pete or Murphy, and she was filled with panic.

Hassan, waiting at the entrance to the cut, quiet and patient as always, seemed to her, at that moment, like a comforting angel, and she ran to him, crying, 'Oh, Hassan, where's me da?'

And he replied soothingly, 'Don't worry; he's a little sick and can't get out, but I'll take you to him.'

When she asked where Murphy and Pete were he said he understood they had gone that morning across the river, where, they'd heard, lay the chance of some odd work.

Rose Angela did not know where her father lodged. On this he had been firm. When she had asked him to tell her in case an emergency such as the present one arose, he had laughed and said, 'Me, I be ill no more now.' Nor did she know exactly what was wrong with him, for he would not talk about himself.

Hassan had called into his eating-house and collected some food, and as he led her along narrow streets and through short, black alleyways where she could see nothing but felt that in the thick depths figures were standing, she began to understand why her father had refused to bring her here; and on reaching the house, his firmness on the matter was made absolutely clear to her. The house was one of a number which led out of a yard, and the yard was approached by a passage from the street. The ground floor was in darkness and silence, but on the first landing pale shafts of light came from beneath numerous doors, and voices in strange tongues came to her. They passed another landing and mounted yet another flight of stairs, and the air, after the freshness of the river, almost stifled her. The prevailing smell was of dirt, dirt such as she had never yet encountered even in the worst part of the fifteen streets. Even before she followed Hassan into the room she was sick at heart for her father, but when she saw him in the rusty iron bed, his back supported against the bare rails, pity and love overwhelmed her. He grasped her outstretched hand, but he did not speak, for he was holding a rag over his mouth.

The beating of her heart stopped for a moment as she saw the red streaks on the cloth—consumption! Oh God! Yet he had no cough, just that little tickling sound in his throat. She imagined all consumptives coughed and spat, like that man who travelled on the Jarrow tram and spat into a bottle. She could never make up her mind which was the worst, spitting on to the floor or into a bottle. But her father to have consumption ... and spitting blood with it! As his eyes looked into hers with unbearable love and tenderness she knew what she must do—she must come and live here and look after him.

During the past four months she had grown to love him with a love so deep it amounted to worship; and each day she was made more poignantly aware of what she had missed by being brought up without him, and of the unnatural load of fear that had been bred in her because of his absence. But now, the knowledge that he was near was building up in her a courage that had already ousted much of her fear. Yet there were always new fears waiting to be born. She had imagined he was getting better, for he looked better and talked as if whatever was wrong with him was now cured; but this—she knew what consumption meant, especially bleeding from the mouth.

They mustn't be separated again ... for the time that was left to him she must be with him, even in this house.

She drew his head to her, and as he leant against her she felt him sigh, and a fresh surge of strength, like the strength that had once been his, flowed into her, and she knew she would need this strength if she was to stick to her decision. First, her mother must be told. To face Bridget and say 'I am leaving home, I am going to sleep in' would be the final confirmation in her mother's mind that she had 'gone wrong'; but far rather let her think she was living with Mr. Stanhope than she was living in Holborn.

The simplest course for her, she knew, would be to tell her mother the truth, but there the simpleness would end, for she felt she knew her mother enough to know that even were there no Uncle Matt to be considered the return of this gaunt Negro into her life would fill her with nothing but pain and embarrassment, to say the least. It would also deprive her of what happiness she had with Tony.... Rose Angela felt a separate pang of sorrow for Tony; he had been so good; he had lived his life just to serve her mother and her. No, things must remain as they were. Her father was wise—he knew the situation was only bearable as it was now. She could not tell whether he harboured any bitterness towards Bridget, for he never spoke of her, but she guessed there were a number of reasons why he did not want her mother to know of his whereabouts.

After a while, when she told James what she intended doing he became agitated, saying, 'No, Rose Angela, me better tomorrow. She not do this, Hassan, eh?'

Although Hassan said no and that it would be unwise to do so, his eyes were telling her that above all things he wanted her here, not in this house, but in Holborn.

Rose Angela was well aware of Hassan's feelings towards her, but so well had she come to know him that she no longer feared him, or resented the fact that he should love her; and at times she thought it a waste and a pity that he should care for her as he did, for never could she return a spark of such feeling. Even if this other great love had not come into her life, she would have never considered Hassan.

To soothe James she had complied with his wishes of last night and had gone home, but she had been borne down with anxiety. This morning she'd had to wait until word was brought to her regarding his condition for she could not have found her way to the house alone. Murphy came in the middle of the morning, and his words 'I'm afraid, miss, he'll soon kick the bucket' had decided her. She told Murphy that as soon as she was finished work she would go home and get her things, and she asked if he would meet her at the cut and take her to the house. She also asked him if Hassan had sent for a doctor, and Murphy said he had.

There were still two more hours before she could leave. She longed intolerably to get away, yet she shivered at the thought of facing her mother.

She was brought from her thinking by her master entering the kitchen. He had not 'thumped' for his afternoon tea—at least she didn't think he had. 'You didn't knock, sir?' she asked.

'No—I thought I'd have it down here—it's warmer. Not in your way?'

'No, sir, of course not.'

She began immediately to get his tea, thinking that if only she hadn't so much on her mind she could enjoy this moment. Twice before during the past few days he had taken his tea with her and talked to her, and she had lain awake at night thinking over the things he had said. She looked at him now, sitting in the basket chair by the little blue stove, and it came to her that he seemed lonely; and another phrase was added to that feeling which she thought could not be enlarged.

He startled her by turning his head suddenly and holding her gaze. 'You look pale today, Rosie. Are you overworking?'

'Oh no, sir.'

'You don't still take notice about that wash-leather business I barked at you when you first came, do you? I always used that technique on the types they sent me from the agency. You see, I was a lone man and I found they always wanted to run me as well as the house; that washleather was a very good way of putting them off.'

She smiled and said, 'You mustn't have been fierce enough, sir; it had no effect on me.'

'I'm glad of that.'

She turned from his eyes and began to set the tray; and he looked into the fire again, and a quietness that was weighed with peace filled the kitchen; and Rose Angela forgot for the moment what lay before her this evening.

'Rosie, would you mind coming in on Christmas Day?'

'Not at all, sir. I expect to.'

'If Mr. Collins is here I won't ask you, for then we'll go out somewhere.'

'It won't matter in the least, sir. I'll come in.'

'Rosie'—he was still looking into the fire—'what do you want most? Is there something that you've longed for and never been able to have? Tell me—I want to give you a Christmas present.'

She stopped in the act of pouring his tea out. What did she want most? That her father should be better. He couldn't give her this; but the other great desire he could fulfil, and him only. Her face began to burn and although his eyes were not on her she turned away in case he should look up and see what madness she had come to. It was one thing to surrender her soul to him in the deep privacy of her being, but it would, she thought, destroy itself through exposure.

'I've ... I've never wanted very much, sir; I have all I want—a job, a very good job,' she added.

'Oh, Rosie, for God's sake don't be so humble.' He was aggressive again, his jaw thrust out and his eyes glinting. 'You shouldn't be humble; there's nothing about you to create humility. Why, you could——' He paused. 'Look; tell me truthfully; is there anything you've ever dreamed about?'

What words he used! She pushed the little trolley up to the fire, and now she was near him, looking down into his face, into those startlingly blue eyes. What could she say? Could she say a wireless? But that would be so expensive. A fur? Oh no ... some little thing—a brooch.

'Perhaps a brooch, sir.'

'A brooch!' His tone ridiculed the word. 'You're a disappointment, Rosie.'

'Yes, sir.'

'Sit down and have some tea with me.'

She hesitated for a moment, and he yelled, 'Go on, sit down, woman! There, you've got me bellowing again ... you shouldn't cross me.'

As she sat down on the opposite side of the hearth to him she caught the glimmer of a twinkle in his eye, and her own was forced to respond, and they laughed together.

'You must think me a funny old man.'

'I don't think you old, sir.'

'Well, I am; I'm nearly twice your age. I'm close on forty.'

'You don't look it, sir.'

'Nice and polite of you. Why are you not married, Rosie?'

The abruptness of the question caused her to stammer, 'Well ... well....'

'I suppose you're waiting until you have enough money.'

'No, I am not waiting.' To herself her voice sounded

cold and unemotional, giving no indication of the inner turmoil. She was conscious of drawing herself up, as if to defend her pride, as she went on, 'I've never been asked.'

He continued to look at her for a time before saying softly, 'There are more damn fools in the world than I thought.' Then he returned to his previous question. 'Now, tell me the truth, what would you like for Christmas? ... Besides a brooch, that is. By the way, I hate brooches, and I can't stand women who plaster themselves with jewellery.' He looked so aggressive as he said this that she was forced to smile again, thinking it was well she knew him.

'There's nothing really, sir.'

'Well, I'm not buying you a brooch. I'll give you the money and you can get what you like.'

'That's very kind of you, sir.' She turned to the table to hide her pleasure at this, for above all things at the present time she needed money.

'You know, Rosie, you are the most formal individual I have ever come across. Tell me, are you afraid of me?'

'Oh no, sir.' Her assurance was so sincere that there was no doubt that it was true; but he went on, 'Then if you're not afraid of me you are of someone or something.'

Rose Angela looked down at her plate and broke her cake into small pieces. 'I have been afraid of many things in my life, but lately they have all gone, or nearly so.'

She said no more, and he did not press the question, but continued with his tea in silence until she rose and went to the oven; and he asked, 'What have you in there? It's a lovely smell.'

She called back to him from the scullery, 'It's your Christmas cake, sir'; and he repeated laughingly, 'It's your Christmas cake, sir.'

When she returned to the kitchen he was standing by the table, and as she readjusted her apron and straightened her cap he nodded towards her head and said, 'It still isn't straight.' There was a quirk to his lips.

She flushed and said, 'It's my hair, nothing will stay on

it.' And she again attempted to straighten the cap.

'That's another thing I detest—caps. Take it off and never wear it again.'

She paused, her hands raised to her head, and at his next words her feelings almost suffocated her.

'You are very beautiful, Rosie.'

As her hands brought the cap from her head she forced her eyes from his in case she should betray herself, and the wisdom of this was given to her as he went on, his tone brusque again, 'Don't worry ... I am merely paying you a compliment.'

He went out in his quick, bustling way, and she sat down by the table, the cap still held in her hands. 'You are very beautiful, Rosie ... I am merely paying you a compliment.' Was that the artist speaking or was it the man? She sat quiet until the chimes of the clock from the hall told her that soon it would be time to go, and there were other things that she must think of; and she wondered why everything should have come into her life at once ... her love for this man, and the coming of her father....

Rose Angela's nervous system was like a highly tensed wire. The fears of her childhood and teens had played on it with such regularity that it responded with a feeling of acute sickness and anxiety when anything of a worrying nature affected her. Now, as she faced Bridget, she felt so sick that it was as much as she could do to stand. She had told Bridget that Mr. Stanhope had people staying and that she was going to sleep in for a little while. She had managed to face her mother's blank stare as she said this, but under Bridget's silence her new-found courage was failing her. She knew that her mother did not believe a word she said, yet she forced herself to go on bluffing. 'It'll only be for a little while. I'll still let you have something each week ... perhaps it won't be so much for the time being, as ... as I'm living in.' It would have been difficult enough to lie if Bridget had believed her tale, but under the circumstances she was finding it almost impossible.

'Are you going to live with your master or the Arab?' Bridget's voice was without tone or colour. It seemed like the voice one would expect to hear from the dead, could the dead speak.

Rose Angela mouthed 'The Arab?' without any sound coming from her lips, and Bridget said, 'Yes, the Arab ... you are going to live in Holborn, aren't you, where you've spent a good many of your evenings these past weeks?'

Rose Angela could only stare at her mother. It was Hassan she was meaning ... someone had seen her with Hassan. But who? It had always been dark when she saw him, except that once by the ferry, and then there had been no one about. . . . Oh, this was worse than anything she had ever imagined. Her mother mustn't go on thinking this. Oh no, she couldn't let her think this. She must tell her about James, no matter what it entailed: Matt's vengeance and Tony's unhappiness; she must tell her. She could have allowed her to go on thinking she was Mr. Stanhope's mistress, but not this. To have married an Arab would have been bad enough, but to casually live with one ... no, she would be foolish to allow anyone to think this, most of all her mother.

Relief flooded her with the knowledge that she was about to straighten things out, and she put out her hand to Bridget, saying, 'It's true I'm going into Holborn, but just to—well, lodge there.'

Bridget did not take the proffered hand, and as Rose Angela, knowing that she was about to give her mother a shock, said gently 'Sit down a minute, Ma', there came to her the sound of stormy voices from the back yard, and one at least brought the sickness over her again.

Within a second Matt and Tony were in the kitchen, and Matt, not pausing from his battle of words, directed the onslaught of his bitterness against the thorn that was forever in his flesh. 'That's the cause of all the trouble—there!' He thrust out his arm and pointed his finger at Rose Angela.

'Don't be so daft, man; she wasn't here when your ma

and da were rowing.' Tony, too, was angry and his nose was twitching rapidly.

'She didn't need to be, but it was through her. She's at the bottom of everything. If me ma goes off her head I swear to God I'll kill her.'

'It'll take a lot to knock your ma off her head,' said Tony, scathingly.

'What is she, then, but nearly daft, running round the streets begging folks to give her books for me da?'

'That's remorse for the thing she did to him, and it'll do her good to feel like that, but it'll take more than that to knock her off her head.... It's your old man you should be worrying about, not her. She's burned more than his books the day.'

Matt was not in the least concerned about his father, but his dauntless, laughing, loud-mouthed mother had always held his respect, and during the last few hours she had shocked him by going soft and begging the silent Cavan to forgive her, promising to get him all the books he could ever read. To Matt, her final humiliation was her actual begging for books, and it was all because Bridget wouldn't put him up for a night. And why wouldn't she? Because of that Arab whore.

'If she has,' he answered Tony, 'who's to blame but that dirty Arab supplier? Whites don't suit her now, she must get herself an Arab.'

Before Tony could bring out a startled exclamation and the sound of Bridget's groan escaped her lips, Rose Angela's voice rang through the kitchen louder than it had ever been raised in that room before. 'How dare you say such a thing! You're a liar! Do you hear, a liar!' There was no sign of fear in her as, for the first time in her life, she faced up to Matt. 'You and your filthy mind! You're like a sewer.' She turned from him and confronted Tony. 'Uncle Tony, do you believe I'm going to live with an Arab?'

'No, lass. I'd never believe that, never.'

'Then why,' put in Bridget beseechingly, 'are you going to live in Holborn, lass? Tell us that.'

The three stared at her, hanging on her reply.

Rose Angela looked from one to the other, and as her lips opened her eyes came to rest on Matt. She had only to say 'because James is there' and she would be clear; yet in doing so she would be handing him over to this maniac. She couldn't do it. She knew from the look in her mother's face that she believed the worst of her, and now even her Uncle Tony's expression was showing bewilderment and doubt at the mention of her going to live in Holborn. She looked at her mother again; then dropped her lids to shut out Bridget's tortured gaze and turned away, saying flatly, 'No matter what I said, you wouldn't believe me. Think what you like, I'm going to get my things.'

Matt hadn't spoken since she had called him a liar. To say the least, her bold front had startled him, and it was strange that he, who in the first place had accused her of going with an Arab, was now the only one to believe her when she denied it, even in spite of having with his own eyes seen her talking to one. He was astute enough to know that it had taken a very powerful emotion to arouse that outburst against himself, for he knew that he could instil the fear of God, as he put it, into her. He stood, his eyes fixed on the staircase door, awaiting her return and asking himself the question, 'Why should she be going to live in Holborn, if not with somebody? And if it wasn't the Arab, then who was it?'

The gas began to flicker, and Bridget, moving heavily towards the mantelpiece to get some coppers from the toby jug for the meter, shoved him aside, and in putting out his hand to steady himself he touched the fretwork pipe-rack on the wall, the hated relic of the damned nigger! His whole instinct was to whip his hand away as if it had come in contact with molten steel, but his hand remained still as something clicked in his brain, and his widening eyes seemed to draw from the pipe-rack the answer to his probing. Slowly his fingers began to move into the holes, until they hung like talons from the rack. God Almighty! Could it be? Who else?

The gas went up with a plop and Bridget came back

into the kitchen, and Matt turned from the pipe-rack and looked from her to Tony. Who else. Who else? They didn't know, they suspected nothing. Nobody knew, only that half-black rat up there. Hadn't she nearly given the game away to clear herself, just a minute ago? She had pulled up only just in time. No, nobody knew but her ... and now him. God Almighty!

Slowly he began to rub the scar on his face. How long was it? Sixteen years ... sixteen years! His fingers nipped the flesh about the scar at the corner of his mouth. Sixteen years he'd carried this, sixteen years of nights he'd lain tossing and turning. He looked back to the days when he had laughed with the lasses. He had wanted nothing from them but to laugh with them, not even to touch them. There was only one woman he had wanted to touch. Yet from when they laughed no more with him a desire to extract something from them had arisen, adding to the torment of his days and the agony of his nights; and now he who caused all this was back. He must be ... that was the only answer to that lily-livered rat up there having the spunk to face him. Perhaps all these years she had been on the look-out for the nigger—she'd had it ground into her enough as a bairn by that blasted fool Tony that her da would come back. He'd heard him at it time and again before he got thick with Bridget. A pain like a knife twisting in his bowels went through him, and his fingers moved up the scar, nipping the silver flesh into momentary redness.... Well, if his surmise was right, Master Tony would soon have the tin hat put on him; he knew his Bridget well enough to follow her reactions to the nigger's return.

He turned his eyes to the staircase door. She would get brave, would she? By God, she'd need to be brave before he'd finished with her. Stand up to him, would she? He'd see about that. He'd plaster her name with the Arab's so thick about the fifteen streets that she wouldn't dare put her nose inside them, much less come home again to live. If her own mother and Tony could believe she was thick with an Arab, how much more gullible would be the neighbours. And what about the painter bloke? Aye, what about him!

And if she was willing to forego what was left of her good name to cover up for the nigger, it would be the crowning thumb-screw on her if he nabbed him—and by God, nab him he would, or die in the attempt.

CHAPTER TWELVE

THE END OF THE WAITING

Rose Angela would have laughed to scorn anyone who would have told her a fortnight ago that there were many worse places to live in than the fifteen streets, and that there would come a time when she would miss them, miss the privacy of a house, of going upstairs to bed, of walking from one tiny room to the other, and miss the streets themselves, and the greetings and conversation thrown carelessly across their narrow widths; for in Holborn the tongues were many and varied, and she never could make out whether the neighbours in the rooms around were rowing or merely talking.

She saw very little of her neighbours, or of Holborn itself, for she went out in the dark of the morning and returned in the dark of the evening, yet the atmosphere pressed down on her and was as strange as that of a foreign country. But her days were too full to allow the change to penetrate farther than the fringe of her mind. What did penetrate and cast a shadow over her days was the rift between Bridget and herself. She wondered if anyone before had experienced so much happiness and unhappiness at the same time; there was James's love and this other love, but they were unable to ease the separation from her mother. She did not much care now what the people of the fifteen streets or of the town thought about her, but she still cared very much what Bridget thought. But for this, she felt there could be no one happier; her da was so much better—it seemed as though her presence had given him a temporary lease of life; and then this impending thing; for she did not hide the fact from herself that something was impending and that she was waiting for it, waiting with her heart racing so fast at times that she thought such emotion could not be borne and that something within her was bound to give way.

What would happen when at last her master spoke? She knew what would happen—she would become his mistress and so qualify for the name the fifteen streets had already given her. If this thought brought with it a sadness, she told herself she'd rather be his mistress than any other man's wife. Two weeks ago she would not have allowed herself to dream of becoming his mistress, for to her mind he had given no indication that he thought of her other than as a very good servant; but from the night he told her she was beautiful there had been a decided change in his manner towards her. For the three days following he almost ignored her, never looking at her, and when he spoke his voice was harsh and more clipped than usual; nor did he stay in the kitchen either for his morning coffee or for his tea, but used it merely as a passage from the hall to the wharf. Although the weather was at its worst, he spent most of his time on the river, and after one severe day he developed a cold. It was the cold that broke down his defence. He remained indoors the following day, and Rose Angela, without being summoned, took up a hot drink to the studio. He was painting on a small canvas, and on her entry he took the canvas off the easel and laid it face upwards on the table in the corner of the room, saying, 'I didn't knock.'

'I know, sir, but I thought you needed this.'

For the first time in days he looked at her. 'What are you thinking, Rosie?'

'That you should be in bed, sir.'

'That all?'

'You have a nasty cold.'

'I know I have—and I'm annoyed. I've never had a cold for years, and you're to blame.'

She didn't ask the inane question 'But why me?'; she just looked at him, her skin growing pink and the brown of her eyes deepening, and he turned from her, saying,

186

'You are either so full of humility, Rosie, that you are not quite woman, or you are so full of the wisdom of the serpent that you are laughing at me.'

She did not at the moment try to unravel his references; only one thing was clear to her and that was she was not laughing at him—whatever feeling he had for her could not arouse her laughter. He said no more, and she went downstairs.

Although, since then, his manner towards her had been gentle, he did not resume his habit of sitting in the kitchen; and she knew he was fighting her, and at times this knowledge filled her with glory and she waited, doing nothing to precipitate the moment yet longing for it to come about.

He was out now, in Newcastle she thought, for he had said he might not be back before she left. Only twice before had she seen him 'dressed', as she put it, and today she thought he looked very grand; and she knew a qualm of fear—his heavy tweeds and large trilby seemed to remove him from her—he looked too grand. Could anyone like him think of her in the way she was imagining? Yet she thought of his words as he left the house. 'Don't wait for me, Rosie, I may not be back before six,' and it seemed to her that he wanted them to convey the opposite meaning—it was as if he were saying 'Wait for me'. It would have been nice to have waited, on the pretext of giving him a hot meal, but she knew how much her da longed for her return, and she never kept him waiting a minute longer than she could help.

It was now half-past five and she went around the house doing the final touches of the day, building up the drawing-room fire, taking the counterpane off the bed and turning back the bed-clothes; and as she left his room she glanced towards the flight of stairs leading to the studio. How empty the house was without him up there ... even if she never heard him for hours his presence would seep down to her. The feeling to be nearer to the things that were part of him now enveloped her and she went slowly up the stairs and into the first studio. She did not switch on the light but passed through into the other, the room where he spent most of his life. She pressed one of the switches on a board near the door and the light appeared high up in the far corner of the ceiling. This was part of the system of lighting by which he worked at night. A reflector directed the light on to an easel, on which stood the small canvas he had been working on for days. She had not seen this picture, for his breadth always obscured it, and once she remembered him taking it down when she was in the room. Now she moved towards it and saw it was hidden behind a covered frame clipped to the top of the easel and leaving only a narrow strip of the canvas visible. Gently she lifted up the frame and stood staring at the picture. . . .

Had she known this was what she would see? Was that why she was drawn up here? Did she really look like that, her mouth half smiling and her eyes sad? But were her eyes as sad as that? And her hair . . . did the coiled plaits appear like a silver and black halo where the light touched them? Surely she didn't look like this. No, this wasn't meant to be the picture of the self that she saw in the mirror, it was rather the picture of what she knew herself to be inside. The little things she laughed at were there in her lips, but the fears of her life were in her eyes. She unhooked the frame from the easel and the light fell full on the picture. And now she was confronted with another aspect . . . she looked superior, or, to use the fifteen streets' term, 'stuck up'. But she wasn't stuck up—no one could be less stuck up—for what had she to be stuck up about? Nevertheless, there it was on the canvas. Was this how he saw her? She moved back and sat down and stared at the portrait, her hands gripped tightly in her lap. No matter how he saw her, he had painted her, and hadn't he said, 'I never paint women?'

'Well, what do you think of it?'

She swung round on the stool, her hands clutching the front of her dress. He was standing in the doorway, still in his outdoor clothes, and the sight of him made her dumb.

She was afraid of having been found here, for this was his sanctum sanctorum, and it was an unwritten law that it would always be held as such.

As he walked towards her she turned to the canvas again; and when he stood behind her and she felt his coat against her shoulders a painful stillness filled her.

'Do you like it?' His voice was unsteady.

Still she could utter no word. His hand came down on her shoulder and moved slowly to her chin, and as her head was tilted back the stillness vanished; the waiting was over, and wave after wave of trembling happiness washed through her as she looked up at his great tousled head.

Now his other hand was on her face, cupping it. 'You know, Rosie, don't you?'

She closed her eyes against the light in his and felt herself swung round and to her feet.

'You know I love you. For God's sake say something! Stop me making a fool of myself. I know I'm a damned fool, but I can't help it. God knows I've tried.' He pressed her clasped hands into his chest. 'Tell me I'm not a fool ... tell me, Rosie.'

Still she could release no words; it was as if her happiness had locked all expression of itself within her; but she leant towards him and all that her being held was in her eyes, and he kissed her, kissed her with a fierceness that met and satisfied the deep demand that lay hidden beneath her calm exterior. She stood crushed in his arms, pressed into him, almost crying from sheer happiness.

'Rosie; Rosie; Rosie——' With each murmur of her name he rocked her gently. 'How I've longed to do that. For months and months I've longed just to do that ... even from the very first day. Do you know you've driven me nearly mad?' He held her from him. 'I'd sworn never to paint another woman, and you see what I had to do?'

Dimly she registered the fact that he had at one time painted women; and a woman was likely the reason why he had stopped. But what did anything of his past matter? He was hers now ... hers ... hers.

She was in his arms again and he was murmuring into her hair, ' "What's your name?" I asked you that first day. Do you remember? "Rose Angela Paterson", you said. Rose Angela. There has never been anyone more like their name, half flower, half angel.'

She lifted her head and laughed at his flowery exaggeration, such a gay, happy, free laugh that she could not believe it came from her; and with a naturalness as if she had spoken it instead of merely thinking it every day she said his name ... 'Michael.'

'Say that again.'

'Michael.' Her lips shyly framing the word seemed to hold it while she drew fresh joy from the utterance. As she was borne away on his emotion, part of her questioned the reality of what was happening. But reality or dream, it did not matter as long as she remained in this state.

'Come'—he took her by the hand and led her to the door—'I've something to show you ... something that you asked for.'

But at the door he stopped; and there was laughter in his eyes. 'What do you want most, Rosie? Tell me. But this time I want the truth, mind.'

And when she gave him the answer she had wanted to give him that night in the kitchen he swung her off her feet and up into his arms and carried her down the stairs.

She made no protest, but lay against him; and as he sat her down in the drawing-room, saying like a boy with his first love, 'I'll never let you walk up or down those stairs again—it will be an excuse to hold you,' she dared to say teasingly, 'Even when you bellow for me?'

His face became serious. 'To think I ever bellowed at you!'

Diffidently she put up her hand and touched his cheek. 'I used to long for you to bellow so that I could come up to you.'

He was on his knees, his arms about her again. 'You

love me, Rosie?'

'Yes ... oh yes. I've always loved you, right from that
first day when you looked down on me from the window
and said, "I don't want a model."'

'And all the time you put me off, by looking either
frightened or aloof.... You'll never look afraid again;
from now on I'll make your life such as no fear will touch
it.'

She moved her hands through his hair. 'It all seems too
good to be true.'

'Nothing will be too good for you.... I'll take you
travelling—I'll show you the world. Not that I think
much of the world at the present moment, but you must
see places. We'll go through France to Germany, and
through the Black Forest ... you'll like that.'

She answered slowly, 'Yes, perhaps ... but I don't know.
I can think of no better life than to stay here in this house
with you.'

'Rosie, your humility is painful, but I love you for it.
Where's that damn box?'

He patted his pockets and dragged the greatcoat that
he had flung on to the carpet towards him. 'There'—he
thrust the small parcel into her hands—'that's what you
asked for.'

She undid the wrapping, and she flashed him a look of
gratitude before opening the black box lying in the palm
of her hand. It would be the brooch. It was the brooch,
but such a one as she had never seen before. In an oval of
finely wrought silver lay a rose worked in stones glinting
with red and purple lights. She had no knowledge of precious stones, but she knew that in this exquisite setting
lay something of great value, something that she was
afraid to accept.

'Well, what do you think? You asked for it, you know;
though what you want a brooch for God alone knows.
You shouldn't wear jewellery—you have all the jewels
you need.' He moved his fingers round the circles of her
eyes.

'It's beautiful; but it's too much.'

"Too much!' he scoffed. 'Rosie you are the only beautiful woman I have met ... in fact the only woman, beautiful or otherwise, who didn't think she was worth the earth. You must put a greater value on yourself.' He pressed her face tightly between his hands. 'After you've lived with me for a while you will—I'll make you know your own value.... Oh, my love!' He laid his head on her breast; and his voice took on a touch of sadness. 'You don't know what you've done for me. I never thought I'd allow a woman into my life again. Years ago I received a nasty knock and it turned me against all your kind, but from the moment I first saw you, you changed that. And then to find you possessed a sense of fair play—you seemed too good to be true.'

He lifted his head, and she looked down into his eyes, the blue now dark and soft, and her mind was awhirl with the wonder of him and his love for her that was making him tremble. At last. At last life was coming right. You only had to wait and be patient and happiness came to you. Oh, Holy Mary! She felt she wanted to go down on her knees and pray. But the thought of praying brought a self-consciousness with it; if he didn't mention marriage—and she was sensible enough to know that there was very little likelihood of him doing so—and she went to him, as she knew she would, what about praying then? It didn't matter ... nothing mattered but him. What was marriage and religion, anyway? Look at the lives the married people led in the fifteen streets ... good Catholics, too! She would let nothing come between them. She would take this love whichever way it was offered and stand the consequences. But the consequences could only be good. And as she listened to his voice she felt the certainty of this.

'That day you told our enterprising Mr. Pillon what you thought of him, you didn't know I was in the boat alongside the wharf, did you?' She shook her head. 'I had started up the river, but found there was some gear missing, and when I came back you were in the thick of it.

You did something for me that day, Rosie: you more than saved me nearly two pounds a week; you gave me back my faith in human nature—the female side, anyway. It was surprising to know that a woman could be honest —a beautiful woman—and just for the sake of honesty, with no ulterior motive behind her action. Oh, Rosie, Rosie, I love you for so many things.' He gazed at her tenderly. 'What are you going to do about it?'

The onus was on her, and it brought the colour flooding to her face. She shook her head and swallowed, and he asked gently, 'Would you ... would you come and live with me, Rosie?'

Her eyes fell away from his and she said simply, 'Yes.'

'Rosie! Oh, Rosie, my dear!'

He held her gently, and a silence fell on them that was not entirely devoid of embarrassment.

He rose from her side, saying, 'We'll have a drink, then dinner, eh?' But he hadn't reached the cabinet before she was on her feet, protesting, 'Not tonight! I'd forgotten the time ... I must go home.'

'What! Now?' He turned in surprise. 'But you can't, Rosie.' He came towards her, his heavy brows gathering into a furrow. 'You don't mean to go yet.'

'I'll have to. Look, it's quarter to seven. He ... they'll be worrying.'

'Surely not for an hour or so? Stay and have something to eat with me, and then I'll take you home. I've always wanted to take you home ... next to keeping you here.' He stood close to her, not touching her, but his eyes tracing each feature of her face.

'Oh, I'd love to stay ... you know I would.' She took his hand and held it to her cheek.

'Then why don't you?' He covered the hand that held his with his own.

'Because they're expecting me.'

He remembered it was Friday and she had been paid, and he surmised it was for this they would be waiting.

'All right, then, but I'm taking you home.'

At this her mind whirled into a panic, and saying she

must get her things she turned from him. . . . He thought she was going to the fifteen streets. What would he have to say to her living in Holborn? And what further would he say when he knew the Negro was her father? He would have to be told, but not tonight. Anyway, she must hurry. What on earth would her da be thinking? He'd be lying worrying. But how was she going to put Michael off?

'It's raining, and you've still got that cold . . . don't come out again.' Even to herself, her effort sounded feeble.

'Don't go out; but let you go alone, and over that road too?' He was his bustling self again. 'I don't know what I've been thinking of all along to allow you to go alone in the dark through that jumble of debris. God knows what might have happened to you.'

She was forced to smile at his solicitude. For months now she had walked through the debris and she doubted if he had even thought of it.

But his next words brought a tenseness to her body. 'I would have seen you to the tram, in any case, tonight, for I had to warn off one of those damned Arabs as I came in. I found him standing at the edge of the clearing, apparently surveying the house. Have you had any trouble with them coming here when I've been out?'

'No.'

As he was shrugging himself into his coat again he said, 'I'll break the first one's neck I find with his foot on my ground—I can't stand the oily blighters.'

Poor Hassan. At one time she had felt that way too. She still did towards most of the Arabs, but towards Hassan she felt nothing but sympathy. But she guessed this feeling would be hard to explain to this love of hers, who in many ways was a law unto himself. She would explain her acquaintance with Hassan after she told him about her da—it really shouldn't come as any great surprise to him to know that her father was a Negro, for he must see she had coloured blood in her veins. It was always a matter of amazement to her that the likeness in the eyes had escaped him. Yet her da had sat for him every day for a week, and he hadn't noticed.

As he insisted on buttoning a mackintosh of his over her coat she probed his feelings on the matter of her colour by asking shyly, 'Michael, do you mind about me being ... coloured?'

'Coloured? Oh, my dear, I wouldn't mind if your father was an orang-outang as long as you were you.' He drew her to him. 'Never mention that again. I adore you ... I always shall. Right from the day I first saw you I knew what would happen to me. Coloured! Where you are concerned I'm colour-blind.'

She laughed. 'Oh, how funny. You're like God, then.'

'God?' His eyebrows shot up into his hair. 'Me?'

'Well, I think you must be the only one besides him in all the world who is colour-blind. Our priest told me when I was a child that God was colour-blind; I've never found anybody else who is. Oh, and I love you for it. Oh, Michael, Michael!'

She kissed him with a fervour that prolonged the departure and made him plead again, 'Stay a little while ... just a little while.'

'I can't. Tomorrow night I will, I promise.'

Yes, she would stay later tomorrow night. She would tell her da and he would understand.

As soon as they were outside she began to talk, as a warning to Hassan, whom she knew would be waiting. Stanhope held her by the arm, her elbow pressed into his side and her fingers laced tightly through his own; and going up the dark bank towards the market-place he pulled her into the deep shadow of a wall and kissed her, a silent, wordless kiss. But as they walked across the steel-glistening empty market-place to the tram it took all her gentle persuasion to counter his voluble insistence that he should accompany her home, and she did not feel safe until she stood on the platform of the tram as it jogged out of the market-place, watching him receding into the distance, the blueness of his eyes seeming to pierce the darkness until he was lost from her sight.

The tram stopped four times before she alighted; then

she stood, uncertain for a moment what to do. She must give him time to get well out of the way before she ventured back to the Mill Dam again.

When she did come to the bank she kept to the shadow of the wall until she entered Holborn and, although she now breathed more freely, her steps became slower, for she had never before traversed these streets alone in the dark.

She had hardly covered the first deserted street when she heard quick padding footsteps behind her and a well-known voice call softly, 'Rose Angela.' She stopped in relief and laughed into the darkness, 'Oh, Hassan! I am glad to see you!'

Hassan made no reply, but walked quietly by her side; and because of his silence she knew that he was aware of what was between her and Stanhope. He would have seen them; perhaps he had followed them. Thinking of the dark bank leading to the ferry, she blushed and decided to bring the matter into the open. It would be the best way.

'Mr. Stanhope set me to the tram tonight, he doesn't know that I'm living down here.' It was difficult to go on, for Hassan's displeasure was as visible as the wet darkness, and as cold. 'You wouldn't believe it, but he doesn't know James is my da. After painting him, too! It's odd, isn't it?'

Still Hassan made no comment, and they walked in awkward quietness until they reached the house, but in the darkness of the hall he spoke softly and rapidly, holding her gently by the arms as he did so. 'Rose Angela. You know I have a great love for you. No, don't say anything yet. . . . I am not as others. I want one woman and one only, and that woman is you. I have money—much money. I can take you and your father away from here and send you both to Switzerland, where the healing air will prolong his life. But above all things I want to make you my wife . . . I want to marry you. The painter will never marry you—he comes of a class that scorns any colour but their own.'

She said nothing. The darkness hid his face from her, but she was filled with pity for him.

'Think it over. I don't want to hurry you, Rose Angela, but...' He did not finish, and they stood in silence again. He was waiting for her to speak; and as they stood it was brought to both of them that their silence was part of an unusual quietness that pervaded the whole house. Usually at this time of night the house was alive with clatter and noise. Only when danger threatened the inhabitants or something unusual was afoot would there be this silence.

Hassan drew closer to Rose Angela and whispered, 'Something is wrong. Go up and stay in the room, I'll be up later. Don't come downstairs again, not until I've found out what the trouble is.'

He gave her a gentle push towards the stairs, and she ran quickly from him, and each door she passed showed no light, nor gave forth any sound. Only from the bottom of her own door did a light shine. She paused, and the ecstatic happiness of the evening became submerged under the weight of a dread. Reluctantly her hand went to the knob, and she turned it slowly and went in.

For the past hour James had lain watching the door. Soon she would be here, and his day would begin. His days for the past two weeks had started at half-past six in the evening, when his Rose Angela came through the door, and ended at half-past seven in the morning when she left him. All day long he lay quiet, reserving his strength for her. He had little to say to Murphy or Pete, or even to the generous Hassan, while they sat with him giving him the news of the river. Only when they commented on the change Rose Angela had wrought in this room did he allow himself to be roused. Yes sir, by Jove ... she wonderful.

He looked now to the corner where her shake-down was curtained off with a piece of gay chintz, and at the window to the side of him where the same material shut out the sight, if not the sound, of the torrential rain; even the

rusty bedrail was removed from his gaze by her neat drap-
ing. His hands, long and bony, with the nails startlingly
pink, moved lovingly to the glass jar of yellow chrysan-
themums on the bamboo table by the bedside ... she
thought of everything. Flowers for him! And the food she
brought him, food that now he couldn't eat. Two years
ago he could have eaten it; how he could have eaten it. If
he'd had food then there might have been a chance for
him. Or if he had waited a little longer and hadn't sailed
in that hell ship, with short commons and rotten boilers
that sweated the flesh off a man. But hadn't he waited too
long, years too long, always hoping that he would strike
the money and come back and shower gifts on his Rose
Angela?

It was strange how the thought of his once beloved
Rose had been thrust into the background by the love for
his child. Had he always known that Bridget wouldn't
wait for him? He supposed so. Yet it came as a shock when
he knew it was Tony she had chosen ... Tony, the boy
who had taken Rose Angela from his arms that night long
ago; Tony, who had always liked him. He did not blame
Tony. Women were the devil—they had always been the
devil, all except his Rose Angela. Yet she played the devil
with men, too, tenfold more than her mother had been
capable of doing. Hassan ... Hassan was mad about her.
But he was glad she no want Hassan. He was good fella
and kind, but he was not for his Rose Angela. He did not
want her to marry any coloured man. No sir. She was
mostly white and he wanted a white man for her. If she
married coloured man all her life she'd be in trouble,
inside of her and outside, whereas if she marry white man
she be protected by his colour alone. The painter man he
like his Rose Angela, there were many signs of that. He
bellow a lot, but not at her; he look at her when she not
looking, and his voice soft and kind when he speak to her.
But would he marry her? Liking and marrying were two
different things. And him a swell.... And his Rose
Angela. How did she feel about the painter man? She no
say nothing, not even last night when he noticed strange

light in her eyes when she came in, and he say to her, 'You happy?' and she replied, 'I'm happy to be back with you.'

'Who bring you?'

'Murphy, and he's practically drowned, but he wouldn't stay—it's blowing a gale.'

Murphy had not brought that light to her eyes, but as yet she did not wish to tell him who had, so he had turned the conversation.

'It blowing great guns all day—river'll be in a temper. I no like wind much. You like wind, Rose Angela?'

'No, I don't.' She touched his brow with her lips. 'That's another thing I've got from you, you know.' She looked lovingly into his face. 'You look heaps better to-day.'

'Me? I'm fine.' And to prove it he had hitched himself up and talked to her as she emptied the basket and set about preparing the evening meal. 'Me? I never like wind, 'cause I don't understand him, how him come about. Harvest—it no mystery; you put seed into earth. You can see the earth and see the seed, but you no can see wind. Only things that it touches you can see. Me, I see it touch one part of tree, other part still as death; and I see it wave one blade of grass—just one. Clever fellow on boat, he say it was worm or insect at bottom. Wasn't worm or insect on the tree. No, I no like wind. I hate fog and I no like wind, yet I love the water. And water and wind are cousins, they say. Strange. Me, I can never understand it. You like fog, Rose Angela?'

'No, I can't stand it either—it makes me afraid. I always expect something strange to loom up out of it.'

He nodded understandingly. 'Me same.'

The tie of kinship seemed to be stronger because she had inherited his fears, and he became silent, content just to watch her.

Later she told him she had seen a little house they could rent, not actually out of Holborn, but away from this quarter, and it pained him to witness her disappointment when he said, 'I no move from here, Rose Angela; Matt not get down this part. If I no sick I not mind, but...' He left the sentence unfinished, then went on, 'I be able to get up next week, and you go back home.' He hung on her reply, and it was like new life pouring into his veins when she said, 'You are my home.'

Was it any wonder he lived only when she was near him? But would he live enough days to make up for the years they had been separated? With the hope that is the heritage of the consumptive he thought he would and longer....

He was lying now, still and unmoving, his great eyes watching the door, but at half-past six she did not come. Nor yet at seven o'clock, and the fear of the wind became lost under the weight of apprehension filling his wasted body. And when half an hour later the noise and clamour of voices that always filled the house became gradually still and into their place came a scuffling of feet on the stairs as if someone was being dragged up them, he hitched himself up in the bed and waited, the sweat pouring down his body; and he fell back almost in a faint when the door was pushed open and a man was thrust into the room by Murphy and Pete.

Across the bed-rails James and Matt surveyed each other, and both for the moment forgot all else but the terrible change that time had brought to each face.

Then the years fell away, and the hate that had reached its destroying climax in Bridget's kitchen sixteen years before filled the room. Matt's body jerked spasmodically with it; he made sounds in his throat but did not speak; only his eyes, riveted on James, spoke for him.

Murphy and Pete released their hold on him but remained threatingly close, and Murphy said to James, over the bed-rail, 'We had to bring him up—the Greek tipped us off he was watching the house. We couldn't nab him in the street, we had to wait until he got into the yard.'

Matt growled again, and Murphy, raising his forearm, warned, 'Mind yersel'.' Then he repeated, 'We had to bring him up; he knew you were here, Jimmy. He would have come up on his own or got the polis.'

James made no comment, but lay returning Matt's

stare, and Murphy asked, 'What's to be done with him?'

The ominous question brought Matt's gaze from James and he glanced from Murphy to Pete, then swiftly around the room.

'Aye, have a good look,' said Murphy. 'The only way out is the way you come in.'

As Matt's eyes darted to the door the sound of running footsteps, intensified by the quiet of the house, came to him; and the other three men also turned their eyes to the door and waited. When it opened, Matt looked at Rose Angela standing there with her hands over her mouth, and a flash of his old power wiped out for the moment his own fear. Where was her bravery now? His eyes held hers as she came into the room and backed towards the bed, and when, without looking at James, she groped for his hand, Matt growled, 'Thought you were smart, didn't you? Well, you weren't smart enough, were you?'

'Shut yer gob, else I'll shut it for yer!' Murphy lifted his hand threateningly, and James interposed in a surprisingly calm voice, 'Let him talk, Murphy. There lots he wants off his chest.'

The sight of Rose Angela's fear seemed to restore Matt's courage, and he cried, 'There's one thing I'm gonna say you needn't think I was fool enough to come down here without lettin' on to anyone, so you can tell these two tykes of yours they better be careful what they're up to.'

'Why you come, anyway?' James asked.

'You know bloody well why I came ... to get you!'

'You too late.'

'I don't know so much about that.' Matt's eyes darted to Rose Angela. 'I'll never be too late as long as that un's about.' Matt's sense of power mounted as he saw James's calm vanish and the hand holding his daughter's visibly shake. 'One of you'll pay for this.' Matt jerked his chin to indicate his scarred face.

James said, 'You no blame anyone but me ... you asked for what you got, you try to ruin ... my wife.' The word wife had a stilted sound, as if stiff for want of use.

'Your wife! A bit of a lass you took down when she was drunk. Your wife! I wonder, if she could see you now, what she'd think of her great, swaggering nigger. You made a mess of me, but, by God, it's a flea-bite to what you look like! That's why you didn't send for her on the quiet, eh? Didn't want her to see what a fool she'd been.'

The jerking of James's fingers within her palm told Rose Angela that Matt's surmise was one of the reasons why her father hadn't wanted to see Bridget; and when Matt went on, 'She knew she'd been a fool all right, long before you went, and you weren't gone five minutes before she had another bed-warmer,' she cried out, 'Don't believe him; he's lying! It was years after, years and years.'

She looked pleadingly down on James, and he, calm once more, reassured her. 'You no worry; that no matter ... makes no difference.' He lay back, and, staring at Matt over the bed-rails, said quietly and pointedly, 'When Bridget took other man I not know, but you did. Must have been very devil for you that!'

The words, like a knife-thrust, turned Matt's face to the colour of dirty silver. 'You black swine!'

He drew his body up as if to spring, and Murphy cried, 'I wouldn't if I was you.' And as he said this Murphy stepped a little to the front of Matt to prevent any movement he might make towards the bed, leaving exposed to Matt's right the little kitchen table, on which stood a lamp, an old-fashioned affair with a painted iron stalk and an oil container in the shape of a round flower surmounted by a tall lamp-glass.

In this tense, passion-filled atmosphere, Matt's mind was attuned to take advantage of any opening, and in the lamp he saw the weapon to his hand. Like a cat he sprang sideways, and in an instant he was at the far side of the table with the lamp in his hand. For a second, surprise made the others still. They stared at him, unbelieving, as if he were some demon capable of conjuring up separate selves. It was Murphy who made the first move, and Matt yelled, 'You stir from there and I'll hurl this on to the bed!' Slowly his eyes ranged from one to the other, and he said softly, 'Now who calls the tune?'

As Murphy made to move again Rose Angela cried, 'Don't Murphy, don't ... he's mad ... he'll do it.'

'Yes, I'll do it ... you know your Uncle Matt, don't you?' He spat across the table at the term 'uncle'. 'But before I do it I'll do something else ... come here, you!'

'You no move.' James was sitting upright, his voice hoarse with fear. 'I go.'

'I don't want you yet, I want her. I'll deal with you later. You come here. If you don't, you know what I'll do with this lamp.'

Wild-eyed and staring, as if her eyes were already fixed in death, Rose Angela loosened James's fingers from her coat, and pressed him back into the bed; and skirting Murphy and Pete, slowly walked towards the table.

'Not that side ... this side.'

Like a marionette she obeyed him, until she was standing less than an arm's length from him, with the table at her back. Now she knew the summit of all fears ... the total fears of her childhood and her teens were one minor tremor compared to the emotion now paralysing her. She felt that all her years had been a waiting for this moment. In the ecstasy of Stanhope's kiss she hadn't told herself, like most girls would, that all her life she had been await-ing such a moment ... that this was what her thoughts and dreams had promised her, but now, standing fasci-nated under Matt's diabolical stare, she knew that this was the moment she had been awaiting, this moment in which he would destroy her face. Every atom of feeling in her was transformed into fear; it was shaking her limbs as if with ague.

'You're sick with fright, aren't you? Go on, spew—you always spew when I frighten you.'

Without taking his eyes from her face Matt spoke to Murphy. 'Stop that dirty nigger from getting out of that bed, and you two listen to me. I'm gonna do something, and if any of you as much as move a finger when I'm at it I'll hurl the lamp into her half-breed face, d'you hear me?'

The desire to destroy both James and Rose Angela was burning its way through Matt like an acid. Inside his tortured mind he sensed that, whichever way things went, this was the end for him, but end or no end he was going to do things in his own way. For the first time in his life the desire for Bridget was lost under a greater desire—he would crash the lamp into her face if it was the last thing he did! But first there was something else he would do. For how many years had he wanted to feel the contact of his fist between those eyes? He could not remember a time when this urge had not swayed him. As he glared into Rose Angela's blanched face he realised that his hate of the daughter exceeded a thousand-fold that of the father.

His body began to sway and his hand with it, and the lamp sent the shadows of Murphy and Pete across the ceiling like crouching demons leaping through space. The room for the moment became strangely silent, with all the figures motionless and stiff. Then Matt, shouting another warning to Murphy, flung the silence into pandemonium.

As his fist crashed between Rose Angela's eyes Murphy sprang. He hurled himself on Matt, or more correctly where Matt had been, for Murphy's hand slid off Matt's twisting shoulders as if they were greased and he measured his length with a thud on the floor.

Pete did not move, but his unblinking eyes never left Matt; not even when James's swaying body rocked towards Matt did he remonstrate. Not until Matt threw the lamp did he spring. Then, like an enraged monkey he hurled himself sideways across the table, knocking Rose Angela flying as she stood swaying and moaning, her hands covering her face. Still with the antics of a monkey, he caught the lamp, and fell to the floor with it, balancing it upright like some circus clown.

Murphy, rising to his knees, clawed wildly at Matt's

legs as he rushed towards the door, but he did not succeed in checking him. . . . It was James, looking more weird and grotesque than ever, his long, wasted legs sticking like props from beneath his shirt, who blocked Matt's way. Once more he and Matt confronted each other, and James's anger was even greater now than it had been on that faraway night, but his strength was as a child's. As his feeble hands were raised to strike, Matt's foot shot out, aiming at his stomach, but catching him on the thigh and sending him sprawling against the wall.

The way clear now, Matt flung himself out on to the landing and down the stairs, rocketing against the walls as he went, and through his brain rocketed only one regret—the lamp had missed her! All through that blasted dwarf! As he neared the hall he knew by the thundering on the stairs above that they were after him, and in the yard, where no vestige of light showed, not even a glimmer from the street lamp, for that had been put out, he knew himself to be running for his life, and that every man's hand was against him. By a stroke of luck he found the alleyway, but in the street, shadows that seemed darker than the night loomed at the end by which he had entered, so he turned in the other direction.

He was running as he had been wont to do years ago, with long loping strides, springing from one foot to the other. He became conscious as he ran of a strange and new feeling of freedom; his body seemed light and young once more . . . he would beat them yet. . . . When had he last felt like this? The night he had run home to see Bridget and saw the black swine for the first time . . . Bridget, Bridget, why did you do it? It was as if the years were being flung off with each flying step until he was back to that very night, walking the black streets and crying like a child as he walked, 'Bridget, Bridget, why did you do it?'

He was now in a maze of buildings, warehouses mostly, and this told him he was near the river. If only he could find an alleyway. He paused in his running and listened. Yes, blast them, he could hear their feet pounding the cobbles.... Where was there a damned alleyway? He groped along one wall and laughed in relief as the wind, rushing up the alley, brought him the tang of the river. Once on the bank, he could make his way to the Mill Dam; he would slope them yet. His legs became infused with revitalised life; he was young again, really young. He had done something he had wanted to do for years—he had bashed that one's face. And now he was going to tell his Bridget that the nigger was alive, but was less than useless. He wouldn't trouble her, but it would put paid to Mister Tony, and his Bridget would be alone again, and would turn to him. Oh, Bridget, Bridget! His running cut through the wind like the keel of a ship through the water, and his head filled with the wind. It swelled and swelled, making his body so light that he was no longer on the ground. The wind became a whirlwind; until finally the roaring of it culminated in a bang and his head burst into stillness.

He came to a sudden stop on the very edge of the wall that hemmed in the river, and below him he could hear the lap-lap of the water against the wall. He put out his hand and felt the walls of the warehouses that closed him in on both sides. He put out his foot and there was nothing. This last action conveyed one thing to the hollowness of his mind—he must not jump down there because he couldn't swim. He lifted his hand to his brow and his fingers groped at the emptiness under them. What had he been thinking when he was running? Had he been running? Yes, he had been running ... but what had he been thinking? He must try to remember what he had been thinking. The sound of the pounding feet came to him again, and they carried another single thought into the hollowness ... he must hide. But there was only the river, with the sheer wall down to it.

It was impulse that made him lower himself over the wall. Alongside the warehouses the shelf of the wall was scarcely more than a hand wide, but the finishing stones had been left in parapet form and to these he clung, and edged himself a foot or so out of the line of the alleyway.

His legs were in the water up to his thighs, and when his toes, scraping against the wall, found a niche where a brick had been washed out, he thrust his feet in, and this lifted the weight from his hands; and he hung there, listening to the footsteps, their coming and their going, and he began to laugh softly.

CHAPTER THIRTEEN

THE FEET OF THE BELOVED

It was ten o'clock when Rose Angela stumbled over the last sleepers towards the clearing, and the white-painted door and windows of the house shone at her like welcoming beacons. Never had she loved the house as she did at this moment; nor needed its comforting warmth and colour so much; and once inside, with Michael's arms about her, all her mental and physical pain would be eased.

She pressed her hand to her brow, where the pain was most acute. How would he take the sight of her face? She must tell him everything ... everything but how she came by the blow. She would say that she fell—she must not tell him Matt did it, for not even to him must she say that she had seen Matt last night, for as yet she did not know what had happened to him. Hour after hour she had sat waiting by the side of James for Murphy or Pete to come back with some word, but they hadn't come. Nor yet had any of the neighbouring men looked in, or the women, and this augured bad, so she must not say she had seen Matt.

The terror of last night would remain with her, she thought, until she died, and after, and the terror had not ceased when Matt had flown, for the scarlet blood pouring from James's mouth had been equally terrifying. But this morning he seemed better, yet she knew that last night's events had precipitated his end, and she had been loath to leave him even for the short time it would take to tell Michael the reason for her absence. Oh to be with Michael just for a few minutes, to rest against him and have his sympathy flow over her. She broke into a run, and when she rounded the narrow shingled path to the back door she could not restrain herself from calling his name aloud, 'Michael! Michael!' If he was up in the studio he would hear her and come bounding down the stairs, to stand horrified for the moment at the sight of her face—yes, she knew her face would shock him.

She turned the handle of the door and, finding it locked, called again, 'Michael!'

He mustn't be up yet, and it was after ten. Likely he had been working most of the night. Automatically her hand went to the beam that supported the roof of the porch, but her fingers, groping behind it, did not come in contact with the key. When she had tried the other side, and been met with the same emptiness, she turned and looked at the blue boat bobbing forlornly against the side of the wharf. She was nonplussed. If he was not down in the morning the key would still be behind the beam, where she left it at night. Again her fingers traced the key's hiding place; then panic seized her. If he had gone out, he would have left the key. Perhaps he had been taken ill and couldn't get downstairs ... perhaps he was dead.

'Michael!' She battered with her fist upon the door. 'Michael!'

When she heard his steps in the kitchen only the tight painfulness of her face prevented her from laughing with relief, and he had barely opened the door before her hands went out to him. But they found no answering grip. His arms did not pull her to him, exclaiming in horror at the sight of her face, nor did he demand in his impetuous way where she had been until this hour. After staring fixedly at her face for a moment, he merely turned from her and put the width of the table between them.

As she stared at him in astonishment her whole body began to shake, and her voice, too, trembled as she asked softly, 'What's the matter?'

He did not answer her immediately, but continued to look at her with eyes so coldly blue that she appealed to him as a child might, saying, 'But what have I done?'

She watched him pass one lip over the other, and his voice was so quiet when it came as to be scarcely recognisable as his.

'Are you living in Holborn, Rosie?'

The racing of her heart warned her of what was to come, and she answered with difficulty, 'Yes, but I was going to tell you ... I ...'

A small deprecatory movement of his hand checked her hesitant words.

'With an Arab?'

'No. No!' She screamed the words at him; and again he checked her, asking sharply, 'Last night you never went to the fifteen streets, you got off that tram and went back to Holborn, didn't you?'

She was unable to answer him—her eyes were fixed on his face like a fear-paralysed rabbit.

'That Arab I chased was waiting for you, wasn't he?'

Still no words would come, and he went on, 'I see he has thrashed you for your duplicity. He has that to his credit, anyway.'

'Michael'—she gasped his name fearfully—'I'm not living with him. It's true he was waiting for me. He's ... he's a friend. He takes me into Holborn. I'm living with my father ... the Negro, the one that you painted.'

She watched his eyebrows rise, then draw into a thick furrow. 'Your father, eh? My God!' He shook his head as if at his own gullibility. 'Rosie, I wouldn't have believed you capable of such barefaced lying.'

She leant across the table towards him and cried beseechingly, 'Believe me, oh, believe me, I'm not lying. I know it looks bad, but I'm not lying.'

'Be quiet!'

At his low-growled command she straightened herself and tried to draw on what little pride and strength she had left to face up to this man, who was now neither master nor lover. But it was no use. Under his contemptuous glance she not only bowed her head but her body also, and she leaned her hands on the table for support as he went on, 'May I ask where you mother comes in, in this scheme of things? Why isn't she with your father?'

'I can explain——' She made to raise her head.

'Wait. If I remember rightly, you told me your mother was a widow, and that your father died when you were a child.'

Yes, he remembered rightly, and she could remember his question 'Is your father out of work?' and her answer, to save explanations and more humiliation, 'He's dead. He died when I was a child.'

She spoke with difficulty from under her breath, 'That was a lie, but it's the only one I've told you.'

'Rosie!' His tone as he uttered her name was quiet but heavy with scorn. 'Don't make matters worse. Look at those.' He placed two letters on the centre of the table. 'Do you recognise the writing?'

She shook her head.

'They are anonymous letters about you.'

'About me?' Her head came up with a jerk, and her mouth hung agape in amazement.

'Why do you appear so surprised? Everyone isn't blind, you know; I happen to be an exception. One of those letters, I know, is from Bessie, who tells me it's about time I found out I was being fooled. Apparently she had her own ideas of why I kept you on. The other is from someone, I should imagine, who knows you very well. One sentence interests me very much. It says you can assume a cloak of timidity and fear so as to hoodwink people. I once said to you that I wasn't sure whether you were so full of humility as not to be a woman or so full of the wisdom of the serpent that you were being amused by me, and, my God, how you must have been amused! What was your game, anyway? Did you think you could get off with it?'

'Please M——' She could not now speak his name. 'Please don't say any more ... you're wrong. Those letters are full of lies.'

'Yes?' He picked up one of the letters. 'This writer points out that you have always been a great source of worry to your mother, and that she tried to stop you from going into Holborn. But you wouldn't listen to her. Is that a lie?'

'Yes ... no ... She did try to stop me, but ...'

'Why didn't you tell her then about ... your father?'

'Because he didn't want me to ... he was ill, as you know and changed.'

'How was it I didn't notice any tender relationship between you during his visits here? Throwing my mind back, I never once remember you even looking at the man. Why, in the name of God, must you bring him into all this?'

'Because I've told you ... he's my father.'

Stanhope scrutinised her for a moment, then said softly. 'And the Arab is just a friend? He waits for you each night and takes you home?'

Knowing her answer would bring down his contempt on her head, she hesitated before saying, 'Yes.'

'What do you take me for? If it had been a white man I would have had my doubts, but an Arab! And to term him a friend. You know as well as I do that no man, black or white, could be merely a friend to you, and an Arab least of all.'

Oh God! It was like the scene of her frequent dismissals over again, only intensified a thousandfold. She had often wondered what her master would be like were he in a real rage. Then, she had thought, his bellow would reach such volume as to scare even the bravest. She had never imagined that his rage would produce no bellows, that his voice would be low-toned and even. Nor had she imagined that his eyes could express such disgust and a disdain that would make her feel unclean, unmerited as it was.

The terrible coldness of his manner was having a numbing effect on her already failing senses, and as his voice went on she had to grip the edge of the table for support.

'And your face ... the Arab didn't do that?'

'No, he didn't.'

In spite of her faintness her words carried conviction. But when he asked, 'Who did then?' and she answered, 'I fell on the stairs,' he made a sound like a laugh.

'Do you take me for a fool altogether? In my young days I used to box, but had I never given or received a blow between the eyes I would know that it was a fist that had hit you.'

Rose Angela knew that there were levels of pain she had not yet probed. What she was suffering now would be nothing compared to the agony that would be produced by the emptiness of a life separated from this man's.... She must tell him about Matt.

'It was a fist. My uncle did it—the one that wrote that letter. He's always hated me and lied about me.'

'Oh, your uncle, now! Is he lying when he says you have been turned out of situation after situation because of your double-dealings with men, and that you've never kept a job more than a few weeks?'

Rose Angela stared at Stanhope without seeing him. What was the use? Living or dead, Matt's work went on. She could do no more; yet through all the turmoil of her feeling ran a thread of bewilderment at what appeared to her a determination on Stanhope's part not to believe anything she said, for only last night hadn't he told her it was her honesty that had altered his opinion of women?

Then, as she stood swaying on her feet, his voice, losing its levelness and sinking into his throat with bitterness, brought her sharply back from the oblivion that was upon her; and she knew part of the reason for his unrelenting attitude towards her, for, as much as he hated her at this moment, he hated and loathed himself even more.

'Last night I asked you to live with me, but after you had gone I knew that wouldn't be enough ... I must marry you and make sure of you. Make sure of you ... that's funny, isn't it? And when this morning I received these two letters it was history repeating itself, for all this has happened to me before. When I was about to be married, twelve years ago, I received such a letter as that.' He flicked Matt's letter with his nail. 'The girl was as beautiful as you, and as practised a liar.' He paused for a while, and ran the side of his finger across his lips as if wiping something distasteful from them. 'I felt a young fool, then, but now I feel an old one. And that I find harder to stomach!'

Now she knew the uselessness of trying to convince him. The giddiness swam over her again, and his voice came to her as if from the end of a long corridor, saying, 'There's a week's wages in lieu of notice. And you may keep the brooch. It is of some value, as doubtless you expected when you asked for such a simple gift.'

When the mist cleared from her eyes she found that she was alone. She hadn't heard him go. His movements, like his voice, were now quiet and final. She leant over the table, her body trembling. Her hand went to her throat, and, groping at the brooch fastening her blouse, she undid it and placed it on the table near the money he had laid there. Then unsteadily she left the kitchen.

Outside, she stood watching the sun's watery rays reflected on the river. It was over—just like that....

She walked on, almost blindly, over the rails and sleepers and she wondered vaguely why she was shedding no tears, for inside she was crying as she had never cried before: in many ways at one and the same time, like a child that had been misjudged, and like a girl who had been spurned, and like a woman who had drunk bitterly of humiliation. The child was crying, 'It's always the same. Oh, I wish I was dead! Oh, I wish I was dead!' And the girl was crying, 'He believed everything in that letter, about the men an' all.' But the woman's cry overshadowed the others, for she was crying, 'It's my colour. If I'd been all white he would have let me convince him, in spite of that other girl. Last night he said colour didn't matter, but I know, I know. It will always matter, and balance the scales; it's still like when I was a child.'

She drew to a halt and stared at the river. The fitful gleam of the sun had vanished, leaving the water a broken mass of steely grey. There was a way out—it was deep by the broken wall, and once in she would never get out. There was only her da to really mourn her; and then not for long, for he would soon go.... Mourning. All her life had been one long mourning; mourning because she was what she was. She was tired, so tired, and her face was like a sheet of hot pain. She had been born to misery, so why had she imagined that anything might come right for her? And of all things, Stanhope's love! She had been like a child, firmly believing that a fairy-tale could become reality.

She started to run over the sleepers, tripping and stumbling like someone drunk. She passed the railway carriage and was deaf to Murphy's voice calling after her. And she had actually mounted the broken wall before she was pulled to a halt.

'Here, here! Steady on. What is it, lass? What you running like that for? ... Look, stop it!' Murphy put his arms tightly about her, restraining her until she suddenly became still. 'That's better. What is it? What's happened to you?'

She leant against him, her head resting on his greasy muffler, and he held her gently until she murmured, 'It's him.'

'Him? Who?' asked Murphy.

'The guv'nor.' She used Murphy's own term for Stanhope. 'He won't believe me. He won't believe I'm not living with Hassan.' She was speaking slowly, with the dull simplicity of a child, and Murphy stared at her perturbed as he repeated, 'Living with Hassan? God Almighty! What put that into his head?'

'Matt. Matt sent him a letter; and Bessie too.'

'Why, blast the pair of them for lying skunks! Look, lass, come inside the cabin a minute and get yourself warmed; you're all in.'

She allowed him to lead her back and into the railway carriage, where he sat her on the backless chair before the fire and began clumsily to chafe her stiff hands, talking all the while and trying to break through the strange light in her eyes. And he looked apprehensively at Pete when she broke in on him, saying dully, 'He was going to ask me to marry him, and I would have been Mrs. Stanhope then, Murphy.'

Murphy pursed his lips and jerked his head approvingly. 'Aye, fit to marry anyone, you are, Rosie ... you'll marry him all right, won't she, Pete?'

Pete nodded, sparing his words as usual.

'Not now,' she said, 'because it's all happened before.'

'There, there then. Are you warmed? ... I'll brew some tea. There ain't any milk, but it'll be hot. Been through a bit too much, you have. Lean back against the wall ... he'll marry you all right, don't you worry.'

'No ... he wouldn't believe about Matt ... about him always being bad.' Murphy's hand became still for a second as he measured the tea into the black can, and his eyes darted towards Pete's; then he turned the thread of her thoughts by saying, 'Not that Pete and me want you to marry and be skedaddled off to some place else, do we, Pete?'

Pete shook his head.

'Best friend we've ever had, you've been. Not many like you about. No wonder yer da dotes on you. It'll be a bad day for all of us when we lose you, I can tell you that.'

Bad day for all of them when they lost her ... best friend they'd ever had. She felt a momentary glow of comfort ... there were kind people in the world—these men were kind. And they believed in her, they who had known her so short a time. Not like her mother, who knew her even before birth, and him who last night had told her he adored her from the moment he set eyes on her and would continue to do so every moment of his life.

The crying and inward sobbing began to mount. It was Pete's unused voice that caused her pent-up tears to break, betraying himself by look and word as he said briefly, 'Nobody's good enough for you ... the Stanhope bloke nor nobody else.'

This was a long speech for Pete, and as Rose Angela looked at the dwarf his love penetrated the mist of her mind, and all the pain within her gathered itself into her throat, and as it found release she covered her face with her hands and sobbed, great tearing sobs that convulsed her body.

The men stood helplessly by, gazing at her bent head. When the sobs, gathering on themselves, threatened to choke her, their hands hovered towards her but did not touch her. It was as if they both realised that this safety valve must not be checked. Twice the crying died down, only to burst out afresh, and it was only when her body sagged almost double that Pete intervened by motioning to Murphy to give her the tea.

Clumsily Murphy straightened her hat, saying, 'Come, Rosie, lass, and have your drop of tea.' He took the mug from Pete's hand and held it to her lips. 'There now, drink that, and we'll get you a drop of water, for your face and hands are in a mess.' His voice was placating, he was humouring her as if she were still the strange distraught child he had pulled from the wall.

But after she had sipped the tea she spoke to him, and her voice was as he knew it. 'I'm sorry, Murphy.'

Murphy's face showed his relief. 'There, there, it's all over now.'

She sat in silence, the two men watching her. Was it all over? Wasn't there more to come?

'Where is Matt?' She asked the question as she stared down into the mug of black tea.

After a pause Murphy muttered, 'We don't know.'

She cupped the mug in her cold hands and the steam rising from the tea wafted about her face. 'What happened last night?' Her voice betrayed her premonition.

There was another pause before Murphy said, 'We chased him and he went down the drop alley.'

'The drop alley?' She looked quickly up at Murphy. 'But there's no way out of there but the river.'

Pete's eyes were fastened on the floor, and Murphy turned his head aside as he replied, 'I know. Me and the fellows waited to see if he'd come back, and Hassan and Pete went along to the sculler steps to nab him if he came up that way. But he didn't come. . . .' He paused, and then went on hopefully, 'He could have swum along the river and come up somewhere, though, and is hiding out, trying to scare us.'

Rose Angela looked through the carriage window to where the river was moving swiftly in black and grey patches. 'He couldn't swim,' she said flatly.

Neither Murphy nor Pete made any comment or movement, and she went on fearfully, 'There'll be an enquiry if they find him, and if there are any marks on his body...'

'Honest to God, we didn't touch him, Rosie,' Murphy put in. 'We never got near enough to him, or I don't know what we might have done at the time ... but we never laid a hand on him, did we, Pete?'

Pete gave the usual reply with his head.

'If there are enquiries, you'll have to be careful.' She was talking quietly now, as if it were an ordinary, every-day topic. For the moment all the turmoil seemed to have been swept away on the flow of her tears, and being thus quiet she asked herself questions, and the answers brought no pain. She asked herself did she hope Matt was dead; and the answer came: Yes, oh yes! She asked herself why she had pleaded so much with Stanhope. Had she stormed at him, as most women would have done under the circumstances, would she have convinced him? Her head shook slowly from side to side. No. Anyway, she could never have stormed at him.

All her life she had been humble because openly and in covered ways she had been given to understand that her mixed blood was like a poster advertising some inferior form of human being, and she had never used the argument, 'Is it our fault we are what we are? Must we go around searching for others like ourselves to form a world apart? The blame lies with them that bred us.' To have taken this view would have meant criticism of her mother and her da. Yet in this moment she dared to wonder what life would have been like had each stuck to his own kind, for it was borne in on her that Stanhope's unrelentless-ness, whether he realised it or not, was due not so much to the fact that he had been duped before but that this time it had been done by a half-caste.... The thought laid hold of her. Last night when he said that colour did not matter it was because he wanted her—men would say anything to get what they wanted. Life had taught her that lesson thoroughly. Last night he and God were colour-blind; now there was, as before, only God.

She surprised Murphy by rising abruptly and saying, 'I'll go now. Don't come ... I'll be all right,' and adding calmly, 'If you are questioned you'd better say you were in with us till ten o'clock. And Hassan too ... we must all say the same thing, mustn't we?'

They did not answer her, and she turned from them and went out of the railway carriage, and together they moved towards the door and watched her walking away with a step that had in it some quality that reminded them strongly of James. And as she walked, Rose Angela herself had the strange feeling inside her, in some depths where no white mind could reach, that most of her father walked with her.

Murphy watched her until she disappeared from view, then he turned to Pete. 'What do you make of it?'

Pete shook his head.

'She was ready for the high jump then, all right. Think she'll be all right now?'

Pete nodded.

'Can't understand the guv'nor taking notice of them letters, can you? He don't take no notice of what nobody says as a rule. What do you think we best do?'

Pete brought his eyes from where in imagination they were following Rose Angela, and said briefly, 'Tell him about Hassan?'

'Aye, that would be the best thing.'

Murphy pulled the door of the railway carriage to, then they set off walking slowly over the sleepers—slowly, as if they did not relish coming to the end of their short journey. Murphy did not speak again until they reached the wharf, when he said, 'What if he's mad?'

Pete's answer was to indicate the door with a motion of his head, which said plainly, 'Knock and find out.'

Murphy knocked four times on the door, but received no answer. It took courage to go round the house and ring the front door-bell; but even this brought no response, and only when they came to the back door again and knocked once more was the studio window thrust up with a bang; and Murphy and Pete stepped back and looked up at Stanhope. No word was spoken for quite some seconds, for Stanhope's expression froze Murphy's tongue. He was used to hearing the guv'nor going off the deep end and to see his face become furious with sudden temper, but the man up there was not in any way connected with the guv'nor he knew. His face was white, almost livid, and he did not yell at them, as usual, with, 'Well, what the devil do you want?' but stood waiting for them to speak.

In keeping with the unusual that seemed to be the order of the morning, it was Pete who spoke.

'Can we have a word with you?' he said.

Murphy looked swiftly from Stanhope to Pete and back to Stanhope again, who asked curtly, 'What about?'

'Well'—it was Murphy starting now—'it's like this, guv'nor. Y'see....' His Adam's apple jerked swiftly and he swallowed and brought out, 'It's about Rose Angela.'

'What about her?' The words seemed to take their time in reaching them; they were weighed with something that chilled Murphy and curbed his ready tongue.

'Well, there's been a mistake made, guv'nor'—he dared not say 'You have made a mistake,' and went lamely on—'about Hassan. The Arab fellow, y'know.'

'Yes?' This word came sharp now, like a rapier.

'Well, she said you.... Well ... you've got the idea——' Murphy hesitated. 'It's a bit of a mix-up, guv'nor.'

'And she sent you along here to explain it away?'

'No, no. But we thought you should know....'

'She's living in Holborn, isn't she?'

'Aye, she is.'

'Who with?' Again the words were heavy.

Once more Murphy brought his gaze down to Pete's. Here was a complication they hadn't given themselves time to foresee. If they said Jimmy, one thing would lead to another and before they knew where they were they would be talking of Matt; then of last night; and the less who knew about that affair the better.

But Murphy was not required to answer this particular question, for Stanhope threw another at him, 'Who gave her the black eyes?'

'What's that?'

Murphy's mouth was agape as he stared up at him. It was as if he hadn't heard, or, having heard, the question did not make sense to him.

This pose of stupidity seemed too much for Stanhope. In a moment he became the guv'nor they recognised, only more vehement than they had ever seen him before.

'Get the hell out of it, the pair of you! Get!'

It was as if he would topple out of the window on to them with the force of his passion.

'But look here, guv'nor....'

'I'll give you a minute to get going. If you aren't gone by the time I come down I'll throw the pair of you in the river!' His voice rose to a yell, and before he had crashed the window down they were off the wharf, for they were too experienced to attempt to reason with anyone in the state he was in.

'What do you think we'd better do?' asked Murphy as they returned to the railway carriage.

'Wait and tell him the morrer.'

'But what will we tell him then?'

'The lot.'

'The lot?' Murphy stopped in his stride. 'Oh, I think we'd better see Jimmy afore doin' that.'

'Aye,' Pete assented with a nod.

'Will we go now?'

Again Pete nodded.

'But how about taking a look round first in case he's...' Murphy did not add 'come up'. And once more Pete's head inclined agreement, and without further words they walked along the river bank, their eyes turned towards the water.

CHAPTER FOURTEEN

COLOUR

The quietness was still with Rose Angela as she mounted the stairs to James, but it was now a frozen quietness, and she knew that when it melted there would be pain to bear greater than ever she had known before.

James's eyes, burning in their great sockets, fastened on her from the moment she opened the door, and his voice came as a hollow, cracked whisper from the bed, saying, 'You not long.'

'No.' She went straight to him and took his hand. 'How do you feel now?'

'Oh, a lot better ... heap better.' He stared up into her face, his eyes searching hers. 'What wrong now? Something more wrong now? They find him?'

'No.'

'Well, what wrong? You been crying mightily.'

'Don't talk any more. Now lie quiet.' She put his arms inside the clothes, then turned from him and took off her hat and coat.

'Your face pain?'

'Yes.'

'Rose Angela. . . .'

'Yes, dear, what is it? She turned at the entreaty and bent over him.

He stared at her in silence for some time before answering, 'I feel in here'—his hand was moving under the bedclothes with its old gesture of patting his chest—'things not right with you. . . . Painter ... Mr. Stanhope, he all right ... him not mad at you staying off?'

She had to prevent her eyelids from closing to shut out

the pain, for now the quietness was melting, and it was a moment before she answered, 'Yes, he's all right.'

'And you hear nothing about ... the other one?' James could not bring himself to pronounce the name.

'No.'

'Sure?'

'Yes. Now don't talk, dear; I'm going to make you a drink.'

'I got to talk. It won't make no difference, one way or other. Sit down by me.'

She was lifting a chair to the bedside when a tap came on the door, and to her 'Come in' Hassan entered, and she saw immediately that he was disturbed.

'You've heard something?' she asked hesitantly.

He shook his head, but said nothing, only continued to stare at her, and James called feebly, 'Hassan! Here!'

Hassan went to the bed and James motioned him to sit down. 'What happen?'

'Nothing.'

'No sign of him?'

'No.'

'Perhaps him get back home somehow.'

'No; they're looking for him.'

'You been up?'

'I sent up.'

There was silence in the room for a time until Rose Angela came to the bed with a drink for James and she said to Hassan, 'Could you stay for a short while? I've got to get some oil and things.'

He nodded, but still he did not speak to her, only stared up into her face.

She put on her hat and coat again, and saying, 'I won't be more than a minute or two,' she left the room.

She had hardly closed the door when James hitched himself up on his pillows and said urgently, 'Something wrong with her—something more wrong. She come in and she been cryin' sore. You know what 'tis, Hassan?'

Hassan looked away, and James urged, 'If you know, you tell me—I not long for top and I want her be happy.'

'Jimmy'—Hassan leant forward and took James's hand —'I want to marry Rose Angela. You know that, don't you, without me telling you?'

James stared fixedly at the Arab without answering, and Hassan went on, 'I can make her happy. I know I can.'

James shook his head.

'I tell you I can. What have you against it? You married a white woman.'

Again James shook his head, and his voice rose above its whispering quality, and for a moment there was the echo of the deep timbre note in it again. 'It very wrong thing for black man marrying white woman. It bad enough for man, for him sore inside all his days, but for white woman it hell. And bigger hell for children. What you think the real reason I no let my wife know I'm here? It because I know she happy with white man. That's as should be— colour to colour. But me ... I not blaming you, Hassan, for wanting my Rose Angela, for only when fellow near death can he be wise. When life leaps inside him no man wise.'

'But Rose Angela's different ... she's not all white.'

'She is'—James was sitting up now in agitation—'she's white. I tell you she is white.'

'All right, all right, Jimmy,' Hassan said soothingly. 'Outside she may look more white than black, but inside she's all you—and that's a good thing.'

He smiled into James's troubles eyes, and James leant back and said between gasps, 'You say kind things, Hassan. I always like you, but I near death and I must speak truth. I no want my Rose Angela marry you. Anyway, she...' James looked down on his hands, almost transparent in their thinness, and went on lamely, 'I think she loves painter fellow.'

'Yes, and he's turned her out.'

Hassan had risen to his feet, his voice harsh and angry, and James's eyes darted up his thin frame to his face. 'What you say?'

'That fellow Matt wrote and told him she was living

with me, and without any evidence he believed it. That's the kind of white god he is. And he turned her out, and she nearly threw herself ...'

Hassan pulled up too late, and James said fearfully, 'Go on.'

'It's all right. She was a bit overdone—I'm sorry I said anything. She's all right now.'

James bent over and gripped Hassan's arm. 'She try throw herself in river?'

'She's all right now. Don't you worry.'

'My God! You say don't worry. Go after her. Don't leave her, and bring her back.'

'But she wants me to stay.'

'Go now—go.'

Hassan turned from the bed; then swung round again. 'If I ask her and she will marry me, what then?'

James closed his eyes. 'I said my say, Hassan.'

When Hassan had gone, James lay back weak and exhausted, and for some time he did not move. Only his fingers clutched and gathered up the white Marcella bedspread. After a while he moved his head to one side on his bank of pillows so that the knob of the bed should not obstruct his vision, and now he could see the three statues standing on a shelf to the side of Rose Angela's shakedown. There was a statue of St. Joseph and one of the Virgin, and another of Jesus. Years ago he had bought them at the door of the church because the man there, who said he was a brother of St. Vincent de Paul, also said that many blessings went with these statues. He remembered Rose Angela, from when she was a tiny child, claiming them as hers, and they were among the few possessions she had brought here. Now, in his mind, he began to talk to the statues, as he had often done of late, but this time with added urgency. 'You not let this come about, you not let the painter fellow believe this. You can't do this. You not let her marry Hassan, or kill herself in river.' He hitched himself a little farther to one side and appealed across the distance, 'I not want to die till she fixed up right. You can understand that. Don't let me die till she fixed up right.'

He waited in his thinking, and a narrow shaft of sunlight, the only shaft in the day that ever found its way into the room, fell across the face of the figure of Christ, and for the moment obliterated it in light; and James became still inside in wonderment.

He lay quiet and at peace now, watching the streak of sunlight narrow before it disappeared altogether. When it had gone he shook his head at himself. 'Me, I imagine things. All my life I imagine things.'

He lay staring at the statues until the drowsiness which was becoming more frequent of late took hold of him, and as he dozed off he wondered whimsically if, when he went into the long sleep, he would meet the people the statues represented.

He did not know what he would find in the coming long sleep. Perhaps he would see God, perhaps not. Perhaps God died when the brain could function no more. Perhaps he had done his work then. But if, on the other hand, he did meet him, what then? What had he to show for his life? Drowsily he shook his head again. Only a kindness here and there . . . and loving. Yes, he had loved. Love had been the driving force, the force that had brought him to this way of dying. Then perhaps it had to be . . . perhaps he had followed the pattern cut out for him. But it did not matter either way. He allowed himself to slip farther down the bed. All that mattered was that his Rose Angela should know happiness, happiness such as he knew existed but which had escaped him. If his daughter could have this happiness, then the pattern of his life had been a good pattern; and working it out was like paying in advance for another life—Rose Angela's life.

Hassan guessed that Rose Angela had gone to a little group of shops off Commercial Road, and he made for there. But as he turned the corner of the street he actually ran into her, and in her surprise at seeing him she clutched at his arm, exclaiming, 'He's not . . .?'

'No, no—he's all right. He asked me to come and help you with the basket.'

She looked at him in disbelief. 'What's wrong, Hassan? There was something the matter when you came in.'

She started to walk rapidly towards the house, and he took the oil-can from her hand and said without looking at her, 'There are two men I'd like to kill, and one's that painter.'

She stiffened, and he went on, 'I must talk to you, Rose Angela. Will you come to the café for a minute?'

She shook her head. 'I must get home.'

'Just for a minute.'

With the appeal of his voice she turned her head towards him and said kindly, 'You know I can't leave him for long.'

They were crossing the yard now, and it was empty of people, as was the dark hallway, and inside he brought her to a halt. 'Listen just one minute, Rose Angela. Tell me, are you afraid of me?'

'No, oh no, Hassan!' Her answer was so spontaneous that it brought a smile to his face.

'Thank you, Rose Angela. Do you ... do you like me?'

'Yes, I like you. No one could help liking you, Hassan.'

'You are not afraid of me and you like me.' He took the basket from her hand and laid it, together with the oil-can, at the foot of the stairs. Then he gathered both her cold hands in his. 'Will you believe me when I say I can make you love me?'

She stared into his eyes and saw there the released fire of his feelings.

'Will you believe me?'

'Oh, Hassan!'

She bowed her head, and he pulled her to him. 'I love you so much, Rose Angela, that I would give my life for you. You cannot believe it at this moment, but there would be no pain with my love as there would have been with his.'

She made a movement to withdraw her hands, and he gripped them closer. 'Listen. All your life you will be colour-conscious. I know, for I have watched you. You feel inferior. Inside you feel inferior ... you, who could be a queen. And could he take that inferior feeling away? No. And however he might have overlooked it, his fine friends would not, and he has plenty of fine friends. But with me you will never feel inferior. Instead of knowing you are looked down on, you will be looked up to—adored, worshipped; and you will want for nothing.... Oh, Rose Angela, look at me. Tell me, Rose Angela.'

She did not raise her head, for his words were finding resting-places in her mind. He was right. Always inside she felt inferior, but never so much as she did at this moment; and as he said, with him it would go. She could believe this, for he did not feel racially superior to her. With him she could stop fighting; once joined to him she could allow the stamp of her colour to rise to the surface and she could accept what she was, and with acceptance would come release.

For a moment the face of Stanhope came before her eyes, as it had been last night, saying, 'What are you going to do about it?' He hadn't thought her good enough to marry, then; only this morning in the midst of rejecting her he could say he had been going to marry her. It was easy, then, when there was no possibility of its taking place. Into the pain and despair that seemed to be finding passage through each vein of her body was mingled a feeling of bitterness against him, and against her mother. Bridget was also in her mind at this moment, for was she not another, the only other one that mattered, who had so readily believed the worst of her? And if she were to marry Hassan she would not have to suffer the shock of breaking it to her, for that had already been endured. And yet another worry that Hassan could relieve her of was money, for she had only a few pounds she had saved up to provide extras at Christmas. All her wages had been spent on James and the room. If she was to support him she must find work; for the short time left she must find work—or else. She raised her eyes to Hassan. He had said, 'You will want for nothing.' Well, she had never wanted very much from life, and the little she had got, which amounted to food and a few clothes, was acquired only through long hours of labour at the beck and call of others. And these had always been punctuated by the fight against men. So what had she to lose if she married Hassan?

Hassan sensed the change in her, and he pressed his point. 'Tell me, Rose Angela.' And although he was urging her answer, when it came he was rendered dumb with surprise.

'Give me time, and I'll try.' And as she said it there swept over her a wave of sound, full of her father's voice, crying, 'You not do this.'

It was done, but as Hassan leaned forward to place his lips on hers she recoiled, saying, 'No, no, not yet.'

'All right, I can wait.'

There was pain in his eyes, and she turned from him and picked up the basket and the oil-can, and went heavily up the stairs.

CHAPTER FIFTEEN

PAYMENT

After Stanhope had rushed down the stairs to carry out his threat to Murphy and Pete, and found he was not called upon to do so, he again locked the back door; then he stood and glared around the kitchen. He looked at the delf rack. The dishes she had washed yesterday were all arrayed neatly and gleaming, and his anger was such that he had to place the utmost restraint on himself not to raise his arm and sweep the lot on to the floor.

He flung out of the kitchen and into the drawing-room. The cold deadliness of his feeling was passing and he was wanting to storm. He caught a glimpse of himself in the mirror, and was brought to a halt. He looked as he felt, wild with temper.

He sat on the couch and, resting his elbows on his knees, he gripped his hair with both hands as if he would pull it out by the roots. God, why had he let himself in for this? The first time was bad enough, but nothing compared with this. She had got into his blood and maddened him, and in spite of her lies, this raving ache would go on and on.... The lies, the bare-faced lies! He might have questioned the truth of that man's letter if she hadn't actually admitted she was living in Holborn. To think he had put her on the tram and she had doubled back into Holborn!

Anyway, it served him right, at his age, falling for a bit of a girl! ... But she wasn't a bit of a girl; she was mature, with the knowledge of life in her eyes; and by God, she must have it, too, living in Holborn! And he had been such a fool as to fall for her simplicity. Living with her father in Holborn!

He lifted his head and let out a staccato laugh. That black he had painted! Why on earth had she to pick on him? Had there been the slightest resemblance between them he would have noticed it ... wouldn't he? It was a pity the painting had gone.... His thinking brought him upright, and before the thought ended he was up the stairs and into the studio. He pushed aside a number of files that stood against the wall, until he came to one with the word 'Hulk' written across it. This he lifted on to the table and flicked over the loose sheets it contained, most of them being rough sketches of a boat rotting in the mud. And when he came to the sketches of the Negro he became still, devouring each line of the drawings. This one was a quick sketch, done when he first saw the man. It was made up of only a few lightning strokes, because, finding he was being sketched, the Negro moved off. Then this one, a side view, showing that enormous ear. And this, just his mouth. Was there any resemblance between that mouth and hers? ... None! But he had done one full-faced. He flung over more drawings, depicting hands and feet. Then he came upon it: the ear, the pock marks, the emaciation, all there. But out of this, James's eyes, almost alive, stared up at him, and for a moment the man became submerged in the artist, and he thought, with a sense of awe, of his own achievement: I got those eyes. Then, still looking down into the charcoal eyes of the Negro, he began to place odd pieces of paper over the face. In all positions he placed them, until only the eyes were left, and as he stared an uneasiness grew in him; and he protested, speaking aloud, 'It isn't so. I would have known; I would have detected it.'

He looked around the room, at the various paintings hanging there, as if they would confirm him in his belief.... 'I would have known.' Yet the eyes looking up at him were the eyes of Rose Angela.

My God! Supposing she was speaking the truth! But the Arab ... he was waiting for her all right. And her face. Who had really done that to her?

He was still staring down into the eyes when a faint tap, tap came to him. There was someone at the back door again, blast them! Murphy come back, perhaps. No....
Then Her? He gave himself no answer, for it would not be her; she would not come here again—his reception having blasted her as far as another continent from him.

Well, who the hell was it, then? He marched to the window, and, flinging it up, looked down on to the wharf and into the upturned face of a woman.

'Mr. Stanhope?'

He found himself answering quietly, 'Yes.'

'I'm Mrs. Paterson. I've come to see my daughter.'

For a long moment he stared at her. Then he said, still quietly, 'Wait a moment, I'll be down.'

He would not allow himself any pondering as he went hastily down the stairs. But when he unlocked the back door he was made to wonder what this woman's visit could portend.

Bridget and he appraised each other for some seconds, and it was she who spoke first. 'Can I see my daughter, please?'

His reply was to step aside and say, 'Will you come in?'

Silently Bridget passed him and walked into the kitchen, into the blue kitchen that Rose Angela had described so vividly. She stood stiffly waiting, and he pulled a chair from the table and said, 'Please sit down.'

She sat down, and looked towards the door that led to the hall, as if expecting Rose Angela to make an appearance.

Stanhope looked at this woman, the mother of Rose Angela, the woman who had married a coloured man. She was a fine-looking woman with a stately bearing, but there was a stiffness about her that wasn't a veneer of the moment. It seemed to emanate from within her.

She looked up at him and asked, 'Is Rosie in?'

'No.' He turned from her and looked out of the window towards the river. 'I'm afraid, Mrs. Paterson, she is not here.'

'Not here? You mean she's gone?'

He nodded.

'When?'

'This morning.'

'This morning,' she repeated. 'Mr. Stanhope'—she was on her feet now, looking at his back—'do you know where she's gone?'

'No.'

He heard her swallow in the silence that followed his answer. Then she burst out:

'Mr. Stanhope, you know something, you know where she's gone. Has she gone into ... Holborn? Is she living there altogether?'

He did not answer her, and she went on, 'Has she been working here all along?' And he said, 'Yes, up to yester-day.'

'And is she not coming back?'

'No.'

Slowly Bridget sat down again. 'If I'd only come yester-day.' She was talking softly as if to herself. 'I knew some-thing was wrong. Mr. Stanhope'—she entreated the for-bidding solidness of his back—'you know more than I do, for God's sake tell me!'

He remained for a moment longer staring at the river. Then, turning slowly, he pulled a letter from his pocket and handed it to her. 'Read that.'

Wondering, she took the letter from him, and he watched her closely as she began to read it. He saw the colour of her face change; and before she had read very far she turned to the back of the letter in search of the signature. Then she said in an awed whisper, 'My brother wrote this.'

She read a little farther, then again she stopped, and the glisten of tears was in her eyes. 'Oh, it's lies, all lies. She was the best lass in the world, she never caused me a moment's trouble. Not until ... these last few weeks. But this about having to leave her places, it's a pack of lies. She left because she wouldn't ... well, the men wouldn't leave her alone, and her mistresses. ... It wasn't her fault.

Matt, my brother, has always hated her.'

She read on to the end of the letter, then folded it slowly and handed it back to him. 'There's not a line of truth in it, except...' She bit her lip and pulled at the fingers of her thin black gloves. 'He ... Matt, my brother ... he said he saw her with an Arab. And then she said she was going to lodge in Holborn. But somehow, knowing her, the more I thought of it the less I could believe it, in spite of what I did.' For an instant her eyes flicked away from his. Then she murmured in perplexity, 'But if she's left here and is ... in Holborn...'

Stanhope pushed his hand through his hair. 'I don't know, I don't know what to think. An hour ago I would have said she was with the Arab all right. Now I'm not sure. And if I'm wrong...' The enormity of his thought brought his movements to a stop, and he stood, his hand in his hair, staring at the table, as if lying there for him to see was some disastrous result of his doubting.

'Mrs. Paterson'—he dropped into a chair opposite to her—'I think I'd better tell you. ... You see, I loved Rosie. I was no better than any of her other bosses, but not up till last night did I tell her....'

'Not till last night? Then she wasn't...?' Bridget caught herself up.

He shook his head at her. 'No, she wasn't living with me.'

'I'm sorry I...'

'Don't be. Last night I was quite willing that that's how things should be; but then, on reflection, I knew I must marry her. I went with her to the tram and saw her get on it—as I thought, to go home. Prior to this I had chased an Arab away from outside. Then this morning I received this letter. And not only this one, but another from Mrs. Grant. Then Rosie came. You can imagine how I was feeling.' He looked away from Bridget towards the window again. 'But I can see now that the distress she was in was genuine. And her face, her beautiful face, was scarcely recognisable.'

Slowly Bridget rose up from the chair. 'What about her face?'

'It was disgured.'

'Disfigured? With a knife?'

'No, no, not with a knife; the blow had been done with a fist, right between her eyes. She said her uncle did it, but I didn't believe her; I thought the Arab had done it.'

'Oh, my God! What's it all about?' Bridget clutched at the front of her coat. 'Matt always said he'd spoil her face. I went in fear for years that he'd do it. And yesterday morning he went out, and hasn't been seen since. My other brother's been looking for him half the night; and this morning we had to tell the polis. Oh, Mr. Stanhope, I'm afraid of our Matt and what he'll do to her. Was she alone last night when he caught her?'

'I don't know.'

'Have you any idea at all where I'll likely find her?'

'Apart from knowing she's in Holborn, I can't say. She said she was...' He stopped and stared at Bridget. 'Mrs. Paterson, is your husband alive?'

Bridget stared back at him, and murmured, 'I don't know.'

'It's some years since you saw him?'

'I saw him last when Rosie was four years old. He had a fight with my brother and he thought he'd killed him, and he ran away. I haven't seen him since.'

'Sit down, I won't be a minute.' Stanhope left the kitchen, and in a matter of seconds was back with a single sheet of paper in his hand. He put his face downwards on the table and, leaning towards Bridget, said gently, 'Mrs. Paterson, this may come as a shock to you..., or it may mean nothing. Do you recognise this man?' He turned over the drawing for her to see. He watched her eyes widen and her lips slowly drop apart; then he saw her body fold up as if it had been released from a spring, and she slumped face forward over the table before he could reach her.

Lifting her limp head he urged, 'Come on, Mrs. Paterson,' but she made no response. He hurried into the drawing-room, and when he returned with some brandy she was raising herself up. And her face was blanched.

'Drink this.'

He put the brandy to her lips, and she sipped it and shuddered, then said, 'I'm all right.'

'Take another drink.'

She shook her head. The drawing was still on the table, and she looked down on it again, but did not speak. Nor did Stanhope, for he was seeing Rose Angela's face as she said, 'I'm living with my father ... the Negro ... the one you painted.'

Every word she spoke had been true, then, and he had kicked her out. He closed his eyes.

Bridget's voice, low and trembling, was saying, 'This is my husband. He's changed ... but it's him. Where is he?'

'If that is your husband, then, Mrs. Paterson, he's in Holborn. And he's been living there for some time. And Rosie is living with him. That is the explanation of it all. The only thing I can't see now is why she had to keep it secret.'

Bridget took her handkerchief and wiped the moisture from her face. Her conscience was suggesting one reason why James had remained hidden. She stared at the drawing again. The eyes were as she remembered them, but that ear and the pox about his chin and the hollowness of his cheeks all spoke of hardship. Remorse and pity rose in her! Oh, Jimmie, Jimmie! And Rosie knew. All the time she knew and stayed with you, and put up with everything rather than let on in case Matt found out. Yes, that would be one of the reasons why she had kept quiet ... in case Matt found out. Oh, Rosie, lass!

Stanhope touched the outline of the drawing with his finger. 'He was a very sick man when I drew that.... You should know he was dying with consumption.'

'Consumption?'

'I'm afraid so. And after I'd finished painting him he seemed to disappear. Murphy and Pete, two friends of his, never mentioned him again, and I took it for granted he was dead.'

Bridget gripped the edge of the table and brought herself to her feet. 'Now I know!' She turned startled eyes on

Stanhope. 'Matt knew about him'—she nodded to the drawing—'about Jimmie being here. He's been queer for the last week or so; he's been queer for some time. But lately he's been saying strange things; I thought he was going mad. Only yesterday morning he said'—she paused as if to recall each word—'he said, soon he'd be able to tell me something and I'd be really free; he said there wouldn't only be one funeral. You see, me father's ill. He had an accident and burnt his hands; then he got soaked sitting on the ... being out one night, and he took pneumonia and we thought he was going to die. But my mother's pulling him through.'

She paused again, and Stanhope could see her mind probing, and for the moment, he knew, she was no longer with him but back in a number of yesterdays, piecing together what well might be a tragedy.

Since coming downstairs this morning his life had been changed completely. Yesterday he was lord of all he surveyed—the house, the wharf—and last night, Rose Angela. In spite of the torment of his growing passion for her his days had been full and smooth; he had his work and material, for it swarmed about him. But now, after a few hours, he was being drawn rapidly into the maelstrom of lives, each converging to a climax that had its beginning when this woman married a Negro. That she foresaw tragedy he could see by her expression—the terror in her face conveyed itself to him—and he thought, I likely could have prevented anything further happening if I hadn't been such a blasted fool and had listened to Rosie.

'If they meet, Matt'll kill him,' Bridget spoke again. 'He always said he would. I must find Rosie. When I find her I'll find him.'

'Likely they have met already. When your brother hit her he must have cornered her somewhere, for it's not likely he'd try it on in the street.'

'But he hasn't come home! You don't know Matt; he'll keep at a thing until it's done.'

'But where are you going to start to look for her? You know the people in that quarter—they can be like oysters if they choose ... Wait! What am I thinking of? Murphy, the man who lives in the railway carriage, he'll take us. I'll get my coat.'

When he returned, Bridget said, 'But it's putting you to a lot of trouble.' And he answered soberly, 'Trouble, Mrs. Paterson? If I can't gain Rosie's forgiveness, then I'm only at the beginning of my trouble.'

They stood for a second longer looking at each other and understanding each other, as if this was but one of many meetings during which their hopes and fears had been laid bare.

He opened the door for her and she went out before him, and as they hurried over the sleepers he took her elbow to help her, and this action thrust her painfully back into the past—Jimmie had done things like this ... Tony didn't. His loving showed itself in other ways; like the men of the fifteen streets, he practically ignored women in public, at least when it meant doing any service that would qualify him for the name of 'Sloppy' and bring derision on him and the recipient of his affection. But, she remembered, Jimmie had not minded. He, like this man, had done these little things naturally. Her heart began to ache with an intolerable ache. Poor Jimmie! She should never have married him; she should have had the courage to have the bairn. But he had wanted her so. And she was young and silly, and ignorant.

And now he was dying; and he'd been living in the town and hadn't troubled her; and Rosie had stood all that scandal about living with an Arab rather than give him away. Would Rosie ever forgive her? What must she have felt when everybody turned against her! Oh, Rosie, lass, Rosie!

Stanhope's tongue, clicking with impatience, brought her thoughts from Rosie. He was looking through the railway-carriage window.

'They're gone!' He turned a disappointed face to her. 'The thing is now, where to look for them, for they may have gone across the water. Yet there's the chance they may still be knocking around the market place or the ferry.'

So, for an hour or more Stanhope and Bridget walked about the market and the ferry and beyond them, but saw no signs of Murphy and Pete. Then Stanhope suggested that Bridget, who was looking very tired, should return home and that as soon as he found Murphy he would send her word.

But Bridget was reluctant to comply with his suggestion, even when he pressed the point that they would likely go on for hours without success. At last, when he intimated that he stood more chance of finding something out if alone, she agreed; and, as he had put her daughter on the tram for home last night, now he did her, reassuring her once more that as soon as he had any news he would send for her.

Alone again, he hurried down the Mill Dam bank; but stopped before turning into Holborn. It would be a good idea to leave a note at the railway carriage telling Murphy, should he return, to wait there for him. Forgotten now completely was the fact that a short while ago he had threatened to throw him in the river.

He was going through the narrow cut, when, to his surprise and relief, he saw Murphy entering it from the river end. Murphy had, however, seen him first, and was already making a hasty retreat when Stanhope shouted. 'Hi there! Murphy!'

Murphy did not stop, so Stanhope broke into a run, calling, 'Just a minute! What's the matter with you, man?' And when he came abreast of him he demanded, 'Are you deaf? Couldn't you hear me?'

Murphy looked at him out of the corner of his eye and cautiously answered the latter part of the question, 'Aye, guv'nor.'

Then, remembering the reason for this caution, Stanhope said, 'I'm sorry about that; I was a bit mad. But something's happened since then, and I want your help, Murphy.'

'Aye, guv'nor.' Again Murphy looked sideways at him.

'I want you to take me to Rosie.'

'What?' Now Murphy was fronting him. 'Take you to

Rosie! Oh, well, guv'nor.' He rubbed his chin with the palm of his hand. 'Well, it's like this. I can't do it ... not right away I can't. I'll have to have a talk with ... Well, you see ...'

He stopped, and Stanhope said, 'It's all right; I know who Rosie's father is. Her mother has just been to see me.'

'To see you,' repeated Murphy. 'But God, guv'nor, she don't know nowt about Jimmie being here!'

'She does now.'

'How?'

'By the drawing I did of him.'

'But he don't want her to know.'

'She knows, anyway, and it's right that she should. And she's worried about Rosie. I'm worried about Rosie, too, Murphy.'

Murphy had never before detected such a tone in Stanhope's voice, and he moved from one foot to the other, saying, 'Well, guv'nor ... I dunno ... I suppose it'll be all right.'

'It will be, I assure you.'

'I wish Pete was here.'

'Where is he?'

'Gone along the river looking for a sign of ...' He stopped; it wasn't likely the guv'nor knew anything about Matt. 'Seeing if there's anything doing,' he ended.

'Take me now, Murphy,' Stanhope urged. 'If you don't, I'll find them anyway. It will take me longer, but I'll find them.'

'Aye, there's that in it.' Murphy again looked sideways at him, and his next words would never have been spoken had he given thought to them. But as he stared at this big, blustering man, they seemed to be drawn to his lips. 'You're a bloody funny bloke,' he said, and his mouth fell agape at his own temerity.

After a moment they laughed together, then turned and went through the cut and into Holborn.

Hassan came thoughtfully down the stairs. His first love

offering had just been refused. When previously he had left Rose Angela he returned to his café and had there packed a basket of delicacies for James, and for her he had selected, from a small hoard of such things, a ring, a very valuable ring. Although he had given a lot of money for it, he knew he had paid only about a third of its real value. Rose Angela, however, had merely glanced at it and shook her head, and instead of allowing him to place the ring on her finger she had placed her fingers on her lips to ensure his silence so as not to disturb James's sleep. And when he left the ring on the table she picked it up and followed him on to the landing and whispered, 'No, Hassan, I can't take it. Not yet, anyway.' And he simply said, 'All right,' and told himself that he must go carefully, and that time was young. Give her a few weeks to recover and she would turn to him; she would be his ... he would make her his; only let her not see that painter and she would forget.

It was at this point that he reached the foot of the stairs, and, as if his thought of the painter had conjured Stanhope up, he saw him. Through the open doorway he saw him and Murphy enter the yard, and as fire will sweep over oil, so a flame of hate swept over him.

He stood guarding the foot of the stairs; and when Murphy, coming first through the doorway, said, 'Watcher, there,' he made no reply. He did not even look at Murphy, but kept his eyes riveted on the breadth of the man protruding behind him.

Stanhope, coming abreast of Murphy, faced Hassan, and he recognised in this thin tall Arab the man he had chased from the house last night. Also, even before Hassan spoke, he knew him to be the Arab whose name was coupled with that of Rosie, and immediately guessed that if rumour was wrong it was not this man's fault.

'What do you want?' Hassan pointedly addressed Stanhope.

And Stanhope tried to override his own dislike, for, after all, this was a man, and if his feeling for Rosie was to be compared with his own, then, whatever his race, he was to be pitied. So, with unusual calmness for him, he replied, 'Don't you think that's my business?'

'No, I do not.'

The English was precise and clipped, not the pidgin kind, and this too impressed Stanhope that he was not dealing with the ordinary run of Arab who manned the cargo ships running back and forth from the Tyne. So again he curbed the hot retort on his tongue and said, 'Well, whether you do or not is beside the point. Now, if you'll move...'

'I'll see you in your own particular hell first!'

'Why, Hassan, man'—Murphy was gaping open-mouthed—'what's come over you? Look, the guv'nor just wants to see Rosie and...'

Hassan turned on Murphy and repeated, 'Just wants to see Rosie! You fool!'

Murphy stood dumb with amazement. Never before had Hassan taken this line with him. To him Hassan was a warm man, and a very decent bloke, better than many whites, for he always had a civil word and would sit and crack with you. But now he was speaking to him as if he was a dog. And no coloured man, however decent he might be, was going to speak to him like a dog! After all was said and done, what was he but an Arab, even if he had money. No, by God, he'd soon let him see who he was speaking to!

'What the hell's up with you! The guv'nor's come to see Rosie, and he's goner see her!'

Murphy's tone now brought Hassan's gaze back to him, and his anger for a moment was touched with sorrow: Murphy was no longer Murphy, he was a white man, taking another white man's part against colour. And Jimmie, in his wilful ignorance, thought Rose Angela could entirely escape this!

Hassan's voice was quieter now as he addressed Murphy, but bitterness lay deep in it. 'A few hours ago you saved Rose Angela from jumping in the river, because of this man's treatment of her. Now you bring him to her. Well, it's too late, she's going to marry me.'

'What'—the loose goose-flesh skin of Murphy's neck rippled—'marry you!' He turned and looked at Stanhope; but Stanhope was showing no surprise at this preposterous statement, for inside he was sick with this new knowledge, that because of him Rosie had tried to drown herself.

'Marry you!' gulped Murphy. 'Why, man, you must be mad.' He knew that Hassan was fond of Rosie, but so was he, and so was Pete. Aye, by lad, Pete was very struck on Rosie. But would any of them think they could marry her? Yet here was Hassan saying he was going to. Why, it was enough to make the guv'nor bash his face in. He looked again at Stanhope, who was looking at Hassan ... not as he should do, in one of his mad tears, but quietly, and what was more puzzling he was speaking quietly too. Funnily quiet, Murphy thought.

'I am here to see Rosie, and I am going to see her! As for what she does, that is for her to decide.'

'You're so sure of yourself, aren't you? You think you only have to see her again and tell her you know now she wasn't living with an Arab and everything will be all right!' Hassan's lip curled back, miming the scorn against himself the last words implied.

And Murphy thought, I shouldn't have told him. I want me head look'n.

'Will you get out of my way?'

Hassan's reply was to remain staring down at Stanhope from the vantage point of the bottom stair. There were now spectators on the scene, some on the stairs above and some in the doorway. Stanhope was not aware of them; he was only aware that his tolerance had reached its limit. With a lightning stroke for one so heavily built his hands shot up, and the Arab and he changed places. In almost the wink of an eye he had swung Hassan bodily from the step. But like lightning, too, Hassan's hand moved behind to his hip pocket in a movement that spoke plainer than words to the onlookers, for whereas before no one had uttered a word, now there were cries of, 'Don't be a fool, man!' 'You know who'll get the worst of it, don't you?'

and 'None of that, now; do you want to bring the polis on the house?'

Hassan's fingers still gripped the handle of his knife as Stanhope turned from him and walked up the stairs, followed by Murphy. And now the people in the hall and those on the stairs came and closed round Hassan, urging him, for his own sake, to be sensible and reminding him of the too swift justice that followed when a coloured man attacked a white.

As Murphy tapped gently on the door, Stanhope stood taut, waiting. His mind was in a turmoil; all he wanted to do in this moment was to savour the thought that he was about to see her again, but the scene just past and the significance of the Arab's statement that she was going to marry him, combined with the thought that but for Murphy she might have succeeded in drowning herself, all added to his confusion. And when the door was softly opened and Rose Angela stood there, a warning finger on her lips, all he could do was to stare at her.

As her hand dropped to her side, Murphy whispered, 'What did I tell you, eh, Rosie? Here's the guv'nor; he wants to see you.'

When neither she nor Stanhope spoke, Murphy went on, 'Is Jimmy asleep? Well, that will do him good.' The silence being too much for him, he moved from one foot to the other, then sidled past her into the room.

Stanhope said, 'I must talk to you, Rosie.'

With a backward glance towards the bed, Rose Angela stepped out on to the landing and pulled the door to behind her. And now they were within a foot of each other. He looked into her face, discoloured and bruised from cheek-bone to cheek-bone, her eyes swollen level and their expression without life; and his love at this moment became purified and selfless. All he wanted was to ensure that never again would she know fear or want; and so deep was the sadness in her eyes that he felt that not in a lifetime could he erase it. That he had put most of it there he knew, and the responsibility lay like a weight on his tongue, making him inarticulate. 'Rosie ... what can I say?'

She did not help him, she only looked at him, into his eyes.

'Oh, Rosie, if you had only told me at the beginning. Can you forgive me?'

He took her hand, and it lay passively in his. 'Can you?' His voice was deep with his feeling.

Slowly she inclined her head, and he sighed. 'Oh, Rosie, I'll never forgive myself ... never.' He looked about the landing. The other two doors were closed, but he felt that behind them were straining ears, and he whispered, 'Come back with me, I must talk to you.'

She shook her head.

'But we must talk.'

He looked at the door behind her, and for the first time she spoke. 'My father is very sick.'

'Can I see him?'

'I would rather you didn't.'

The listlessness of her voice perturbed him, and he said, 'There's bound to be some way in which I can help.'

Again she shook her head, and it seemed to him she was growing more lifeless each moment.

'Rosie'—he meant the demand in his voice to stir her—'go back to last night; try to forget what has happened in between. I will make you forget. I'm to blame, at least for this morning.... Will you?'

Still looking into his eyes, she answered him, 'A short while ago I promised Hassan....' But what she had promised Hassan she could not go on to explain. Instead she shook her head pitifully and Stanhope's brows gathered into a furrow and his jaw stiffened. 'You can't do it! You didn't mean it. You did it on the rebound, you know you did. And perhaps, naturally, to hurt me.'

'No. I did it because'—she looked away from him as if she was seeing the reason for her action beyond the walls of the house—'because I'm tired of fighting.'

'Tired of fighting?' He echoed her words in perplexity.

She nodded, her gaze penetrating the future. 'With him

there'll be no need to fight; I won't be ashamed any more of being what I am.'

'Rosie, you're mad! You don't know what you are saying. You, ashamed of what you are! You're tired and ill. You're not thinking rationally because of all you've been through.'

She turned and looked at him again. 'It's strange, but my mind is clearer now than ever before in my life. I've always been fighting inside myself because I felt inferior. I've always felt inferior and tried to hide it; and only Hassan could see it, for he, too, knows what it is like to be looked down on. But now there won't be any need to hide it.'

'Stop it!' Stanhope's voice had a touch of the old arrogance in it. 'You cannot compare yourself with him.'

'You don't like Arabs, do you?'

'No, I don't!'

'Yet I'm coloured too.'

'Rosie'—he swallowed hard and inhaled deeply in an endeavour to retain a hold on his calmness—'why all this talk of colour? What's come over you? Last night you didn't take this line.'

'No, I didn't; I was still hiding from myself. But now I know it was because of my colour that you believed the worst of me.'

'My God, Rosie, you can't believe that! It never entered into it. Can't you see it was because, as I said, when I was to be married before, I found out about this girl, and the circumstances were pretty much the same? Rosie, Rosie, for God's sake get that out of your head!'

'But I kept telling you the truth, and you wouldn't listen to me.'

'Yes, I know, I know. But I was mad with jealousy because I loved you so much. Look'—he pulled her to him—'you're not going to do this. You wouldn't only be wrecking your own life, but a number of lives. There's your mother—she's worried to death.'

Her face was close under his and she whispered, 'My mother?'

'She's been to see me. She knows about your father, and she's worried because your uncle hasn't returned home. And she's afraid he'll do you both further harm.'

'My mother been to see you, and she knows?'

'Yes.'

He felt a sigh of relief pass over her, and the despair for a moment left her eyes.

'She's coming here?'

'Yes, as soon as I can get word to her.'

She looked towards the door of the room in which James was lying. 'I must warn him.'

'Rosie, let me speak to him.'

She hesitated a moment, then said dully, 'All right.'

'And Rosie'—he pulled her closer—'listen to me. I love you and I'm willing to spend my life trying to convince you of it, but I'd rather see you dead than married to that Arab. You love me, don't you? ... Look at me. You can't look at me and say you don't. Look at me.'

But she did not look at him. Her eyes, wide and staring from her head, were looking at something beyond him. And he flung round from her, expecting to be confronted by the Arab. But he faced a man whom he had never seen before, and who was staring with a diabolical stare, not at him, but at Rosie. And before he had time to think, the man had sprung past him and at Rose Angela, and they were borne to the floor together.

Matt had lain all through the night and most of the day concealed between the wall of a warehouse and a rubbish dump. He had slept fitfully through the night, and each time he had woken he had groped at his head. Once he woke up laughing and punching at the air. When daylight came he kept awake, but did not move from where he was. He could not tell himself why he was staying here, but instinct was telling him that he must hide. There was a pile of shavings among the rubbish, and after a while he burrowed into this and lay trying to find something to hold on to in the hollowness of his head. He could not remember his name, nor where he had come from; he only knew he had been running ... running, running. But when he thought of himself running he felt disappointed, and groped at the feeling, but the reason for this, too, evaded him.

Although a drizzle of rain was falling, he did not feel cold, only hungry. But he was loath to move, until the fading light of the afternoon urged him to get up. And he had to struggle out of the shavings, for his limbs felt heavy. He gazed about him, but did not know where he was. The river meant nothing to him, and he turned from it and walked with dragging step to where an opening showed in the wall beyond the refuse heap. It was an alleyway, and at the farther end he could see people passing in the street; and, strangely, he did not fear them now, but had an urge to be near them. Yet, once in the street, he walked close to the wall, keeping his head down. He turned the corner and crossed a road as if he knew where he was going, and he had walked quite some distance before he stopped. He was beside a short passage leading into a yard. Some way beyond, on the pavement, two men stood talking to an Arab. He turned his back on them, and as though he had done it before he lifted his eyes to the tin plate nailed above the arch and read 'River Court, 1, 2, 3 and 4'. Then he went along the passage and into the yard, and looked from one to the other of the four doors leading from it.

In the centre of the yard a woman was emptying slops down the drain, and as she banged the bucket to dislodge some filth she turned and glanced at him, and he hung his head. She took no further notice of him, but went to a tap near the wall, rinsed the bucket, threw the water on to the yard, then went through an open doorway.

Matt looked around the yard, selected a door, and went towards it. As he reached it his hand went to his head again, and his fingers moved over his scalp. Two children coming through the doorway looked up at him, then continued on their way; and he walked into the hallway and up the stairs without meeting anyone. But when he reached the second landing he heard voices, and he stood still, listening. First a man's voice, then a woman's. The woman's did not come often, but he waited for it. It was soft, scarcely above a whisper, and his mind clung to it, and he knew that he knew it. It began to form a substance in the hollowness, yet he could not pin it down, for when he groped at it it evaded him, moving away swiftly, almost becoming lost in the void again, until the whisper was renewed. Then he could feel it, the something that would bring him back. But when, for a seemingly long time, the woman's whisper did not reach him, he began to mount the stairs, pausing on each tread to listen. He was half-way up when he saw the feet through the banisters. They were close together, the woman's and the man's. He mounted still farther, until now he could see the back of the man's head. Then he was at the top of the stairs, and the woman moved her head and he saw her face, and he knew.

Now he knew what he had been trying to remember: his life that had been wrecked, his days bare and his nights empty, and all because of her. And he had come back to level things off. Once he had done this he would be happy, and the remainder of the void within him would be filled again. The woman saw him and became petrified, so petrified that she could make no sound, and at the sight of her fear he experienced a feeling of pure glee. And when the man who was shielding her with his body turned, the way was clear, and he sprang.

His hands clawed at her flesh, and he felt her body under his as they went down together. He heard the rattle of pails and tins as they were scattered about them. Then he was no longer on the landing but swinging into the air. And as he fell the second time he clung to the thing that had lifted him and bore it with him. He was fighting now like a mad-man, with his teeth, his fists and his feet, until fresh hands tore at him and fresh faces milled around him ... white faces, dark faces; and hands, thousands of hands; and voices, crying and screaming. Then as suddenly as the void had begun to fill, so it emptied again. He still fought and struggled, but now only to get away, because he had become afraid of something, not of the pain from the blows, but from something welling inside him. Above the noise and stamping of feet he heard a high scream; then the struggle ceased abruptly.

He was on his knees, and the front of his coat and shirt were ripped away, and on his bare chest there were spatters of blood. Someone was holding his arms, and someone else had hold of his hair and was pulling his head back. The strain on his neck was excruciating, and from this angle all he could see was an Arab standing some distance from him. His eyes strained from the face down the man's side to the knife clutched in the brown hand.

Then the grip on his hair eased, to fall away altogether. And now his eyes were looking at the floor and the dirty boards spattered with blood, and he felt a rising gurgle of laughter moving up through his stomach. But before it reached his lips it changed. He saw it changing. It was in the centre of the great empty void that was him. He saw it disintegrate, then form again. And it formed into a sorrow that he knew was his life. And the weight of it became so great inside of him that he felt he must tear it out. But he had no means of doing this, and he knew it. Then into the stillness came a terrifying sound. It was the thing that had frightened him, the thing that he feared. It was the sound of his own weeping.

Stanhope looked from the sobbing man to his arm. The long gap in his greatcoat, coat and shirt looked like a series of jagged red lips. He was feeling no pain; from the moment when a red hot needle seemed to rip his skin the arm became numb. His main feeling was one of amazement. Even in the heat of the fight he had felt this amazement, when he realised that the Arab was trying to knife him. When he first saw the knife gleaming in the Arab's hand he wanted to protest against its use on Matt, but the milling of six bodies, for by then Murphy and two other men had joined the fray, made it impossible. When the knife slit the front of his coat he thought it was an accident, but not when he felt the prick of it between his shoulder-blades. He had untangled himself from the arms that were trying to hold Matt down and turned, filled with fury, yet still amazed, to where he thought the Arab was, for in the dimness of the landing it was fast becoming difficult to distinguish one figure from another. Almost at the same moment as he heard Rose Angela scream he felt the knife go down his arm, and he was thrown against the wall by the force behind the blow.

And now there was quiet on the landing; even the people crowding the stairs were quiet; and Stanhope thought he must be light-headed when, in a matter of seconds, the stairs were emptied of people as if a hand had wiped them away. Doors on the landing, which had been open and filled with shouting women, were now closed. He saw the two men who had been very prominent in the mêlée glide like vapour down the stairs. And now there remained only Murphy, who was holding the kneeling Matt by the arms, Rose Angela, who was pressed tight in the corner of the walls, the Arab and himself.

He looked at the Arab, whose face appeared a dull grey, its expression a mixture of hate and bitterness, and he thought, The dirty greaser! He tried to do me in. And he'll try to pass it off on to the madman there. A flame of intense anger swept over him, and he knew that if he himself had a knife handy at this moment he would ram it home into the Arab's chest. His anger impelled him from the wall, and, shouting a gabble of words, he lunged at Hassan. But before he could reach him, Murphy was between them. He struck at Murphy with his good arm until, without any warning, his strength left him and he had to lean on Murphy for support. The sweat ran into his eyes, blinding him for the moment. Then again he was looking at the Arab. But the Arab was now staring at Rose Angela, and she at him. For a seemingly long time he watched them stare at each other, until he pulled himself from Murphy's hands and stumbled towards them.

Hassan, turning his eyes from Rose Angela to Stanhope, seemed to be on the point of saying something; but, instead, he allowed his curling lip to convey the contempt he was feeling. Then, unhurriedly, he walked across the landing and into the black well of the staircase.

There seemed to be nothing left now but the sound of the crying. It was like the crying of a lost child, with snuffles and breaking sobs. And again, from the support of Murphy's arm, Stanhope gazed down in stupefaction at the man sitting on the floor, his clothes torn from his body and his face and chest spattered with blood. He could not reconcile this whimpering heap with the maniac he had been fighting, and to his disgust he felt a faintness overcoming him, and he retched.

James lay with his eyes closed. His heart was beating rapidly, but not so rapidly as it had done two hours ago. Then he had thought that each beat would sever the slender line with which he was holding on to life. His heart was pounding now because of what was to come, for at any moment the door would open and Bridget would be in the room.

He had thought he did not want to see her, but now he knew he had been lying to himself by way of comfort. What she had done with her life since he left her did not hurt him any more, nor was he worrying about what effect his changed appearance would have on her; not for much longer would he suffer from vanity or pride or whatever it was that had made him hate the idea that she should see him looking anything but ... the big fine Negro man.

The murmur of whispering voices floated to him; Rose Angela's and the painter's. He was a man after his own heart, that painter, stubborn and generous. The doctor had been stubborn man too; he say the painter must go to hospital, and the painter, he say he not go. The painter was worried in case Hassan come back, but Hassan no come back, and that good thing. Yet he was sorry, very sorry, for he liked Hassan, and he wished things had worked out different, for he no want Hassan or any man to hide like he had to hide. But now Hassan think that painter put polis on him, and he lie low for time. Yet painter generous, for he had the chance when polis ask him who stab him, and he say he not see man who did it. And when polis ask could it be Matt, painter still say he not know.

James had always felt that life was full of strange contradictions. Things had puzzled him, and when he groped into the deep depths of himself in search of answers, he had only become more puzzled. Yet he would have stood by the theory that once you love, you always love, and once you hate, a groove is seared in the mind, a groove that can be filled with nothing but itself. He would have rejected the idea that he could allow pity to fill the groove, yet the groove of his hate for Matt had been filled with pity when he watched him for the last time through the open door and saw him propped against the banisters, crying, ceaselessly crying. There was something improper in a man crying like that, but instead of arousing his scorn, pity for this man who had directed his life into tragic channels rose in him; for, to all intents and purposes, Matt was a dead man. He was gone now; they had taken him away. And the doctor was gone. And Murphy was gone too . . . to fetch Bridget.

Life was strange. A man wanted something, and he got it; and he thought it make him happy; and he thought all things that came of it must be good things because it made him happy. He had wanted Bridget, and he had got her. And he was happy for a time. But it was not good. For sixteen years he paid for that bit happiness. And others paid too. . . . Rose Angela, she paid; she paid too much. And Bridget, she paid; just how much he did not know. But she paid all right. And now Hassan, he pay. And Matt; yes indeed, he pay; he was bound to pay in some way. Everything in life must be paid for, but some things were charged too big a price. He had wanted the painter for his Rose Angela, but this, too, would have to be paid for, and by her.

The hoodwinking of himself, the pretence, the day-dreaming, all fell away, and in a moment of illuminating truth he knew that because of his folly his daughter must pay and go on paying, for, as Hassan said, inside Rose

Angela was black, and the tragedy of his race lay buried in the blackness. In what way she would be called upon to pay he did not exactly know: perhaps with babies who would be black outside as well as in.

She had a saying that the priest had told her. It went: God is colour-blind. He had always had his doubts about this saying; he thought it would be better if God could see colour, for then he would see the black man as the white sees him, and seeing him so, and being God, he would certainly have given the black man some power wherewith he could command of the white and of all races their respect; for surely it was an indignity for a man to desire the flesh of his flesh to be a different colour from that of his own. God should not allow a man or a woman to be born to despise the seed of their body like that; he should not ask such a price for a life.

He raised his tired lids and looked at Rose Angela. She was bending over the painter as he sat in the old armchair by the fire. The strained look was gone from her face, but the sadness still remained. He watched the painter's hand go up to her cheek. Then she saw him rise and come towards him. He looked up at this man into whose keeping Rose Angela was going, and he knew a measure of contentment ... if anyone could, he would make the payment easier.

He put out his hand, and the painter grasped it, and they gazed deep at each other—the need for words was past.

As the sound of a car came to them from the street below, Rose Angela bent over him, and softly and tenderly and with love she kissed him. Then with the painter she left the room, smiling at him before closing the door. And, his heart pounding again, he lay watching the door, waiting for it to open into his past.

CATHERINE COOKSON NOVELS IN CORGI

☐	10916 9	The Girl	£1.25
☐	11202 X	The Tide of Life	£1.50
☐	10450 7	The Gambling Man	95p
☐	11204 6	Fanny McBride	95p
☐	11261 5	The Invisible Cord	£1.00
☐	11087 6	The Mallen Litter	£1.00
☐	11086 8	The Mallen Girl	£1.00
☐	11085 X	The Mallen Streak	£1.00
☐	09894 9	Rooney	75p
☐	09596 6	Pure As The Lily	£1.00
☐	09373 4	Our Kate	95p
☐	09318 1	Feathers In The Fire	£1.00
☐	11203 8	The Dwelling Place	£1.25
☐	11260 7	The Invitation	£1.00
☐	08980 X	The Nice Bloke	85p
☐	08849 8	The Glass Virgin	£1.00
☐	08700 9	The Blind Miller	£1.00
☐	08653 3	The Menagerie	85p
☐	08601 0	Colour Blind	95p
☐	08561 8	The Unbaited Trap	85p
☐	11335 2	Katie Mulholland	£1.50
☐	08493 X	The Long Corridor	85p
☐	08444 1	Maggie Rowan	85p
☐	08419 0	The Fifteen Streets	85p
☐	11336 0	Fenwick Houses	£1.00
☐	08296 1	The Round Tower	95p
☐	08251 1	Kate Hannigan	85p
☐	08821 8	A Grand Man	75p
☐	08822 6	The Lord And Mary Ann	75p
☐	08823 4	The Devil And Mary Ann	80p
☐	09074 3	Love And Mary Ann	85p
☐	09075 1	Life And Mary Ann	85p
☐	09076 X	Marriage And Mary Ann	70p
☐	09254 1	Mary Ann's Angels	70p
☐	09397 1	Mary Ann And Bill	85p